Destiney Fulfilled

Destiney Fulfilled

Sweet Destiney Book 2

Vivienne Paul

Hibiscus Tea Publishing

For the hopeful romantics.

And for my real-life sibling bestie.

Cherished readers,

Thank you for diving into the pages of this story!

I can never express enough gratitude for your support.

I truly appreciate it.

This is book two of the Sweet Destiney Series.

To fully enjoy this story, be sure to check out book one, *Chasing Destiney*, first!

It was a pleasure to write about Destiney and Micah, and I sincerely hope you enjoy reading this as much as I enjoyed writing it.

xoxo,

Vivienne Paul

One

DESTINEY

"Can I kiss you, Destiney baby?"

"Yes."

Micah captured my lips with the softest of kisses, making my eyes flutter. Then he kissed me again, and neither of us held back this time. It was a hungry kiss—frantic—so very fitting for a moment like this. And our tongues seemed just as happy to be reunited as we were.

He drew back, leaving only a whisper of air between us. "Baby?"

I was breathless. "Yeah?"

"Pack an overnight bag. I want you to stay with me. Will that be alright?"

I nodded, agreeing without hesitation. "Yes. Come on in. I'll just need a minute."

He softly kissed me again.

And I didn't have the slightest clue why the hell I **ever** spent a moment away from him.

I was up in my room now. I threw a few things in my bag. I hardly paid attention to what I was grabbing. I wouldn't need much anyway. I'd just need some panties, night clothes, and something for work tomorrow. That was easy. I could show up to work in whatever. I didn't mind getting paint all over. We hadn't yet discussed what would happen after that, but I wasn't even worried about it. I knew I'd be with my man.

My man.

Nothing else mattered.

When Micah arrived, I'd barely just got home myself. And I couldn't open the door quickly enough- couldn't get to *him* quickly enough. Once nothing was separating us, I closed the space instantly. I was swift, throwing my arms around Micah's waist. I held on tight. Inhaling his scent. Basking in his warmth. Losing myself in his refuge. Micah embraced me securely and just as frantically. Rubbing my back softly.

And we stood just like that.

Right in the front doorway.

We held each other for a long time. No idea how long it was exactly. It seemed like several minutes. We didn't need to talk. There would be plenty of time for that.

Damn. It felt so good to be back in his arms. Any reservations I had at one time now seemed... *so trivial.* Frivolous. Nominal. Unnecessary. I had it in my mind that I would make up for all of the time wasted. Time *I* wasted.

Reunited with Micah, I felt... *all* the things. Certitude. Familiarity. Serenity. And, also, I felt sexy. Free. Powerful. And significant. I loved everything I felt with him. I wanted to be with him all the time. I wanted to see him as often as he could stand to see me. I wanted to be in his space and his arms. It felt like no other place I'd experienced. This was precisely where I was meant to be.

With Micah, everything was right in my world.

He's such a gentleman. Damn... so thoughtful. To a fault. Earlier, I kinda needed to remind him that he didn't ever have to ask for what was already his.

Including me. I was his.

He asked for another kiss before I descended the hallway to pack my bag.

"Beautiful Destiney baby… can I kiss you? Please?"

"Yes, please." When we broke apart, I said, "Micah."

"Yep."

"Kiss me anytime. I don't mind." My sweet Micah, ever the gentleman, had asked for permission each time he wanted to kiss me. It was so sweet and incredibly thoughtful, but we were way past that now. "Anytime you want to, you can."

*Micah nodded. "You **sure**?" He had a sly grin, and I couldn't help the cackle that escaped me.*

"Yes, I'm sure. I love it when we kiss."

"You gone eat them words, girl!" If you can imagine, he said it in an overly exaggerated Southern accent, and we laughed at that. He could be so silly sometimes.

I returned to the living room, and Micah was sitting on the couch, his phone in his hand. He appeared immersed in whatever he was reading, but as soon as he saw me, he stood, greeting me with another kiss.

I could get used to these.

"Everything good?" I checked.

"Yep. Just looking over a document, but I can get back to it once we're home." I didn't say so, but I liked the way he said "home" so casually as opposed to "my house." He gently took my bag off my shoulder, tossing it over his own. "Ready?"

"Baby. I want to tell you something. First."

"Indeed." He nodded. "Should we sit?" His brows high expectantly.

"Uh…no. No. This will be quick." I took a deep inhale to calm my nerves. I was all over the place but desperately wanted to share this with him.

Right now.

This moment felt like the perfect time to do so.

I was feeling super-duper shy, so I reverted to what was familiar. "I'm going to close my eyes."

I saw that his smile grew before I closed them.

"Okay."

My eyes closed now; I prepared to reveal my heart to him. I took another moment, and finally, forging ahead, I told him, "I'm in love with you. I love you, Micah."

There was complete silence between us.

I didn't need him to say it back, not right now, at least. After all, I derailed everything we'd built the day he told me how he felt. I didn't take for granted or even expect him to return the sentiment. I just wanted him to know where I was and how I felt. I figured, eventually, we would find our way back.

Anyway, my eyes were still closed, and I was too shy to open them and face Micah now that everything was out in the open.

I heard him put my bag down, and he reached for my hands. Capturing both, he began a gentle caress of my fingers.

Still nothing, but *damn*, if I knew Micah like I thought I did… *any* second now, he'd say…

"Open your eyes, baby." He gently squeezed my hands, patiently waiting.

I opened them to his comforting gaze, and before I could look away, he said, "I love you too, Destiney baby."

I smiled real big. "You still love me?"

"Indeed. I'm still in love with you."

"Wow. Okay." It was music to my ears. For reasons I cannot explain, my eyes started welling with tears, falling before I could stop them. I've always been highly emotional. Some days, I can be so moved by things. Crying at the drop of a hat, hearing a song. A movie. A tender moment between loved ones reunited at an airport. Add to that, I'm so damn sensitive. Got it all from my father.

"Why are you crying?" Micah wiped a couple of my tears and then held me close. "These are happy tears, I hope."

I nodded my head. "You're just so amazing. And I'm so happy." I didn't have my wits about me, and there wasn't nearly enough time to pour my heart out. Instead, I told him, "I'm so glad you're mine."

"I was always yours." He gently held me in his arms. After he kissed my forehead, he said, "And you were always mine. We just had to find each other." He kissed my forehead again. "And now that I've found you, I have so many plans for us, baby. This is only the beginning. I plan to give you something so special. I love you, Destiney baby."

"I love you too, Micah."

two

MICAH

"Thank you for the analysis. Based on that, I'd suggest rebranding is best. An acquisition wouldn't be ideal with this practice."

A team of executives and I were trying to decide how we would move forward on a proposal. A struggling Urgent Care approached us, hoping for an acquisition. They were in serious financial trouble and at risk of closing their doors-*after* going bankrupt. We never wanted to see medical facilities close, especially in the more rural areas. Which this one was located in. Access to quality healthcare mattered a lot, particularly for the vulnerable communities. I was tempted to move forward on that strength alone. And though we could make all of *their* financial problems go away, *we* would garner significant financial problems of our own if we moved forward with an acquisition. Essentially acquiring their debt where there was no return. After my analysis, rebranding and a potential partnership, like a joint venture, would help them get to a better place financially. Possibly, then, we could revisit depending on how the numbers looked.

My hard work and dedication to building my expertise had truly paid off, and my opinion was considerably valued and not just due to my position.

When I joined the company about six years ago, I didn't set out to climb the ladder per se. I just wanted to gain experience, use my MBA, and build my savings. I really wanted a family, and I figured securing these things would put me in the best position to obtain that.

Just over two years ago, I was approached to apply for the System Vice President position. I was the System Director of Mergers and Acquisitions then, which kept me fairly busy. I was hesitant because I wasn't interested in adding unnecessary stress to my life. Though *very* enticing, the money wasn't worth it to me. Not entirely. But after talking with Daddy and Mal about it and praying about it, I decided to apply and leave the rest to God. At thirty-two years old, I was the youngest person to have reached this level in the company's history. It was a lot of pressure initially, but thankfully, things have gone pretty smoothly. I am incredibly grateful, as I know things can be quite different for a young black man in corporate America in a position of leadership and authority. Not many people take so kindly to that. Especially my contenders.

Anyway, it's been about two years now. I've been focused on leading my department to accomplish great numbers, close successful acquisitions, and continue to grow and develop professionally. In my personal life, I've been saving my money, being the best steward possible, and preparing for the wife and family I desire and for which I've prayed.

And now, here she was—just a few feet from me.

I peered over my shoulder.

Destiney was dozing off on the loveseat I had in my office. Guess baby girl was tired. She wouldn't be comfortable sleeping there, and I had no clue how long I would be. We'd already passed the thirty minutes scheduled, and they were still talking. I had to jump on a conference call when we walked in the door, so I didn't get a chance to give her a tour.

7

Besides, she'd been stuck right next to me like white on rice. I didn't mind either, but it was clear she wasn't comfortable enough to venture off on her own. That was fine with me, and we'd get to that.

The director of our region started going into another spiel, and I took that time to encourage her to head upstairs.

I tapped Destiney on her thigh softly. She gave me sleepy eyes. "You head upstairs and rest, baby. The room at the very end of the hall. I'll be up to join you as soon as I wrap this up."

The call lasted another half hour. When it finally ended, I informed my assistant that I'd be logging out for the day.

Then I changed out of my suit. I kept a few things in the closet in my home office, which worked out perfectly.

I headed upstairs to my bedroom to find Destiney sleeping on top of my comforter. She was likely hesitant to get underneath the blankets, but we would work on that.

I took in my sleeping beauty and couldn't get enough of the sight before me.

I couldn't even move.

It wasn't so much that she was so beautiful; it was the fact that she was finally in my bed. Mal told me years back that he'd stand by Gabe's crib and watch him sleep once they brought him home from the hospital. Maybe this sentiment was something similar.

This shit was fucking with me.

In the best way.

Destiney was the first woman to be in my home. In my bedroom. In my bed.

She would be the last. She was the only one worthy.

Earlier, I told her I had so many plans. And I do. For her. For us.

Seeing her in my bed, was... a mind fuck. It was arousing, of course, but so much more. Hell, I don't even know how long I stood there watching her.

Destiney stirred slightly before opening her eyes. "What?"

Destiney didn't have the slightest clue. I shook my head. Then I laughed at myself—I tended to do that a lot. "You have no idea how special this moment is for me, do you?" I finally spoke.

"Tell me," She said around a lazy grin.

Shaking my head, I struggled to form a sentence. "You... being here. *In here.* This is...this is like..." I chuckled. "Damn. I'm so glad you're here, baby. That's all."

A beautiful smile spread across her lips, her captivating eyes blinking slowly. "You make *everything* so sweet, Micah."

"It's easy to be sweet whenever I handle you, baby." I stepped closer to the bed, asking, "Any room for me?"

Destiney flashed an incredulous glare. "This bed is huge, Micah." Glancing on both sides of her and looking back over at me.

She was right. I had an Alaskan King. I'm a big man. I wanted to ensure I had plenty of space to stretch out and that my wife would still be comfortable. I even thought that babies or toddlers would eventually like to or need to join us in bed some days. For example, if they weren't feeling well, I know they sometimes feel extra clingy when they're sick and fussy.

When I had this home built, I made every customization, every detail, and every decision with my wife and children in mind.

"But can I join you?" I could always sleep in one of my guest rooms. I was just glad to have her with me under my roof. I could wait on everything else.

9

"Of course, you can," she said sweetly. "This bed is *yours.*"

Ours.

Nodding, I made my way to my side of the bed and sat down, exhaling a breath. I was beginning to get hard, and his ass needed to chill. Laying back, I turned my body towards her, leaving plenty of space between us, about an arm's length. "Please go back to sleep if you're still tired. I won't disturb you."

She turned her body toward me. "I'm good for right now. That cat nap helped."

"Indeed."

Destiney was lying on her side, facing me. And we held each other's gaze for a while. I wanted to hold her in my arms badly, but we would get to all that. We had been affectionate while we were vertical, but horizontal would take a little time, I was sure. I would keep my hands to myself until she made it crystal clear she was ready.

"Tomorrow after work, I want you to come back." I quickly continued because I didn't want to scare her. "Or I can come stay with you. Whatever you're most comfortable doing. I just don't want to be apart." I meant that shit. I wanted to stay up under her. I wanted her to be under me. I just liked being near her. I loved it. Her energy. Her vibe. Her essence radiated from her. Destiney would have to put in some serious work to get rid of me.

Destiney bashfully gave me a real big smile. "I don't want to be apart either."

"You don't?" I volleyed playfully.

She shook her head. "I don't."

"And you are sure you ain't gone get sick of me?" I asked sarcastically.

She released a hearty laugh, and I swear it was the cutest thing I'd heard in a while.

"I'm the one you're gonna get sick of. I've warned you that I have attachment issues, and I can be real clingy."

"That's cool with me. I want to be close to you. Once you're comfortable enough, I'll *always* be up on you. You just wait, baby." I'm incredibly affectionate but I knew how to control that shit. Especially since there was a lot at stake. The last thing I wanted was to come on too strong and scare her.

"It's going to happen soon. I'm getting more comfortable with you, Micah. You've been amazing." She reached her hand out to mine, and we threaded our fingers. "And I appreciate you being so patient with me."

"My pleasure baby." That shit had two meanings. All in due time.

"We can stay here." She said after a beat.

"You sure? I promise I don't mind."

"I'm sure." Destiney nodded in agreement.

"Alright, that's cool. I don't plan on trying anything, but I can sleep in a guest room if you need me to. I want you to be comfortable."

That must be the word for the day. Comfortable.

That was probably the fifth time I said it in the past hour alone. In the grand scheme, I'd said it *ad nauseam*. But I was serious about this. I was handling Destiney like a rare, delicate flower. I wasn't going anywhere, and we didn't need to rush anything.

She shook her head. "We can sleep in here together." *Damn.*

"I trust you. Besides, your bed is huge. There's plenty of space for us without worrying about personal space. And I'm not a wild sleeper."

11

That bashful smile of hers was back and I could feel my dick rising. *Chill man. Chill. Not right now.* I nodded my agreement. "Alright. So, we're staying here, and we're both sleeping here?"

"Yes."

"Yeah?"

"Yeah."

"Sounds good to me," I said casually. I think I did a convincing job containing my excitement. I was beside myself. You'd think I had never shared company with a beautiful woman before.

But this wasn't just any woman. This was *my* woman. Destiney.

No one compared to her. "You can shower in here, and I'll take one in the bathroom down the hall. Not sure exactly what you packed, but Gabby has some shower stuff and body lotion she keeps here whenever they stay over. You're welcome to use it. Unless you want to smell like me, you can always use mine."

She laughed. "Thank you."

There was comfortable silence between us. We were still facing each other. Eyes on eyes.

I continued my soft caress of her fingers. She was doing her own thing to me with hers… can't put into words the things she be doing with her soft, sexy fingertips. Yep. Those were sexy, too, simply because they were *hers*.

"Can I feed you?" I pressed.

"Yes please!"

I chuckled. "You sound excited."

I felt the vibration of her quiet titter. "What can I say? I love food."

I thought over the ingredients already in my fridge. I planned and prepped meals when I knew I'd have a more hectic week. So, I didn't go too far with groceries unless I knew I'd have Gabe and Gabby over. If everything went according to plan, all of that would change soon. My ultimate desire was to have Destiney with me all the time.

"Remind me. Is dairy alright?"

She beamed. "Yes baby. And thank you for checking. I'm vegetarian, not vegan, so dairy is fine."

"I got you. How's pasta sound?"

"I love pasta. That sounds perfect."

"Indeed. I'll head downstairs and get started. I want to give you a tour, so you know where everything is. But you're welcome to stay up here if you want. Or you can hang out downstairs with me. Either way." I stood to my feet and rounded the bed. She stood too, coming into my arms and placing hers around my waist. I kissed her forehead and remained there for a moment.

"Can I help you with anything?"

"Not a chance."

She cackled and lifted her head, kissing my lips softly. Then I spoke into her ear, "You just relax and look beautiful." She threw her head back, blessing me with low lids and a lazy grin.

Yep. I was already growing even stiffer in my joggers.

"If you insist."

"I sure do."

"Actually, I'm gonna sketch while you do that, so I'll be at the island. I like being close to you."

I smiled in contentment. "I love being close to you."

After giving Destiney a tour, I was in the kitchen, pulling out the pans I would need.

Moments before, Destiney padded down the hall to use the restroom, and I watched her till she disappeared. I was sure to take a moment to adjust myself. Destiney was unbelievably sexy, and I wanted her bad. When we were lounging in my room earlier, she looked amazing. She'd changed into some biker shorts and her thick ass thighs were on full display. Most of all, she appeared relaxed and comfortable. That's exactly what I wanted for her. She was worth every ounce of the restraint I was practicing. We shared intimate space while upstairs, and I swore I could smell her. She always smelled like coconut and vanilla, and I loved that scent on her. But I could smell *her* too. I was convinced I'd end up with blue balls for real. While I showed her the place, I was hard as fuck. To the point that it was painful. Then, while she was changing, I had it in my mind to stroke one out in the toilet downstairs. I locked the door behind me, and I was seconds away, but I restrained at the last minute. Honestly, keeping my hands to myself wasn't as difficult when I kept my distance, so cooking for her was a welcome distraction.

"I'm back." She announced sweetly as she walked around the kitchen island.

"I get another kiss?" She was already walking into my open arms, and I pressed my lips to hers.

"You get as many as you want, baby." She managed around a smile. A few closed-mouth pecks and she was off again, sauntering into the next room where my home office was. When we arrived from her place earlier, I told her she was welcome to use my office space to work in anytime she needed to. I didn't work from home as much as I had the latitude to. I was home alone so much that it was almost depressing. Anyway, Destiney's eyes lit up, and she retrieved a canvas backpack from her trunk. The bag was teal with a funky, whimsical floral pattern that fit her adorable personality perfectly. And it was filled with at least two dozen paintbrushes. Tubes of paint. Pens, pencils, markers, and a few sketchbooks.

After bringing out the pans I would need, I washed and then filled a stock pot for the pasta and set it to boil on my back isle. I mulled over options in the pantry, finally deciding to go with linguine. I was out of penne, which was my preferred choice of pasta whenever I made Florentine. I had a little rigatoni, but not enough for both of us. Linguine would do just fine. I grabbed the other ingredients I needed and headed back to the kitchen.

I found Destiney sitting at the island with her sketchbook open and a few pens spread out neatly in front of her. She was deep in thought, adding detail to an elaborate peacock feather.

"That's amazing," I said, placing the ingredients on the counter and then turning on the water to wash my hands.

"Thanks, baby." She said, her head down as she continued working. "Just a little doodle that turned into something I'm actually beginning to like." She cracked up.

"Do you take your sketchbook everywhere?" I placed the pasta in the boiling water and then pulled out my cell to start my playlist.

"Anywhere and everywhere. I never know when I'll be inspired. Second, if I need to pass the time, it is a fantastic way to do it. You would not believe the amazing things I've created waiting around in the doctor's office and in that damn DMV."

I released a deep chuckle at that. "I bet." I pulled a few more things from the fridge. The smooth sounds of Goapele surrounded us as I whisked together some flour, vegetable broth, milk, salt, and pepper and set it aside. I minced two garlic cloves and then rinsed and sliced some portobello

15

mushrooms. In a large skillet, I added some olive oil over medium-high heat, and once it reached the desired temperature, I sautéed the sliced mushrooms. I added fresh garlic a few minutes later and sautéed it until it began to brown.

"Mmm. Smells good!" She said, looking up from her sketch.

"Thank you, love."

"Do you cook often?"

"Yes and no. I like to cook, but it's no fun dining alone. I mainly cook when I have Gabe and Gabby girl over fairly often. Now and then, Malachi and Ella will come by too, and we'll all enjoy a meal together."

"Same. Daijah is hardly home these days. She spends every free moment with Julian, so it's always just me, eating by myself. My best friend India comes by every blue moon. But she's always busy."

"Well, would you look at that?" I casually said after a beat, adding my whisked flour and broth mixture with the mushrooms and garlic. I lowered my fire to a simmer.

She furrowed her brows. "What?"

"We're both alone most of the time. Sleeping alone and eating alone. I think we just solved that problem." I pretended to play it cool and never looked at her directly, wondering what she thought of my comment. Now that we had shared space, I wanted to do it as often as possible. If I had it my way, Destiney would never leave my side.

I loved having her under me. I loved having her in my arms. I loved the peace and calm she brought. I loved the sight of her sitting at my kitchen island, looking beautiful. I loved talking to her face-to-face.

I stirred the sauce and checked on the pasta as Kem's soulful voice came on, and I grooved to the tune. I was a huge fan of his.

"I'm not much of a cook, but… we should take turns hosting. If you're down… I'd love that," she said, seemingly out of nowhere. I did my best to hide my grin as I headed to the fridge to get the gouda. After locating my cheese grater, I added some to the sauce.

I looked over at her. "You like a lot of cheese?"

"Yes!"

She was so cute. "Indeed." I grated a generous amount into the sauce, then stirred. "And… I would love that too." I walked around the island and kissed her forehead.

I returned to the stove, removed the pasta from the fire, and strained the water.

"You look like a professional moving around this kitchen."

I chuckled. "I do okay. Pasta and me, we go way back. I always asked Mommy to fix me pasta when I was little. When I was about seven, she started teaching me to cook. Pasta is one of the first things I learned. Been hooked ever since. I could easily eat it every day. Easily."

"That's me, but with rice and potatoes."

"Carb city on your plate? Sounds like my kind of party."

We laughed.

"Hell yeah. Where you think these thighs came from?"

Destiney's thighs were perfection. I really wanted to be between them.

I mixed fresh spinach with the sauce and then tossed the sauce in with the linguine. It looked and smelled great.

Mushroom Florentine was an excellent choice tonight, and everything worked out perfectly.

three

DESTINEY

"Would you like wine with your dinner, love?"

"Yes please."

Micah strolled over to a wine chiller against the far wall of his living room. I could see it from where I sat. He called over to me, "Red or white?"

"Hmm. You pick. A little sweeter if possible."

Micah and I had been wrapped in each other for the past few hours.

Not literally. But we'd been side by side, hand in hand, since he met me at my house earlier. Honestly, there was nowhere else I'd rather be.

He was taking such good care of me. Emotionally and physically.

When he started cooking, I had to go to the bathroom. And my panties were just as wet as I expected. Micah was talking sexy in my ear, and I was getting so worked up. My ass was about to lose my resolve, if I'm honest. He was about to be my undoing.

I had never felt this way at this intensity before. It was as if things were beginning to wake up. And I wasn't sure what I would do with it. It didn't surprise me that Micah wasn't trying to get into my panties. He was so respectful, keeping his hands to himself. He didn't imply or allude to sex. But it was all over him. The energy. The way he kissed me. The way he moved with agility. I was convinced he was a sensual lover. The artist in me saw that. I was excited to experience it.

When the time came.

I sent a text to my group chat with Daijah and India. I had to inform them that I was at Micah's house. And I would be spending the night.

I'll see you at work tomorrow, Indie. Girls, I'm spending the night with Micah!

Sibling Bestie: Well, well, well... Don't do anything I wouldn't do Sissy

Indie the Bestie: YASSSSSS!!!! Let him blow your back out Best!

These two were just too much. I'd have to respond later.

"How about I open both. You can try a glass of each." Micah approached the island with two bottles.

"Which one are you having?" I asked.

"Red. But either of them pair nicely." He placed a tall-stemmed wine glass in front of me and poured a generous amount of white wine.

I sniffed the contents, swirled briefly, and took a quick taste. "Mmm."

"Trebbiano di Lugano." He said, handing me the wine bottle. I always admired the design of imported wines. As an artist, I've always seen beauty in everyday things. It was the way I viewed the world.

Micah opened the red wine and poured a hefty glass before handing it to me. "Try this one."

I took a sip and closed my eyes as it went down slowly.

"Oooh, I love this one! What is it?"

"Nerello Mascalese."

"I love it! I'm not as versed with reds, but this one is lovely."

"I thought you'd like that one."

"What other bottled goodies you have over there?" I asked, referring to his stocked wine chiller.

There were at least two dozen bottles of mixed reds and whites. "I didn't take you for a wine drinker, Mr. Walker."

He chuckled. "Funny, I'm not. I'll have a glass of wine on occasion here with my dinner. I love a glass whenever I want to grill a steak. But I rarely have more than a glass or two, and I end up tossing the rest of it out."

My eyes grew wide. "So why the stocked wine chiller?" It was state-of-the-art and quite impressive looking.

"It was a housewarming gift from Malachi and Ella when I had this home built. They also added a wine club membership, paid for two years. Every month, I'd get a shipment with six bottles. I filled the chiller, and the rest started to pile up so quickly I had to start gifting bottles as Christmas and birthday presents." We both laughed at that. Then he took a drink from his glass. "You take some home; maybe Daijah would like a few bottles."

"That's why you were so eager to open both of these," I concluded.

"That's part of it. But I already told you. You get anything you want from me. Anything baby."

"You're so sweet."

"You make it easy being sweet with you." He leaned in, placing a kiss on my forehead right before he headed back to the kitchen. After a moment, "It's ready."

Micah pulled a chair out for me, and after I was settled, he brought our bowls to the table, gently placing mine right in front of me. He topped off my wine before taking his seat. There was even a candle lit in the center of the table. I wasn't sure when he managed to do that. But it was so thoughtful. I'd say romantic… and it was *very* romantic. But romantic is too cheap of a word to describe everything he had been doing for me. Especially this.

Thoughtful is the best word I can think of.

Everything he does is with so much thought, intention, and consideration.

Aside from the fact that this was the first candle-lit dinner I ever had, in the history of ever… no man had ever cooked for me. Aside from my father, of course. I don't know… it may not have been a big deal to him, but it was a *massive* deal to me.

"Wow, Micah, this looks amazing." I eyed the creamy sauce with the hearty amount of portobello mushrooms. I couldn't wait to try it. It smelled just as delicious as it looked.

This man.

This *man.*

This man.

Damn.

"Thank you for all of this."

There was a light titter. "You thanking me before you even have a taste?" He teased.

I didn't even try to stop the wide grin that quickly spread across my face.

Micah didn't understand. It wasn't just the food. It was everything.

He was everything.

"It's my pleasure, love. Thank you for joining me." He grabbed my hands and prayed over our meal. Once he was done, I took a forkful and blew. When I finally tasted it, I was blown away by the flavors exploding on my pallet. The pasta was cooked to al dente perfection, and the mushrooms had a smoky, umami flavor. I could have eaten a whole plate of mushrooms by themselves.

But the sauce. It was delectable. I was amazed because I watched him make it entirely from scratch. I was the person who bought my sauces in jars.

Micah must have seen my facial expression because he asked, "Good?"

"Superb!" I gave him the chef's kiss. Then I took another forkful and blew. "Let me find out you're a chef."

"No way, but I can cook a thing or two. I've made this many, many times. I'm sure that's why I'm so good at it. I love pasta. I'd eat it every day, but I had to scale that back and only eat it in moderation."

"Yeah, I hear you. Pasta can be dangerously addictive."

"Like you." He returned with low lids.

I took a sip of my wine.

Because, well, honestly, I didn't know what to say to that.

I also crossed my legs tightly under the table because *she* was starting to do that thing she did whenever *he* said the things he said.

And in other news, I couldn't wait to thank his mother for teaching him to cook so well, among many other things.

I needed to meet this woman. I wanted to wash her feet in gratitude. Seriously.

***

My first night staying with Micah couldn't have been more perfect. It was so perfect that I went to work the next day, barely even present. Just going through the motions. Distracted the entire time. Counting the minutes until I could be back in his arms. My thoughts were saturated. Musing over the day before.

We enjoyed the finely prepared dinner he made us. We watched part of *Hustle & Flow*, then took showers and got ready for bed.

He had a playlist going, and we were chilling, just being together. We lay in his bed; he held me in his arms, and we talked and talked and talked. And kissed too. A whole lot. Wet. Sloppy. Nasty. And I was having the time of my fucking life. I'd like to think Micah enjoyed himself, too.

No, we didn't have sex.

Which was fine. It was perfectly fine.

There was this unspoken thing. This understanding. It was like neither of us expected the other to move like that. Not quite yet anyway.

It was close to midnight when we finally fell asleep. I'm pretty sure I fell asleep first.

Yeah.

All of this was surreal.

As soon as I woke up, I was keenly aware of my surroundings. I was at Micah's house. In his bed. Waking up to the gloriously distinct aroma of French toast. My *very favorite* thing to have for breakfast. Micah told me he remembered that detail from a long time ago.

I remember the conversation well myself. It was one of our late nights. We laughed so much, getting lost in the newness and bliss of learning more about each other. We were asking each other *this or that* questions.

Mini-golf or bowling.
Movie night or game night.
French fries or onion rings.
Comedy club or poetry slam.
Scavenger hunt or escape room.

Then Micah said, "I have a good one! Pancakes or waffles?"
"That's easy. French toast."

I remember him cracking up at that. *That's not how you play! Gotta pick between the two options!* But I was firm on my answer.

Anyway, I remember Micah telling me that his mom taught him the French toast secret, and I just *had* to try it.

He hadn't lied. Micah makes the most decadent French toast I've ever had.

My favorite part was that he had me sit on his lap and he fed me. Then we fed each other when we made a plate of seconds.

And Micah was such an early riser. I always knew that about him, but observing it firsthand was another thing. After we ate, he informed me he'd already finished his workout. He had a home gym just off of his garage. Talk about discipline. Micah got up early enough to work out, shower, and fix me French toast and an egg white omelet for himself.

And now that we were kissing, we kissed all the time. We can't seem to stop kissing.

Always in make-out mode.

Being with Micah was the most organic thing. Seriously. As natural as breathing. I could not believe how easy it was. He made me feel so comfortable. Right at home.

I realized he had seamlessly curated an environment where I could express myself with exuberance. Free of inhibition. That was perfectly fine with me, too.

When we parted ways to head to work, we joked about just playing hookey and spending the day in his bed. And hell yeah, I was with it. But I'm glad he acted as the person responsible at that moment. Left up to me, we'd be laid up right now.

I didn't like being away from him. I wanted to lie under him and never move. He made me feel *so* at ease. Relaxed. Contented.

I wanted to give him *all of me*. I knew I would be ready soon. And I appreciated that I didn't feel any pressure from him.

While we lay in his bed, he'd had his hands everywhere, caressing me all over. Micah had to know each of my curves by now. My breasts were the main attraction for the time being, especially my right one, which was the one with the pierced nipple. Daijah thought I was silly for only getting one nipple pierced, but one was plenty for me. I liked a little variety. I remember the day India and I went together; she got one, and I got the other. That fucking pain man. One was all I had in me. I had no plans to get the other one.

Micah discovered my piercing the night those months ago when we were in the shower. I remember he ran his fingers over my breasts then stopped abruptly, rubbing my nipple again and again. I heard him gasp, followed by a low growl. Later, he told me in my ear that he was pleasantly surprised and that *"I was a gift that kept giving."* That shit turned me all the way on.

And speaking of being turned on, Micah had been touching me everywhere, rubbing all over my ass but stayed away from my pussy. I sensed he wanted to go there but was waiting for me to tell him it was all right. I knew he was getting aroused just like I was. His bulging erection made that abundantly clear. I could feel the stiffness, girth, and weight through his basketball shorts. We were chilling for now, but I came close to taking a hold of it—a few times. I got the feeling Micah wouldn't mind. We got really close and very familiar without going all the way. I was either sitting on his lap, lying between his legs, or him lying between mine.

And. Yeah. I wanted to feel his hard dick in my hand.

I wanted to do things. Things I'd never done, but I wanted to do them with him. I had grown so comfortable in his space, all thanks to Micah ensuring so.

I couldn't believe I was running from this.

Being with him, even in silence, was so easy. And I would miss his absence even if he was just in the next room. I loved being around him, in his company. I couldn't quite describe how I felt. It was just… there weren't any words. I felt special, and I could feel his desire for me. But not in an aggressive or over-sexualized way. He respected the hell out of me, and I respected him, too.

And he was hyperaware, asking about my mental state all the time. That was so thoughtful.

The way he got me going when we kissed. My pussy would ache and thump and get wet as a damn faucet. I was always wet for him. My. Freaking. Goodness.

Generally, doing things impulsively wasn't my style-for the most part. That would all depend. And anyway, there was a conversation we needed to have. I knew Micah was waiting for me. To say something. The fact that Micah was waiting so patiently somehow had the opposite effect.

Subtlety and gentleness go a long way with me. And lately, I've been feeling like I want to forget the talking. I wanted to take my damn panties off.

No one had ever made me feel the way he did.

Like, Micah oozed sex appeal and BDE. Yet never alluded to trying to persuade me to give up the drawers. I've concluded that he was waiting patiently for me to make a move. He would follow my lead, only going as far as I did. And from the beginning, he communicated everything so there was no room for confusion. I realized that he needed me to offer him the pussy.

And I planned to.

On a silver platter.

Soon.

Anyway, his home was beautiful—expansive, immaculate, and tidy. I loved his living area, which had high ceilings with black wood beams, a fireplace, and a wet bar. Plush white area rugs over white wood floors and a deep grey velvet sectional.

I'm no cook, but I love his kitchen, which had gunmetal appliances and white cabinets.

I loved the smell of his home, too. It smelled pleasant, like fresh laundry. It wasn't what I expected, but I don't know exactly what I expected. There was minimal décor, which added to the charm and beauty of his home. His neutral walls were bare. Free of hanging pictures and artwork. Of the entire house, only two art pieces were hanging. An oversized black Lord's Supper hangs over his dining room table. Then, an oversized, black and white close-up of two hands embraced in the foreground with a sunset in the background. I'd say maybe twenty-four by thirty-six inches. My first time in his downstairs hallway, I was struck. It was breathtaking. Later, Micah told me it was his parents. Micah took the picture on his phone, which was so beautiful that he had it blown up.

But his bedroom.

First of all, it was huge, the size of two of my living rooms. It was tastefully decorated but the opposite of mine. Minimal décor, just the essentials. No television.

The smell was an aphrodisiac. Masculine and clean, a woodsy mix of cedar and mahogany teakwood. His enormous bed sat against a wall he painted black. It was the only wall painted in his entire home. Some oversized pillows. I love pillows. An ottoman at the foot of his bed. Dark cherry oak side tables. Black sheets, a black down comforter, and a blackout curtain.

When I noticed how big his window was, I was beside myself. I love big windows. There was a sitting area in front of the window with a black leather couch. The couch in his bedroom matched the loveseat in his home office. Two doors, one leading to a walk-in closet, where I assumed the entirety of his wardrobe was as his bedroom didn't have any dressers, and another to the ensuite.

The ensuite was oversized too. His and her sinks. A huge jacuzzi-style bathtub and a separate walk-in shower.

Something else that caught my eye were the floating shelves in his bedroom. The lower one had about ten books across genres, including memoirs, autobiographies, and self-help books. But then, the upper shelf was lined with what appeared to be journals.

Get the fuck out of here.

"Micah." I softly called out to him.

"Hmm?" He came to stand beside me.

I pointed at the shelf. "Are those…"

"Journals? Yes. All of them." There had to be at least a dozen hardcover journals lined neatly.

"You… you keep a journal?"

"I do. I have since I was a kid."

Wow. He really couldn't be more perfect.

"Me too." Journaling is what got me through the loss of my mother. I still have many of those journals from that time in my life.

"That's amazing. I think it's a great idea to journal often. I try to as often as I can."

"Totally agree."

I did my morning pages in my journal to clear my head and balance myself—not every day, but several days a month. I loved *The Artist Way*. I bought the book back in college, and it remains one of just a few self-help books I own.

Anyway, I was so in love.

Micah was a whole vibe. Like, the entire thing. It really made no sense. I was convinced this amazingness we had was unlike anything I would ever have with anyone else.

I didn't want to find out either. I was all the way in this.

I loved everything about Micah, but his personality was just unmatched.

Seriously had the dopest personality ever.

I couldn't believe he'd been single all this time. And knowing Micah as well as I do now, I'm not surprised. I know he has options. He's an attractive man with all the things women want. A great career, fancy cars. A big ass house. Child-free.

But Micah's the type to take his time and wait for what feels right. He doesn't rush about anything. He doesn't mind waiting when things take time. But not in a fuck boy way.

He practices active listening. He accepts what he can't change and rolls with it. Extremely humble.

Even-tempered. Incredibly mindful. His mindfulness shows in every space he dwells.

He was perfect. Quite literally.

Handsome. Charming. Respectful. Thoughtful. Sweet.

He encouraged me, especially when I was dealing with my situation. That was tough. But Micah never made me feel like a freak or pity me. I never wanted to be pitied. He made me feel sexy and desired, which was huge for me.

Simply put, Micah was a great fucking catch, and meanwhile, here I was still trying to figure out what the hell I ever did to deserve this. Imposter syndrome was wildin, fucking with me for real.

I love myself. I know I'm unique and proud of that shit. But there wasn't anything *extraordinary* about me.

A man like Micah could have any woman he wanted.

And he wanted me.

He wouldn't dare let me forget it either.

And I wanted him too. *In all the ways.*

four

MICAH

We helped Daddy pull quite a few things out from the garage. The church was doing a rummage sale and swap, and Mommy wanted to donate a few things they no longer used. Mal, Gabe, and I knocked it out within a few hours.

Now, we were hanging out near the grill talking, and I was quite distracted. I tried my damndest to at least seem engaged in the conversation Mal and Daddy were attempting to have with me. In any case, Mal knew what was up. He'd been brought to speed and sent us all the good vibes.

Just last night, he texted me to check in. At that exact moment, I happened to be lying in Destiney's lap.

Brother: Everything good in the hood baby brother?
Perfect. She's been rubbing my head for the last hour
Brother: Which one?
I fell out at his clowning ass.
CTFU man stop!
Brother: Lol
Anyway, shit felt so good she put my ass to sleep while ago. She's invested
Brother: I just fell out laughing. Got my wife asking me what's so funny. I'm asking her to rub my head too but unlike y'all we ain't on restriction
Goodnight
Brother: Yes Lawd it will be
Malachi was a damn fool.

So, the women were inside. In addition to the seven-layer dip, Ella made spaghetti, and Mommy made a peach cobbler for dessert. It was the end of the summer, and it had been such a lovely day out. We planned to eat in the backyard once the food was ready.

Destiney was on my mind the entire time I was working. We talked all night and kissed just as much. Actually, we may have kissed more. She went home last night, and I told her I might not be able to see her today. We'd seen each other four days in a row, and we were both bummed that today may not work. I would still try, but that depended on when I left here. I was busy helping with all the work in the garage and whatever else Mommy and Daddy needed.

One of the nights she stayed over, I can't remember which- I watched her sleep.

She's extremely beautiful. She hypnotizes me. Graceful. Epicene. Soft spoken. With the sweetest soul and the kindest spirit. I was enchanted from the start. Then I thought about how much peace she brings me just being in my presence.

Her aura is soothing. Mesmerizing. Blissful.

The way she sits while she's creating art. The way she draws you in when she's telling you something she's passionate about. The way her eyes light up when she's sharing something that interests her. Her laughter and her voice.

I study her. Every little detail. She's very sexy. So cute. Adorable. A genuine goddess.

I love her so much. Destiney is the jovial spirit we all appreciate in any space she dwells.

This morning, after my workout, I took a shower and called Destiney to say good morning. I told her that I'd be taking her out tomorrow night. I couldn't wait either. I may have been more excited than she was.

It would be our first official date.

Anyway, I was bricking up just thinking about our conversation this morning. I definitely missed her. That, and the intense chemistry we had. All the kissing she was doing to me last night. All the kissing she was letting me do to her. Had she been in my bed and not on my phone, I may have asked her... no... maybe I wouldn't have. My mind went there though. Plenty.

When I called her this morning, I was convinced Destiney felt just like I did. Her voice was extremely telling. I picked up on it immediately. When I told her I missed her, she told me she missed me too, and I took a chance calling her on it.

"You're in rare form right now."

Her light chuckle cruised through the line. "There's something about you... how can I put it? You do things to me, Mr. Walker."

"Yeah?"

"Oh yes." Her sultry voice brought my dick to life. I loved it whenever she called me Mr. Walker.

"Good things?"

"Great things."

"Yeah?"

"Yes."

"Tell me, baby."

She chuckled again. "I'm always wet when you're near me."

"Is that right?"

"Mmmhmm."

"Mmm."

She faintly groaned in my ear. "You don't even need to be near me. It's the way you handle me and the way you talk to me."

"Yeah?"

"Oh yeah. My mind starts to wander... thinking about all the things I want to do with you."

I growled. After a beat. "She wet right now?" I quizzed.

"Yes."

"Hmm. You do the same for me, beauty."

"Hmm. You hard?"

"Hard as a brick."

"Yeah?"

"Yes baby. Only for you."

"It's such a shame we can't take care if each other right now."

I growled at the thought. "Soon."

"Not soon enough. I can hardly stand it."

"I hear you baby." More comfortable silence encased us. Regarding her words, I desired to explore something different with her, and this was the opportune time. No doubt my baby was making strides. That shit was evident even right now, but she still held a level of trepidation. I was good with that when it concerned anyone else, but I didn't want her to feel she needed to hide from me. Her sex kitten was living and breathing underneath these layers, and I planned to bring her all the way out to play. "You been touching your pussy?" I spoke gently with candor. She held in a breath. "It's just me and you talking baby. Have you?"

An audible sigh escaped her. "No. I've come close but haven't in a good while."

"Hmm." Hesitating, I went back and forth the more I pondered.

Fuck it.

"Touch her for me baby."

"Okay." I heard shuffling on her end, followed by a slight moan a moment later. I listened as she continued moaning lightly. Meanwhile, I was hard as fuck thinking about how swollen her bud had to be by now. Nonetheless, I resisted the urge to take hold of my shaft.

"Destiny baby?"

"Yeah."

"I'm connecting us on FaceTime. I want to watch you while you please your pretty pussy."

"Okay." Moments later, her face filled my screen, her bright doe eyes looking back at me.

"Hey Beautiful."

"Hey." She smiled shyly and looked away.

A throaty chuckle left me. "Don't do that. I already know you're getting bashful on me."

"You had to see me **right this second**?" She quipped with a smile.

"You were just talking a big game a second ago!"

"Yeah, but you weren't watching me!" Destiney was so damn sexy. In a class all her own.

"Try not to feel shy. It's only me watching, baby." I reassured.

"I'll try."

Her sweet smile bore into my soul. "Put your phone nearby so both of your hands are free."

She propped her phone on something beside her and lay on her back, giving me a full side view.

"Remove your t-shirt and your bra."

Sitting up, she pulled her shirt over her head, tossing it aside, then reached behind her back to unclasp her bra. I licked my lips, observing the way her heavy breasts fell freely.

Damn.

"Take your panties off." I softly commanded. She lifted her hips, pulling them down, then discarding them. And returned to her back, looking over at me, naked from head to toe.

"You are so beautiful, Destiney baby," I murmured. "You know that? **So** beautiful."

"Thank you, baby." She softly purred.

I could see the gears shifting. My baby was nervous. "I know this is new for you, but I want you relaxed and comfortable. I hope I've proven that you're safe letting go when it comes to you and me."

"You have. Thank you for being patient with me."

"It's my pleasure baby."

Leaning back against the tufted headboard, I placed an arm behind my head, holding my phone in my other hand. I needed to keep both hands occupied before I got any ideas.

"Spread your legs apart and rub your clit beauty."

She closed her eyes and got to work rubbing slowly.

"Rub your breasts with the other hand."

I growled, watching her and getting harder by the second. "You keep your sexy ass just like that. Don't speed up either. Take your time, alright?"

"Yes baby." She murmured.

Fuck. I watched her intently as she pleased herself, rubbing over her nipples and grabbing and squeezing both of her breasts. I wanted to be inside of her. Bad. My dick was throbbing. It was so hard. Still, I didn't touch it. I needed to focus on the site before me. "Keep rubbing her baby." I could hear how wet she was, noting how freely her fingers slid back and forth over her slick center. I wanted to eat her pretty pussy like a peach.

She released low moans, and it drove me wild.

"Tell me how it feels."

"Feels so good." She purred.

"Yeah?"

"Yesssssssss."

"Put a finger inside."

"Mmm."

"Add one more finger." I almost blasted in my boxers watching her. "Taste yourself, baby," I instructed a moment later. I watched her suck and lick her fingers. Got damn. She sped up her strokes, and I saw her facial expressions shifting. Her moans grew in succession and volume, and I knew she was close. "Make her cum for me baby." As if on command, a beautiful sound emitted from her as she reached her peak. "That's my good girl."

She tittered, covering her face with both hands.

"Let me see you, Destiney." After a second, she rolled over on her stomach and peered into the camera with a look of satisfaction.

"Better?"

"Much better." She sighed, "But you're not. I just know you're hard as fuck right now." Her mellow voice brought me the calmness it always had.

"I'm a big boy. I can handle myself."

Her eyes widened, and I saw a subtle grin lifting at the corner of her mouth. I chortled, "Not like that."

"Go head." She purred. I almost lost my resolve right then.

"I can wait baby. I'll only release if I'm deep inside of you… as soon as you're ready for me."

"Oooh. Is that a fact?" She asked me with low lids.

"It is." I reassured.

She sighed again. "I don't like being apart."

"I know baby. Me either."

"I just want to be with you. I'll follow you anywhere you lead me."

Destiney had no idea. I planned to lead her to ecstasy and beyond.

Something else on my mind; especially after hanging up with her... sexual tension was mounting. And maybe we needed to talk about this.

Going all the way. Or not.

From the moment we reconnected there was an intense sexual energy between us and the intensity was growing very quickly.

This was not going to be an off-the-cuff, spur-of-the-moment situation we somehow stumbled into. I had way too much discipline and resolve, plus an insurmountable level of respect for her. And I loved her way too much. I like spontaneity, but this wasn't that.

I planned to only make love to the woman I married. I told her I wanted to marry her. Although I hadn't yet officially asked, she said she wanted that, too. We were on the same page there.

I wanted *her*...wanted to *give it* to her. Make the sweetest love to her.

But I wanted to do it the right way. Marry her first.

We could mess around... though that also gave me pause. But penetrating her, I wasn't so sure about. Yet.

Shit, I didn't know. I was having an internal battle.

Ultimately, I decided to hang back on broaching the subject. Should Destiney come to me, we would talk about it.

"Uncle Micah! It's time to eat!" Gabby brought me from my thoughts.

Mal laughed heartily at me, shaking his head as Gabby and I walked back toward the picnic table.

"Sorry Gabby girl. Just a little distracted."

Everybody else had already taken their seats. The food was brought out from inside just as Malachi's famous ribs came off the grill. There was barbecue chicken as well.

"Oh, we figured that!" Mal jeered playfully from his seat at the table next to Ella. Everyone laughed but I didn't mind.

Just after Daddy prayed over our dinner, Ray walked through the back gate. *How ironic.*

Mal and I shared a glance but didn't say anything.

"Hey Uncle." Ray gave Daddy a fist bump. I stole a glance and Daddy looked just as irritated as Mal and me.

Ray walked around the table speaking to Ella and then the kids.

"Momma Josette!" Ray didn't call her aunt anything. Ever since forever she's been *"momma Josette."*

"Hey baby! Nice to see you. Already eat? We're just about to have dinner."

"No, I haven't. Glad I wasn't too late." He took an empty seat and promptly began filling his plate. Generously.

I rolled my eyes and didn't bother to hide it.

"You mean you ain't still full off that lasagna?" Mal shot.

I snorted under my breath biting back a laugh.

Ray looked up at Mal in surprise, and Mal gave him a look daring him to say something. Ray probably didn't know we knew about that. I don't know why he was so surprised. We would have found out eventually.

A moment later, Ray said, "I'm glad I get to have some of your spaghetti, Ella. This seven-layer dip is good, too. Too bad you didn't fix any of your macaroni and cheese. That would have gone perfect with this barbecue."

Mal snapped, "Man... don't go putting in requests with my wife! The fuck out of here with that!"

"Malachi Walker! Do not use that language in my presence. You know better." My mom spoke sternly as she could, though she spoke delicately.

"I'm sorry Mommy." Mal said immediately.

"Mal, you know my bride doesn't like those words." Daddy kissed Mommy's cheek. "Try not to forget that whenever she's near."

Mal nodded.

"Ray." Daddy said sternly.

"Yes sir?"

Daddy took his time proceeding, "*You need your own woman*, if you call yourself wanting anything specific. In case you forgot, these two are spoken for. That includes anything in my fridge. Your name ain't on shit so be grateful for *whatever* you get. You can always take yo tail on down to McDonalds."

"Yes sir." Ray sounded like a scolded child.

I looked up and Mal was already looking at me. Stifling chuckles, we tried our best to keep a straight face.

Ray was quiet after that.

After dinner we all enjoyed some peach cobbler. I loved Mommy's peach cobbler and was lucky enough to get one of the corners today. We all loved the corners and if you did the math, there weren't enough of those to go around. Today was my lucky day though.

Mommy told us all goodnight and went to her room to lay down. I couldn't blame her. We worked hard today getting that garage cleared out. Once the kitchen was straight Mal decided they would head out so I figured I would head home too. I needed a shower and my bed. Gabe and Gabby had gone out to the car after hugging everyone and saying their goodnights. Ella, Mal, and I had congregated by the front door and Ray was still sitting on the couch looking comfortable. Guess he missed the hint.

Mal cleared his throat. "Ray, we're all about to head out. You need to be leaving too, so my parents can enjoy the rest of their evening in peace."

Without a word, Ray meandered toward the door.

"I also need you to apologize to my baby brother," Mal said expectantly.

Ray glared at Malachi with a quizzical expression.

"You don't call his woman a bitch. *Ever.*" Mal was eerily calm, talking through clenched teeth.

Ella gasped in surprise, and Ray shot me a look expressing the same. I gave him a look of indifference. I was so done with Ray and all his bullshit. I knew Mal would bring it up at some point, but I didn't expect him to do it in front of Daddy and Ella. Oh well.

Daddy cleared his throat. "Now Ray…" Turning in his direction from the comfort of his massive recliner. "I'm hearing a lot of things concerning you as of late. Things that I'm not too fond of."

Ray hung his head.

"Apologize now, and don't let me ever hear that again. You are about to have a problem with me. *I promise you don't want that.*" Daddy was calmer than Mal and that shit was scary even to me.

Ray turned to face me. "I'm sorry, Micah. I was out of line." He put his hand out. I briefly glanced at it before returning mine.

"Apology accepted." All I could do was shake my head. *Freaking Ray man.*

Mal and I exchanged glances, and I just shrugged. I did accept his apology, but whether things would change remained to be seen. I wasn't holding my breath. It was always something with him and I planned to take a page from Mal's book and finally leave Ray the fuck alone.

I walked out to the car, and Daddy followed me, stopping at the porch. Mal, Ella, and the kids had just taken off; Ray left right behind them.

"So, you've found her." It didn't sound like a question.

Looking back at Daddy, I couldn't help the grin that swept my face.

Daddy cackled. With a nod, he said, "That's my answer. That. Right there."

I couldn't help but laugh myself.

"When do you plan to introduce your sweetheart to Mommy and me?"

"A couple weeks?"

Dad's eyebrows were high on his head, coupled with a sly grin. "We'll be here."

"Indeed." I was sporting a grin of my own.

I guess Mommy decided to keep our conversation between us. That was fine.

I knew Daddy would tell her they'd meet my sweetheart the second he reached their bedroom.

That was fine with me, too.

five

MICAH

"I don't know what I was thinking, ordering potatoes." Destiney laughed while taking a drink of her spiked lavender lemonade. As she lowered her glass, she yawned real big, then rested her brilliant eyes on mine. Her eyes were glassy after her yawn yet bright and brilliant as always. I loved her eyes. "I knew they would knock me out. But I love potatoes and just couldn't turn them away."

Holding her gaze, I quipped, "You ready to get out of here or what?"

"Oh no! I'm loving this band way too much."

I was so pleased she was having such a good time. I knew this was an excellent choice for our first date. "Close your eyes for a few."

She moved closer, resting her head on my shoulder. I put my arm around her, pulling her even closer to me. After settling, she said, "I hope you know you're stuck with me."

"I want to be stuck."

"Well, that's good. I love it here. With you. I'm never leaving."

"You're so cute, baby," I told her, kissing her forehead.

We'd been having an amazing time together at *HomeGrownSol*, enjoying the vibe and grooving with the band, Smoke. This band was bad. My boy Solomon was on the Saxophone doing his thing. He was incredibly talented on the

Sax, having played since middle school, I believe. I was so glad we got to hear them tonight. We had great seats, too. Sol came by to say hey earlier, and we spoke briefly. I took the opportunity to introduce him and Destiney as well.

We had dinner when we first arrived, and Destiney raved over their rosemary balsamic baby potatoes and Brussels sprouts. It smelled amazing, and I knew it tasted just as delicious as it looked. Their entire menu was a hit. Anything you ordered would exceed your taste buds. There were quite a few vegetarian options for Destiney, too.

The band was on a break, and we'd been chatting for the past fifteen minutes with an older couple sitting beside us. I'd say around my parents' age.

"Alright, young man. Enjoy yourselves, and you get your lady home safely, " the older gentleman said, tipping his hat toward me. They'd decided to call it a night but said they thoroughly enjoyed themselves. Like Destiney, this was their first time at *HomeGrownSol*.

"Yes sir. You two get home safely as well."

"Actually, Micah, I'm going to use the ladies before I get comfy. If our waiter returns, please ask for more water?" Destiney asked, standing.

I stood with her. "Sure thing baby."

She smiled sweetly at me. "Thank you."

Destiney looked so lovely tonight. Stunning.

She wore a black halter dress; the top of her back was open. I loved that detail. Her dress was perfect for this setting. Long, and sleek, about to her ankles with thigh-high slits on either side. Her thick thighs would peek out with each step she took. Very sexy. Had me licking my chops.

I was beginning to grow obsessed with her thick ass thighs.

She returned as the band picked up again, and I stood to greet her.

"You good Destiney baby?"

"I'm all good baby." She settled beside me again, grabbing my hand and threading our fingers. I kissed her forehead again, sighing in contentment.

"For this last set, we're going to slow it down for all the lovebirds in the house tonight." Cheers and applause erupted all over the place. "Thanks for hanging with us here at Home Grown Soul and always showing Smoke so much love," the lead singer said into the microphone. Various couples began making their way to the dance floor. The band played a few great ones: Babyface, Kem, and D'Angelo. But when the band started playing a cover of *Slow Wine*, I *had* to get closer to her. I kissed the top of her head again. "Dance with me, beautiful."

She peered up at me, eyes wide. "I'm not much of a dancer, Micah. I have two left feet."

I chuckled. "Slow dancing is easy. Just hold on to me, and I'll handle the rest."

She hesitated for a moment with a look of doubt. "I'd only embarrass you."

"You could never embarrass me, baby. You trust me, right?"

"Yes."

"Then you have nothing to worry about. Come on." I led her to the dance floor, which wasn't too crowded. Just a few couples enjoying themselves. I embraced her, and we swayed together, quickly falling into a natural rhythm like we'd done this many times before. I held her close to me, leading us in a gentle glide. She was doing well and seemed like a natural at this. I'd be sure to let her know that later. I knew telling her right now wasn't best. I didn't want her to get bashful on me.

I closed my eyes, and I wondered if her eyes were closed, too. I held her even closer and got lost in her reverie. I deeply inhaled her scent, which I'd grown to love. Destiney felt so right in my arms. Everything about this felt so right. It had been such a long time coming. And the lead was killing it, just like D'wayne Wiggins. The band was grooving, and I loved this song.

> *Slow wine gotta keep it nice and slow*
> *Slow wine gotta use your body and soul*
>
> *Slow wine, so fine if I can wine you in my arms*
> *From left to right slow wine*
>
> *Slow wine, so fine hey girl all my body's yours*
> *…now it would be, now it could be, so nice*
> *If we could…*

In my interpretation, the lyrics were an ode to sensuality. They spoke to letting the mood of slow music take control of your body and moving and feeling whatever came naturally to you. But most of all, they spoke to embracing intimate moments, existing in them, and focusing on deep emotional connections.

As I held Destiney close to me and slow-wined with her, I got to thinking that I've heard this song millions of times. I played it repeatedly, but this hit differently with Destiney in my arms.

> *'Cuz I've finally built up the nerve to just slow wine with you…*

But slow plus a four-letter word is the one thing on my mind
Slow wine, so fine if I can wine you in my arms
Yeah, just let your body flow

"You enjoying yourself, baby?"

"I am. Thank you for bringing me here, Micah."

"It's my pleasure. Thank you for joining me."

It was a sultry song, but it wasn't about sex. Yet and still, Destiney turned me on so much, and the mood was set just right. I knew there was no way I could hide the bulge in my pants. His ass was showing out, growing by the second. I tried not to focus on that too much as we swayed. I heard a slight moan, and in my mind, that was confirmation she felt the brick in my pants.

We danced to the next song, after which I led us back to our seats.

We'd been sitting for a short while when she asked, "Can we go home, baby?" Her question held a sultry tone.

I looked at her as she peered at me through low lids. It was then that it dawned on me that her question had a double meaning.

It was difficult not to go there. This place was thick with lust, heat, and passion. There was dry humping going on all over the dance floor. I'm willing to bet most of these folks were gone get some tonight. No doubt in my mind. The lights were dim, candles were lit, the music was right, and drinks were flowing.

"Yeah, we can do that."

She gave me a smile, blinking slowly. She was so fucking beautiful. Irresistible. Best of all, *she was mine*.

I wasn't sure what she wanted to do once we got back to the house, but the way I was feeling right now, I was willing to give her whatever she wanted from me. I'd follow her lead; all she had to do was say it.

We both stood to leave, and I could have nutted in my drawers right then. My shit was hard as hell and growing in anticipation. Before I could even take a step, I had to adjust myself. The strain against my zipper was intense. My mind wandering. Especially if Destiney was telling me what I thought she was telling me.

six

DESTINEY

I caressed Micah's fingers as we cruised through downtown Sacramento, headed back to his place.

I was floating.

I could not believe I had been slow dancing on a dance floor. I *never* did that. Daijah and India would get a kick out of this when I told them.

All I know is, Micah had me wide open for him, ready to receive whatever the hell he wanted to give me.

When Micah told me he would be taking me out, I was giddy with excitement.

He asked me to spend the night, so I packed a bag and headed over. Then I showered and got ready for our date at his place. He was ready before me and waited for me downstairs.

When I came down, he marveled at me. At my dress. How nice I smelled.

Then he pulled out a gift bag with a signature bright blue box inside. My eyes grew wide. I told him I felt bad because I didn't have a gift for him, but he insisted it was no big deal.

I opened the box, and it was a beautiful Tiffany Bracelet—sterling silver links with a heart tag. I love it. It's so cute. I wore it on our date, and I planned to wear it all the time.

And then we go out, and Micah was so… he's just a gentleman. Well beyond the things like opening my car door and pulling out my chair. I'm talking all *new* stuff. New for *me*.

He asked me to sit next to him instead of across from him. He confirmed what I wanted and ordered for me. Micah stood when I left the table and stood again when I returned. It's the little things. They defy everything, in my opinion. Little things are in the everyday. He held my hand the entire time or had his hand resting on my thigh. He kissed my forehead about a million times. I love his forehead kisses.

I loved HomeGrownSol. The food was so good, and the vibe was grown and sexy. The band was top-tier. I met his friend, Solomon, from high school. He was cool and so talented at the saxophone.

Meanwhile, my mind was gone in the gutter, and my panties were soaked. That sexy ass song we danced to was my undoing. I don't know if I'd ever heard it before. If I had, I wasn't paying attention. I loved the lyrics; they were beautiful and flowed like poetry. I knew that *Smoke* was a cover band, and they did a fantastic job, but I *had* to hear the original. I only remembered a few words, so I pulled out my phone and went to Google to search for *slow wine song*.

I gasped. *Tony! Toni! Tone!*

I should have known. I added it to my playlist immediately.

"I like that song too."

I looked over at Micah, who had an adorable grin.

"Same. Just added it to my playlist."

"Was that your first time hearing it?"

"You know… I can't say. I feel like I'd remember, so I think so."

"You spend more time at my house, you'd have heard it eventually."

"You're a fan?"

"You kidding me? They're one of the best to ever do it."

I nodded in agreement. "Ever seen them live?"

"Yeah. Mal took me to see them at Yoshi's in Oakland for my thirtieth birthday."

My eyes grew in surprise. Yoshi's was a well-known jazz club and restaurant right on the waterfront of Oakland. It was right in the heart of an entertainment district called Jack London Square. The club couldn't have had more than about three hundred seats. I could imagine it was a task snagging tickets to see them. "Wow. That must have been a great show."

"It was. I never enjoyed those big arenas, but I enjoy smaller venues. It seems so much more intimate and personal. It was wild, too, because they only did one show, and it sold out within a couple of hours or something ridiculous like that. Mal earned big brother of the year for getting us those tickets."

I laughed, "Absolutely. I know they usually do something special for their hometown whenever they have a show in Oakland. Whoever got a seat that night will never forget it."

"Yup. We had a great time and made great memories."

We pulled into his driveway and chilled after he killed the engine.

It had been a beautiful day earlier, and the evening was turning out to be just as lovely. The sunroof was still open, and I sat back content. I had such a great time tonight with

Micah. I looked at our hands still intertwined, then to my left to find him smiling.

"What?"

"Nothing. Just admiring you."

"Aww." I smiled back, squirming just a little under his gaze. "So, you're still into me?" I asked, trying to talk myself through my jitters.

"*Hell yeah*, I am."

He lifted our hands and kissed the back of mine. Leaned over to kiss me on the cheek and gently turned my chin, kissing my forehead. I leaned in closer, meeting him halfway as our lips connected. We pecked sweetly on the lips a few times, and I was sure he heard the light moan escape me. After our lips parted, I leaned forward, connecting our foreheads.

"Baby?" I crooned just over a whisper.

"Yes?"

"Can we do stuff?" My embarrassment was stifled by a mischievous grin. I had a tiny bit of liquid courage from my spiked lavender lemonade, which was delicious, by the way.

I could feel the furrow of his eyebrows. "Stuff?"

"Yeah. *Grown folk stuff*." I returned

"You're so damn cute." He released a boisterous chuckle. "Grown folk stuff huh?"

"Mmmhmm..." Sitting back, I gave him a bashful smile.

"So. Tell me. What does one do exactly when they're engaging in grown folk stuff?"

My hand was back in his. "Things with their mouths?" It came out as a question, though I didn't mean for it to.

Micah nodded. So, I continued, "I want to do more than kiss you. I want you to do more things to me. But I'm not the most experienced."

Micah reassured me, peppering kisses into my neck. I know that's what he was doing. Murmuring, "We can absolutely do things with our mouths, sexy girl." He held my face in his hands. I felt his smile against my neck. "I'll learn from you, and you'll learn from me. No experience necessary." Still kissing my neck and gently sucking there too. "That cool with you?"

"Yes."

"Indeed. Shall we go inside?"

"We shall."

seven

DESTINEY

"Can I taste you, beautiful?" Micah kissed me softly, trailing down my chest, kissing each nipple and down to my navel. Lingering there, he rubbed his thumb over my heated center from the outside. My panties were done for. I was sure he'd have to peel them off me.

We entered the house through the garage, and Micah took my hand, leading me up the stairs and to his bedroom. His home was dark, with the faint glow of a few plug-in night lights along his hallway.

Now we were in his expansive bedroom in his huge bed. The room was semi-dark; he had a lamp on at the lowest setting. I was laying on my back with Micah settled between my legs. We kissed for such a long time; our tongues were always happy being with one another. I could seriously kiss this man for hours. Vivid thoughts occupied my mind as he lifted again, hovering his frame over me, kissing my neck and my chin. The sounds of smacking and light moans were the only things piercing the darkness. I was incredibly anxious when he first brought me into his bedroom, but making out like we had was a great way to calm my nerves. Micah spoke softly in my ear, "Destiney baby." He pressed, patiently awaiting confirmation.

I had five incisions on my abdomen. They were quite visible, but my doctor said they would fade in time.

Honestly though, I'm most insecure about my vagina. It was the source of all my issues at one point. Having Micah down there between my legs was tripping me out. I told him about my insecurities once we made it to his bedroom, and he got me out of my dress. I told him that I was feeling self-conscious.

In response, he kissed me all over my body, from head to toe. They were open kisses—my favorite kind—the ones that left light moisture in their wake. He spent the most time kissing my stomach, gently scattering kisses all over it, his strong hands securing me around my waist, humming softly as he did it.

"Your body is beautiful, Destiney baby."

"Thank you love."

"I want you to always know that. Whenever you feel insecure, remember how much I adore this temple."

I smiled as I peered down at him.

He kissed each of my scars. "These are a sign of your strength and resilience. And I'm so proud of you, sweetheart."

Damn.

"Micah."

"Yes baby?"

"I want you." I could hardly wait anymore. I moaned as I reached for him. "Can I touch it- can I touch *you*?" I wanted to feel him. Please him. Had to. Even though he balanced his weight while on top of me, I felt his erection brush against me a few times.

"Mmm. I want you too. And you never have to ask. But you know me better than that..." He resumed kissing me, descending lower. "Ladies first." More kisses. "So, can I taste you now?"

I'd never felt a man's mouth on my lower lips before. But I'd fantasized plenty.

Lately especially. My desire for Micah saturated my thoughts.

I wanted him.

And I wanted him to have me.

"Yes."

"Yes, what baby?"

"That's alright with me." I knew he wanted to make sure I was comfortable, but all this talking took me out of the zone. I'd finally gotten to where I was ready for the taking. But now, my thoughts were in overdrive again, and I was losing the battle of calming my nerves. I pulled at his arms, gesturing him up to kiss his lips again, keenly aware this was the best remedy. He understood, taking my bottom lip into his mouth tugging gently.

Micah broke our kiss to lift his shirt over his head. When he got me out of my dress right before he laid me on the bed, he removed my bra too. I was still wearing my black lace panties. Within seconds, we were connected again, skin to skin. Now his large hands ventured upward, cupping my breasts. I had more than a handful, but they fit perfectly in Micah's massive hands. I loved how warm his hands felt. The gentle callous of his palms, his thumbs teasing my nipples into stiff peaks. His periodic murmur articulating his delight. He lowered himself again, caressing me all over, his large hands kneading my skin like a skilled masseuse. Moving down to my stomach, kissing and caressing, then my inner and outer thighs. Repeating the same.

Shit. His touch, his lips. It was intoxicating.

Settled between my legs again he deeply inheld then kissed my pussy from the outside. He growled, and I noticed he did that when he enjoyed something. That shit was hot. I propped myself up on my elbows, watching as he moved in front of me, coming to a rest on his hunches.

"Lift up for me, beautiful." I did as I was told. Unhurried, Micah pulled my panties off, then leisurely parted my legs, surveying with low lids. He carefully spread my legs further, and I was promptly overcome with a sense of self-consciousness. Fully aware he was now facing *her*.

Completely unguarded.

"Hmm." Micah moved closer, emitting a gruff, animalistic lumber. Just as he descended, my nerves got the better of me, and I jolted upward, inching back on the bed and out of his grasp.

I could see that his expression immediately shifted from perplexity to apprehension. I knew he could see the brief expression of apprehension on mine. "Am I moving too fast?" When I said nothing, he asked, "Should I stop?" His tone even and definite. There was comfort there too.

"No, no, not at all." I sighed, flustered with myself.

He regarded me, composed, awaiting an explanation.

"I'm just wondering... is it okay?" I sat up straighter, peering directly at him. He was still back on his hunches. "Am I okay... my area..." I gestured. "Is it what you expected?" Shit. I was rambling now. This was the most intimate thing I had ever done, and I was in my head. Bad. I felt vulnerable, and I wasn't sure how to process it.

Great way to kill the mood.

Micah held my eyes with those warm brown orbs of his. His voice was tranquil and soothing when he asked me, "Have you been pleased this way before?"

I was speechless and certain he could sense my anxiety. I didn't feel an ounce of judgement but certainly abashed by my inexperience.

"Tell me."

"No. Never." I sighed audibly. "I feel so silly. My inexperience is always in the way. I feel like an inexperienced teen. This is weird, and I am too damn old to feel this way." Micah's eyes were trained on me, and in this moment, they were the kindest eyes I'd ever seen. So, I continued, "With my condition, there was so much I couldn't let happen. No one has seen me down there. *Ever.* I worry about it, and I'm self-cautious." Embarrassed as *hell*, I looked away.

Micah waited a beat. Then, "Destiney."

"Yes?" I found his eyes peering back at me.

"I need you to always tell me how you're feeling and what you need. Don't be shy with that. Please. *Don't ever be shy with that shit.* Whatever you're feeling, know that they're totally valid feelings, and you aren't *weird* for having them."

I silently nodded.

"Aside from when you're self-pleasing, have you had an orgasm before?" I knew Micah wasn't judging me. But... I was... *mortified.* And I felt so pathetic.

"Tell me." He reassured, soft yet firm.

I was silent. Unable to form the words. "I'm embarrassed," I revealed.

"Don't be embarrassed, beautiful."

I said nothing.

"So, you said you felt a safe space with us. Am I right, sweetheart?"

"You're right."

"It's only you talking to me. I would never ask you a question, I wouldn't be open to sharing with you myself. And every single thing we discuss will remain between us."

I sighed, nodding my understanding. "No. I haven't," I returned simply.

Nodding, Micah said, "I'll change that."

My eyes grew wide.

"Being intimate with you is a privilege. And a man doesn't leave his woman unsatisfied."

"You always know what to say, don't you?" I chuckled leisurely, suddenly feeling immensely comfortable. "You have it all figured out, Micah."

"Just being honest, sweetheart."

Micah gently grabbed my chin, caressing it with his thumb, "All I want to do is please you Destiny baby. But if you need more time, please say so."

"I don't need more time."

"Indeed. If at any point you want to stop, you tell me. We can always try this again." He grabbed my hands and interlocked our fingers. "Promise you'll tell me, sweetheart."

"I promise."

Micah grabbed his cell phone from the side table, and as soon I heard the unmistakable melody of the angelic songstress, I recognized the song immediately. "Hold on", The Internet. The music was at the perfect volume, setting the mood just right. It was loud enough for us to hear it if we were completely quiet, so low that I knew the sounds would eventually blend into the background.

This song was made for this moment, and I was absolutely Micah's for the taking. My anxious ass was going to lay my head on this pillow and relax.

Micah was on this same type of time. "Try your best to relax for me. I'll take care of you, baby." He settled on his knees again, carefully spreading my legs. And I did as I was told, tensing up again in anticipation but I instantly mellowed when Micah said, "Mmm...such a pretty pussy Destiney baby."

His voice was smooth and laced with comfort. I felt his warm breath. I heard him inhale deeply, and when he connected us, I felt the wetness and warmth of his tongue. I stifled a moan, but he heard me loud and clear.

"How's that feeling, baby?" He licked my folds as I slowly rocked my hips.

"It feels good." I managed.

"Hmm. You are *delicious* baby." He continued to feast on my pussy and still trepidatious, I fought the urge to express my pleasure. I was failing at that; whimpers and erratic breaths escaped me anyway. And it was no wonder. I was on a cloud high above any place I had ever gone. I had no point of reference, but it seemed Micah was very, *very* good at this. My breathing and rocking increased, and eventually, I arched off the bed as he increased the speed of his tongue.

Micah took his sweet time kissing my pussy with his tongue like she was kissing him right back. Fuck. It felt incredible.

"Does it feel good to you, baby?" He murmured against my pussy.

"Oh yes." I purred.

"Mmm. Don't be shy. Let me know baby." Micah sucked and licked.

Flicked and slurped.

Sucked and licked some more and kept going. Flicking and slurping.

Goodness, his tongue game was vicious. I was in euphoria, releasing a drawn-out moan.

"There's my good girl." He continued feasting. As if he was famished. Hell, I clearly had been. "Mmmhmm…" He slowly pressed a finger into me. "Damn. You are *so* wet baby."

Micah was right. I was embarrassingly wet. Between my moans, his grunts, growls, and wet sounds from below that music had *been* drowned out. His playlist was going but we couldn't even hear the music anymore, we were making our music now.

And another thing; I *loved* how he talked to me while he was eating. That shit was sexy as hell. Micah had been strumming me like a guitar. His finger felt amazing stroking me. Gently he rubbed his thumb over my clit too. That shit was… fuck.

His tongue, his fingers, his kisses, moans, murmurs.

I felt a sensation. My legs began twitching. "Micah." I managed. My voice was thick with pleasure.

"Yes baby."

Moaning, I repeated his name.

"You're ready to come for me." He stated between sucks and licks and kisses. "Go head baby. Give it to me." Talking me through it, Micah's deep register sent me crashing over the edge. As if on cue, I released, feeling the most intense orgasm I'd ever had. A wave of ecstasy taking over my entire body and I moaned in satisfaction.

"Mmmhmm. There you go, my sexy girl. Give me what I want. I got you." *Fuck.* I was in pure bliss. Everything felt so good.

As I came down, Micah gently licked a few more times. Aware. Methodical and calculated. *Gentle.* Much gentler than he had been. I didn't even need to tell him I was extra sensitive there now.

Micah ate the entire fuck out of my pussy.

He slowly moved up the bed, and I felt his hardness as he brushed me.

Embarrassed to face him now, I turned the other way, burying my face in a pillow. "Oh my gosh."

He chuckled, moving closer. "Look at me baby."

I hesitated.

"Don't be embarrassed," he stroked my shoulder. "Give me your eyes."

Finally turning to face him, he wrapped me in his arms, kissed my nose and lips, and lingered there. I could smell my essence on his lips. I closed my eyes and heard him whisper, "Destiney, baby, you turn me on so much."

"Really?" Still shy but so relieved hearing those words.

He kissed my forehead, "Oh yes, sweetheart. *So much.* You taste amazing. Just as amazing as I thought you would."

"You *felt* amazing," I revealed. "No way I would have expected *that*." I cuddled closer. "Your tongue… where the hell did you learn tricks like that?" Seriously. His firm tongue felt amazing, better than any battery-operated toy.

Micah laughed. I felt him shrug against me. "Can't say. Just good like that. You have a wicked tongue too. Since we've been kissing, I've learned a few things from you."

I giggled as a memory came to mind. "Daijah and I read in a magazine; I think *Cosmo Girl*- we were teenagers- that if you unwrap a Starburst in your mouth, it will improve your French kissing skills." I cracked up. "We'd buy Starburst specifically for that purpose. I don't even want to admit how many we unwrapped."

Micah cackled too. "For real?"

"Yep. I'd say it worked. You have to unwrap it with your mouth only. So basically, just using your tongue. We got pretty quick. Could do it in just a few seconds."

He released a light titter sarcastically saying, "It's *all* making sense now."

"Hey, don't judge me! We were teenagers." I playfully nudged him with my left shoulder.

"No judgment here baby. You like it I love it."

***

I stirred, restless and unable to find sleep. I felt Micah's arm tighten around me. He moved closer and I felt his hardness poking against my back.

We stayed up talking for a while, and then I eventually dozed off. Now I was up again and couldn't fall back asleep. It had to be at least three a.m.

I knew exactly why.

"You okay?" Micah inquired his deep voice, nocturnal and husky. We were both pretty light sleepers.

"Yes baby."

I was more than okay.

Micah had been so gentle with my heart, my feelings. My body.

He'd left the bed to get a warm towel to clean me up. We'd made a mess. I didn't have to move. Eventually I did, because I needed to pee. But he took such care, probably more than I would have.

Earlier when I alluded to touching him, he evaded that. Albeit with a persuasive distraction. *Well played Micah*. But I wanted to. Still.

I desired so much to please him too. It had been on my mind since we left HomeGrownSol.

To please him.

And right at this very moment, Micah wasn't playing fair, pressing his hard dick into me.

I wanted his dick. At minimum, I *finally* wanted to hold it. Feel it... maybe even...

Anyway, there was only one way to quench my thirst. I wanted to please my man. But I also wanted to satisfy this urge.

Fulfill desire.

Return the favor.

We were under his blanket. And it was completely dark in his bedroom. I honestly didn't know if- wasn't sure I was feeling extra bold because of that. Or if I was driven by desire. Still high off the satisfying orgasm he gave me. My clit was still tingling.

Who knows and who the hell cares.

Now it was his turn.

I turned, facing him, and without warning, I moved my hand down and into the front of his basketball shorts. Gently taking hold of *him*.

He was velvety smooth. Thick. Long. And *heavy*. I could feel prominent veins as I slowly stroked him, getting acquainted.

"Destiney baby..." Micah groaned. His voice thick with desire. He shifted his body just a little and I heard another deep moan. I maintained my soft grip and continued stroking as he came alive in my hand. Growing harder than he had been just seconds before.

Yeah. I kept going. And so did he. Growing harder and moaning louder. *Sexy*. I stroked his dick for a good while and my man liked that.

I knew it was time so I moved into positioned and in one swift motion, pulled him into my mouth before he could react. I couldn't take much, but I gripped him with both hands as I began sucking slowly.

I was glad the room was dark. I'd never done this before and may have been too self-cautious otherwise.

He seemed to like it. His deep glutaral moans left me no doubt this felt good to him. Micah moved slightly again shifting from his side, now laying flat on his back.

Feeling even bolder, I gradually straddled him, never removing him from my mouth.

I took as much of him into my mouth as I could, using both hands I gently twisted and squeezed, maintaining a moderate tempo. I felt him lifting his hips beneath me. I placed both hands on the bed on either side of him.

He had this under control.

"Mmm." Micah sounded pleased and that's what I wanted. His moans of pleasure drove me wild. I moaned too as he moved faster, his hard dick gliding in and out with a mixture of my saliva and his precum. Resisting the urge, I kept my hands planted at his sides. A deep rumble escaped him as he moaned in satisfaction.

I liked that.

"Yeah... suck your dick baby girl." *This dick was mine alright.* I moaned in agreement. "I hear you beautiful. You enjoying yourself?"

"Mmmhmm."

Yeah. He kept going.

"Baby..." he growled fucking my mouth with deliberate strokes all the while moaning with pleasure.

"Hmm?" My sloppy mouth dripping each time he lifted his hips.

His moans growing louder, he gently placed his hands on the sides of my face tugging softly.

"Baby…" he sounded pressed. His hard dick sliding in and out of my slick mouth. "Destiney…I'm bout to cum in a minute. You must move baby." His voice was laced with pleasure, and it was incredibly sexy. I was so turned on; my pussy getting wetter by the second. I brought my mouth as close to him as I could, now feeling him hit the back of my throat, saliva dripping down his shaft, and my chin.

"Fuck. Destiney, I'm close. Where you want it baby?" His voice was husky and resolute. "Where?" He urged.

I broke away for just a second, "You know where love."

"Baby… you sure."

I wasn't going anywhere. I wanted all of him.

He emitted a low pleasure-filled rumble, which had to be the most beautiful sound I'd ever heard come from a man.

Milliseconds later I felt his warm squirts at the back of my throat.

I swallowed every drop.

I was just as satisfied as he was and so pleased I could please him. He grabbed me with both arms as I climbed back to my spot beside him.

"Come here beautiful." Micah kissed me with incredible fervor.

I lay on his chest as he asked. "I take it you couldn't sleep?" Content laced his voice.

"Nope. Way too distracted."

eight

DESTINEY

The mural at the Elementary School in Downtown Sacramento was completed. It looked amazing. The theme was growth, and it came together so nicely. We painted flowers, butterflies, vines, and trees. The star of the show was a big vibrant sun with various shades of yellows, oranges, whites and reds. That was my favorite part of the mural; it was front and center, lively and colorful. The sun is lifegiving and went perfectly with the growth theme. We added a few quotes from some of the students. I loved the way everything came together. Of course, it was hard to say goodbye to everyone at the end of the project. We'd often become like a family. It's easy to do. Spending hours together day after day, working toward a common goal.

So, this week I started a new project, a gig in Roseville, California. About a forty-five-minute drive from Land Park where I lived.

This was a different clientele. Not a community effort.

A brand-new state-of-the-art childcare center had been built. Privately owned. In an upscale neighborhood. The proud owner, a *privileged* white woman, wanted an ocean theme. The rooms inside would have mural art with exotic fish, bubbles, some submarines, and scuba divers. You get the idea.

This project would take a while.

Fortunately, *and* unfortunately. It was a large childcare facility, twenty-five hundred square feet. The team of artists was much smaller than I would have suggested for a facility this size, but I wasn't the Artistic Director. I was just here to do my thing with a paintbrush.

Anyway, the owner was already on my nerves, and this was only like day number three. She was constantly coming in and interrupting us. Asking us to redo an entire sketch because *"it doesn't quite fit what she had in mind."* The thing is, the Artistic Director will run the designs by the client first. Once it's approved and to their liking, we sketch them out on the wall and then paint them. The sketch on the wall is more than ten times the size of a draft we'd show her for review. It sounds like she shouldn't have approved the sketches. It wasn't as simple as just erasing it and starting over. That would only delay the project.

I can't work like this. Respectfully, I don't have to.

If *Becky* wouldn't let us do our thing, *I'm* not the artist for her.

When I complained to India, she reminded me that it would pay handsomely. And to *get the bag*. That's to be expected with these private clients. But... I didn't revel in working with private clients. Especially these privileged ones. Not even a little bit. I took on private clients *sparingly*.

This constant over-the-shoulder micro-shit is precisely why.

And I'm not sorry.

I almost passed on this gig when I was contacted and asked to join the team. I saw the writing on the wall. The promise of a nice check is what sold me, especially since my past couple of gigs were community projects on much smaller budgets. Meaning smaller payouts.

And India had to pass on it. She couldn't commit to a gig outside city limits for an extended period. Not right now. Her parents took priority, and they needed her nearby. I was so bummed about that. I loved working with her.

India and I planned to pick up a three-day project for fun doing sidewalk art for *Chalk it up! Sacramento*. I couldn't wait. It's an art and music festival, Labor Day weekend, right around the corner. *Chalk it up! Sacramento* happens every year, celebrating local artists and the artistic community. It's been a Sacramento tradition for more than thirty years. I've participated a few times over the years. It's so much fun. Artists get three days to create artwork on two sidewalk squares, and then, during the festival, people walk around the park's perimeter to see the art. I've seen some incredible work. Artists of all levels are encouraged to apply. It's even open to kids. You only have to be in seventh grade to enter. You can join for free, and premium chalk is provided to the artists to use to their heart's content. It's always held at Fremont Park in Midtown, a prime location for an event such as this. There's plenty of shade, thanks to the mature oak trees. There's usually a live band, food trucks, vendors, and a kids' area for families.

I left the childcare center, stopped for gas, and hit the road. The commute was a pain in the ass too. Anyway, the gas station was in a bustling plaza, so I had to wait a few minutes. I looked up and swore I saw a man come out of the gas station resembling my dad.

That couldn't be him.

He was with a woman.

And they looked pretty familiar. I saw his hand at the small of her back.

There was no way that was my dad. He didn't date.

69

So many of our friends who had single moms inquired about him over the years. It never failed. Dad is handsome. Kind. Turning fifty-three at the end of this year. And he looked great for his age. I was never surprised that the moms on our sports teams always asked about my dad. Women at the church. Every damn where we went.

The more I looked, the more he looked like my dad.

It *was* my dad.

I saw them approach his car. After he opened the passenger's side, he climbed into the driver's seat.

My chin hit the floor, and I felt a dagger piercing straight through my heart. I frantically dialed Daijah, my heart pounding in my chest. It rang three times before she finally answered.

"Day!" I yelled before she could even offer me a greeting.

"Hey Des- you, okay?"

"Dad! I saw him coming out of the gas station with a woman! They were close and holding hands! I mean, *who the hell is she?* And what the hell is going on? He never mentioned he was dating! How can he do that behind our backs?" There was silence on the other end. I pulled my phone away from my ear to make sure the call was still connected. It was. "You there Day?"

"Yeah." She was oddly calm, and that's when it clicked. *Oh, ain't this some shit.* "You knew."

"Yes. Dad told me he'd been seeing someone. I also met her briefly when I went by the house to pick up some mail he had for me. She's a nice lady and sweet. They seem to like each other."

"Wow! So, you knew and didn't tell me? I would have told you immediately!" I said through tears. At this point, I felt betrayed by both of them.

"I couldn't say anything Des. Dad swore me to secrecy. He wanted to tell you himself."

"Oh please! Like that shit *ever* mattered. We've always told each other everything Day." My eyes were full despite the heavy crocodile tears falling one after the other.

"I know Des. I'm sorry."

The line was quiet.

"Don't cry Des."

"Too late for that," I said through a forced chuckle, though wasn't shit funny. "Dad still hasn't told me, yet he introduced *you* to the woman. How is that supposed to make me feel?"

"It seems that way, but it could have been either of us. In his defense, I went by the house a day earlier than I said I would. He wasn't expecting me."

Daijah had a point. We both had keys to the house and came and went as we pleased. Dad had a predictable schedule, and we knew his comings and goings. We didn't even have to call first, but most times, we did anyway. I guess all that would change now that he was entertaining a woman.

I wonder if they were…never mind.

"Des, please don't take this the wrong way…"

"I'm listening."

"Knowing Dad, he's been a mess over having this talk with us. *With you especially.*"

"With me? Why?"

"Come on Des. You know you're Daddy's girl."

"You are too!"

Daijah laughed. "Not like *you*. You two have such a sweet bond."

I smiled and got emotional all over again.

"Yeah. I guess we do."

71

We had a few beats of silence, and I knew she was thinking of Mom.

"You had something special with Mom. I figured if either of us, he may have been a little more anxious to share this with you."

"Maybe so."

Silence filled the line again.

"I want him to be happy, Des. You know? He's a great man. So selfless. He gave us so much of himself. Aside from losing mom, we never wanted for anything." Daijah sounded emotional now too.

"Yeah. I want him to be happy too. I guess I didn't think the day would come when we'd have to share him with another woman. It never seemed like a concern of his."

"Maybe it wasn't. But we've got men now. Great men, who will move heaven and earth for us. I think he feels like he can focus on himself again."

I nodded. "Yeah."

After a few seconds, Daijah said, "Call Dad now."

I let out a boisterous chuckle. Daijah knew me well because that's exactly what I planned to do as soon as I hung up with her.

***

"Hey Dad!" I waited for him to lift the garage door for me. His two-car garage wasn't for parking cars. He had a pretty cool setup in here. A flat-screen mounted to the wall, a pool table, and two vintage arcade game machines, *Pac-Man* and *Street Fighter*. Off to the side was a table that sat six people.

"Hey Princess." He kissed my forehead as we embraced. When I felt his arms loosen around me, I held on tighter, burying my face into his chest. Before I knew it, the waterworks began, and I didn't bother trying to control my shaking or sobbing.

I didn't need to. This was always a safe space.

When we first lost Mom, the grief was as unforgiving as it was unpredictable. Daijah and I had taken the loss so hard and had cried so much. The crying only seemed to stop once we finally had no tears left.

But that took years.

Years of patience with ourselves and years of grief counseling and therapy.

Dad held me in his strong arms, rubbing my back as I cried. He'd always done that since Daijah and I were little, and I swore that always made everything better.

When I finally gathered my bearings, I stepped away, wiping my tears.

"Has something happened, princess?" His voice was laced with urgency, and I felt terrible because he was always the fixer. I knew he was on high alert now.

I shook my head. "No. But... can we sit down? I want to talk to you."

"Of course we can." Dad pulled a chair out for me and pushed me in. He consistently demonstrated exactly what a gentleman looked like for Daijah and me. Grandiose things, the little things, and everything in between. "Is there time for tea?" Dad asked, and I immediately smiled real big.

Over the years, we have had many talks over tea, sometimes over two or three cups. My love for tea was all thanks to Dad. He was a tea enthusiast who exposed me to the infinite world of many delicious and vibrant teas. He always says there's beauty, history, and culture behind each cup of tea.

"Yes! That's *always* a yes."

He turned on the electric kettle he kept in the garage, then reached overhead, pulling down his stash of options. "What are you feeling like princess?"

"Surprise me. You have so many that it would take me too long to decide." He had an elaborate variety and constantly added tea bags, loose-leaf mixtures, and whole tea leaves.

He chuckled lightly. "Alright."

After gently placing my favorite mug in front of me, he joined me at the table. "I think you'll enjoy this one. May become your new favorite." I looked up as he winked at me.

I cracked a grin. "You always say that."

Dad chuckled again. "Taste a sip of mine, too." He offered after he steeped and stirred in a few cubes of sugar. I took in the steaming aroma. It was *lovely*.

I used my spoon to ladle out a sample. "Oh my! I love this one! Lavender… and peppermint." It was heavy with spice, my favorite notes for warm tea.

He nodded. "Very good." I'd been getting better at identifying notes in teas. My dad is an expert at it. He told me we mainly taste through smell. Professional tea tasters smell the dry leaves before and after steeping.

I took a sip of his, "Yes. *I love that one! Chamomile?*"

"Yep. Chamomile, rose petals, and white sage. Wait till you try that one iced. Even better."

"I bet!"

"Alright princess. What was that about earlier? Is everything, everything?"

I stirred my tea as I nodded slowly. "Yes. Everything is everything. Just had a moment, I guess."

Dad nodded in understanding. He was one of the most understanding people I knew, and I loved that so much about him. Over the years, Daijah and I have always been able to come to him *about anything and everything.* If he didn't know the answer, he'd say so and promise to help us figure it out.

That was tricky sometimes because there were things he may not have understood as a man. Regardless, he never made us feel bad. Or weird.

We always had an open relationship. He was our human diary, and we shared so much with him. It was a fact that Daijah and I talked with Dad about things many girls wouldn't typically talk to their fathers about.

But nothing about our relationship was ordinary. He was a widowed father of two growing girls right at the start of adolescence. Dad had no choice but to rise to the occasion. No topic was off-limits. Boys we had crushes on, bras, periods. Friendship drama. The whole nine. Even when I fucked up, he was the first person I wanted to talk to. He'd always say, *"I'm glad you told me."* We kept occasional secrets from Dad, but we shared so much.

After talking with Daijah, I headed home, planning to call Daddy when I arrived. I was mid-route when I decided to go see him instead. I'm so glad I did, too. I felt better already.

This conversation was meant to be face-to-face.

Daddy pulled me from my thoughts, "You said you wanted to talk."

I regarded Dad's warm smile, all the reassurance I needed. Holding Daddy's gaze, I bravely said, genuinely, "Today, I saw you coming out of the gas station. And I saw you with a woman. Since you two were holding hands... I would love it if you told me about her. And I would love to meet her."

Seemingly disarmed, Dad sat back a bit in his chair. He put his face in his hands a moment later, and I was sure I heard a slight whimper. Once I heard a sniffle, I knew he was crying. "Dad, please don't cry." He willingly gave me his hand as I reached for it. He looked at me with eyes full of tears, but he had a smile on his face. "These are tears of joy, that's all Princess."

"Tears of joy?" My brows furrowed. Dad nodded as he stood and walked over to a corner where he had a few shelves. He kept a handful of tools in here, though most of that stuff was in the shed out in the backyard. After rummaging through a few boxes, he brought a shoebox and placed it on the table. Removing the lid, he took out a few Polaroid pictures. He glanced through them, stopping at one, and then handed it to me.

My eyes grew wide, my hand flying to my mouth. I gasped, and just that quickly, I got emotional again. It was a picture of my parents decades ago. I'd seen many pictures of my parents back in the day and old pictures of my mom, but this was a picture I had never seen. It was a bright sunny day, and Dad was sitting in a lawn chair with Mom on his lap. They were young and vibrant. I could see the love in their eyes, appearing not to have a care in the world. Daddy looked handsome as always, with a head full of dark hair and a small goatee without the salt and pepper. But my mom. *She was gorgeous.* She had her hair in long braids and wore a green tank top and a pair of shorts overalls. I chuckled. She had a very nineties style. Her smile was breathtaking. It was bright and beautiful. Her big brown eyes sparkled, and I saw Daijah and me all over her. We were her daughters. I hadn't realized how much we favored Mom. I'd always heard we looked like her, and I seemed to hear it more the older I got. Yet, I still hadn't realized just how much we did until I saw this picture.

I continued to study the picture. Everything about it. There was something special about this one... it was ineffable like she had a glow. "Dad... wow," I said, finally finding my voice. "Where was this picture hiding all this time?"

He smiled at me as if he knew everything I had been thinking. "There's a few you two still haven't seen. I'll share them with you in time."

I nodded. I was good with that.

"This is one of my favorite pictures of your mom."

"I can see why. My goodness, she was so beautiful." I kept studying the picture, committing it to memory.

"She was. You know... we'd just found out we were expecting you."

My mouth formed into an O, and I looked over at Dad. "Really?" My eyes filled with tears again.

"Really. She was so happy. We both were. We'd been trying for a while, and when we finally had you, it was like you came at the perfect time. It's the reason she chose your name. *You were Destined.*"

I knew there was something about this moment. The lightly tattered and aged photo somehow exuded so much radiance.

"We lost her so suddenly, but I promised her that even in death, I would continue to be the best father I could be and raise you two the way we said we always would. Along this journey, I made Mom a few promises. You two were most important to me. More important than anything or anyone else. And all I wanted to do was make sure you two were happy and safe. As you've gotten older and you've met gentlemen I would have drawn up, I finally felt like I could release that. They're good men. I know they would look after you two, love and care for you. You'd be moving from my covering to theirs."

"I talk to Mom in my dreams, and sometimes she comes to me briefly. Or I'll hear her voice. Over the years, Mom has urged me to find love again. But I didn't want to. I still love Mom very much. She's the only woman I've ever loved. And I felt this pressing thing as if she was urging me forward to move on. Even visiting me less. I didn't like that. Some months ago, I went back to counseling. And then I prayed, asking that God give me a sign. I needed a sign and confirmation from God and a sign from both of you girls to let go of my reservations.

So, two weeks ago, when Daijah came over unexpectedly and saw that Natalie was here, I knew I still needed one more confirmation from you. I wanted to come to you and tell you. But I think part of me knew what that would mean. Especially if you are open to this. As much as I wanted to avoid those thoughts, part of me knew you would be. I've had such an internal battle with all of this. I love Mom. And I miss her so much. But the fact you saw us earlier clear across town, then came here to tell me you want to know more about her and meet her, gave me confirmation. So, the tears of joy were because God and Mom answered me. That was their way of confirming."

Wow. This was all so much. My dad had been dealing with this, and Daijah and I had no idea. I wish he'd shared this with us. It seemed it was a lot. So much so that it sent him back to therapy. Maybe we didn't give him a safe space to share with us. I felt horrible about that. Today was a new day.

"Yes Dad. I talked to Daijah, and you have both our blessings. We want you to be happy. You deserve it. You gave us so much. And I'm sorry if we didn't give you a safe space to share how you have been feeling openly."

"I had reservations, and they had nothing to do with the two of you. Quite the contrary. You've both done so much for your dear old dad."

"Are you sure?"

"Positive. This is all so new for me. And it's a process that I'll continue to work through with God's help, my therapist, and the two of you."

We stood and hugged. "I'm so proud of you, Dad, " I said into his chest.

"I appreciate you, Princess."

We retook our seats, "So, Ms. Natalie, is it?"

Dad tried to suppress his smile, but it was too late for all that. "I see that grin, Dad! It's alright."

"Ms. Natalie is wonderful, Princess. We've spent some time getting to know one another and I enjoy our time. I look forward to introducing the two of you."

"Tell me when."

"Hmm. I'll check with her to see what works. We can all have some dinner. Maybe the end of the month?"

"Wouldn't miss it. I'll pass the details to Daijah and Julian too."

"Alright. I'd love to have Micah join us. Is he also vegetarian?" Daddy asked with furrowed brows. I brought Micah to formally meet Dad several days ago. They're pretty fond of each other. They talked for hours, jumping from topic to topic. Later, Dad said, "He loved Micah for me."

That made my year!

Micah also got to hang out with Julian. Those two fell into lockstep like old friends. Of course, I wasn't surprised. Julian is a great guy, and Micah is too. I got the feeling they'd get along well.

Some days before bringing Micah to my childhood home, I told him about my mom.

Specifically, that she was no longer here. Physically. That was an emotional conversation, lots of tears, for sure. And Micah held me until I was ready to let go.

"No, he isn't. He'll love your beef kebabs if that's what you plan to put on the grill.

"He's my kind of man."

I chuckled.

"Thank you for coming by and having tea with me."

"Of course. I'm so glad we can always talk, Dad."

I'd probably hang out with my old man a little longer. And have another cup of tea while I'm at it.

nine

MICAH

Glancing at the time, I decided I was done for the day. I closed the document I had been reviewing and shut down my computer. I was reviewing it at the office and decided to take another look when I got home from work about an hour ago. I think I'd been staring at it for too long because the numbers were beginning to run together. That wouldn't work for what I needed to accomplish.

I've been working from home much more lately; I considered going remote full-time. Destiney was coming over almost every day after work. Sometimes, she spent the night too, and I loved having her nearby. I couldn't go anywhere in this house without smelling her scent, *especially my bedroom*, which was fine with me.

I went to the kitchen to get some water and found Destiney leaning against the counter. "Hey. You, okay? I asked, taking her into my arms and kissing her lips and then her forehead.

"Yes baby. How about you?" She embraced me around my waist. Since I was so much taller, that was where she mostly held me.

"I'm good, Destiney baby. Thank you." I loved this. Having her in my home. Being near her all the time. Indulging in her sweet kisses whenever I wanted them. Passing her in the kitchen and smacking her ass. Holding her hand when we shared space. I never wanted to go back to life before Destiney.

I had to go to Glendale, California, for work at the end of the month. One of our corporate offices was out there, so I went there a few times out of the year. It wasn't far, only about an hour-long flight, and I'd just be gone for four days, but still. I wasn't looking forward to being away from Destiney. I considered asking her to join me, but I knew she'd just started a new project. Anyway, I was planning to take her to San Luis Obispo soon. Once I confirmed her schedule for her current project, I would get something planned. One night, we talked about a few places we'd like to visit, and she mentioned seeing the central California Coast. That was easy. And no doubt, it was breathtaking. I loved living there when I was down at Cal Poly during college. I'd love even more to take her there.

Destiney stepped to my side to put her water back in the fridge. After she closed it, she hugged me again and let me go on her way out.

"Hey, come back here baby." I pulled her back to me, then quickly picked her up, placing her on the kitchen counter right in front of me. I planted my hands on the counter on either side of her, dipping my lips to her neck, smothering her with sloppy kisses. She loved it when I kissed her neck but was extremely ticklish there.

She squealed in delight, *"Micah!"*

I went for the thick band of her leggings. She squirmed in protest, placing her hands on top of mine. "Micah!" She had a silly giggle, and her tiny hands were no match for mine.

"What? Is it shark week or something?" I asked her. Destiney told me she called her menstruation shark week.

"No, it isn't."

I resumed what I was doing, ready to get a taste of her.

"Baby." It sounded like a plea, but she moaned too. "I just took a shower."

"Okay." My mouth was still pressed into her neck, and my hand was in her panties. Cupping, then swiping.

"Micah...mmm. We have to leave soon. I won't have time to take another... mmm..."

My fingers were inside of her now. I used my other hand to yank her leggings off gently but with haste.

"I'll be quick."

She laughed. "Micah."

I lowered myself in front of her. Arriving at my final destination, just before I pressed my face into her wetness, I said, "Mal's house is a ten-minute drive from here." Destiney leaned back, resting on her hands. "Mmmhmm." I went to work with my tongue, and she moaned in satisfaction.

"We'll just make a... *messsss*... You know how wet I get. *Baby*...mmm."

"Don't I know it." I was right back at it. Licking her clit, sucking her lips. They were both swollen. I hummed again. Once I'd ridden her of her leggings and panties, I noticed she was already glistening for me.

Yeah.

We've opened Pandora's box.

I got in that pink. Tasted her honey. And it was *on* after that.

Destiney's pussy was beautiful. Fat and meaty with a clit peeking out the second she got excited. Once I got her aroused, I wouldn't have to go searching. I planned to always keep her aroused. It smelled delicious, and it tasted even better. Her clit was long, and I loved that shit. I took it between my lips and tugged it gently. She must have enjoyed that because I got a reaction out of her. Audible and physical. "You like that baby?"

"Hell yeah. Shit, that feels nice."

"Good. Keep telling me what you like sweetheart." I captured her clit again, humming this time as I tugged, and she writhed in response. I wrapped my arms around her thighs to hold her in place. "You stay right here, baby."

The first night I tasted her, I focused on pleasing her. Simply appreciating her. It was a big deal. Monumental. She was in her head so bad, and I didn't want that for her. I wanted her to enjoy it just as much as I was. And man, *was I.* Enjoying. Relishing. Appreciating.

I'm a pleaser, so pleasing her had me painfully hard. I was gentle with my tongue but also intentional. Deliberately licking and sucking and slurping, thoughtfully at a slower pace so she could savor the moment. I was savoring it right along with her, audibly expressing my satisfaction. As pleasure-filled as the moment was, I didn't take any of it for granted.

This was a sacred space.

The gateway to her womb, and I knew this was a privilege to be able to please her in this way. This was the most intimate part of a woman, not just physically but emotionally. So much more than what's on the surface is connected to the apex of a woman. In my mind, this was a step above the level of intimacy than penetration. It was much more personal. It was easy to get your dick wet, but taking the time to please a woman orally was beyond that as far as I was concerned. I was totally fine being the only person who had that opinion.

Before that moment the other night, I used to try to imagine how she would sound when she was pleased or whenever something felt good to her. Destiney exceeds my wildest expectations. She wasn't very verbal *yet*. She spoke back whenever I talked to her, which was sexy as hell. But my baby was a moaner. And my goodness, those moans drove me over the edge *every single time*. And feeling her, no- watching her pussy contracting as she came. That shit... *fuck*.

Like right now.

I'd brought her to orgasm, then helped her down off the counter once she gathered her bearings.

"I'm gonna clean up real quick. *Again*." She playfully told me as she headed back toward the stairs.

"You're welcome." I tossed back in a playful tone of my own.

Then, later that night, after I tasted her for the first time, I felt her lips around me. It was a *very* pleasant surprise. I let her know how much she satisfied me. How great it felt. I didn't hold back telling her any of that. I knew she had to be incredibly brave to do that for me. And I wanted her to know precisely how I felt. Sparing no details.

And speaking of penetration, we hadn't gone there yet. We'd just been putting mouths on each other, which seemed to be plenty for now. *Shit*.

**

We headed to Malachi's house, holding hands and listening to music. Destiney turned it up when Anita Baker's "Angel" came on. "I love this song!"

"You're an Anita fan, huh?"

"Oh yeah. My dad loves Anita. I grew up listening to her."

"Same here. She's a legend."

By the way, I met Mr. David Evans some days ago, and he was such a great man and an incredible father. I couldn't imagine having to raise two daughters while grieving the sudden loss of your wife. He was laid-back and funny. He was just a great guy and easy to be around. I looked forward to getting better acquainted.

Destiney will meet Mal, Ella, and the kids tonight, and then my parents this weekend. I was so excited for them to meet her finally.

"You know what, baby? As nervous as I am, I look forward to meeting Gabby girl the most, I think. Gabby girl is my best friend in my head."

"Best friend in your head?" I lightly chuckled.

"Yeah."

"Can't say I've heard the expression."

"I just like her a lot, even though we haven't met. Just based on what I've heard. Which are all great things."

I nodded.

"Plus, I owe her *big time*."

"Do you?"

"Uh-huh."

"Why's that?"

"Had she not asked you to stop for supplies, I'm not sure I'd ever have met you. I don't think we would have ever crossed paths. We don't frequent any of the same places. Our circles aren't connected at all. Our meeting is all thanks to her. Sac is small but not *that* small." She leaned in and kissed my cheek.

"I've never thought of that. You're right. I owe her too."

Destiney smiled brightly. "Are we almost there?"

"Yes. About three minutes."

"Okay."

I looked over at her, already knowing.

"What is it baby?" I asked her.

"Just nervous. I'm excited to meet them. I know how special they are to you, but I can be awkward as hell around new people. Shy too."

"No need to worry. They'll love you. Just like I do." I pulled her hand to my lips, kissing it softly.

I rang the doorbell and quickly heard the locks disengage.

"Brother."

"Hey, you two."

Malachi and I slapped hands and shared a quick embrace. Destiney stood closely beside me.

"Come on in." Mal stepped aside, and we crossed the threshold.

I grabbed Destiney's hand and led her through the entryway. We followed Malachi as he headed through their spacious living area into their expansive kitchen.

"Ella and the kids should be back any minute now."

"Indeed."

He checked one of the pots simmering on the stove. Whatever it was smelled amazing. Malachi leaned back against the kitchen island. His eyes were trained on me with a knowing expression.

"Destiney, I'd like you to meet my *shorter*, older brother, Malachi. Malachi, my lady Destiney." I hoped to lighten her mood, albeit at Malachi's expense. He was always a good sport. Mal rolled his eyes playfully, lightly punching my arm. I punched him back, and he followed with dramatics, grabbing his arm and feigning injury.

Destiney giggled. "Nice to finally meet you. I've heard so much about you." She put her hand out to shake, but Mal immediately pulled her in.

"Come here, girl, we some hugging folk!"

Destiney continued to laugh.

"Pleasures all mine, baby sis. Can I offer you anything to drink?"

"Water is great, thank you."

"Of course."

I retook Destiney's hand, pulling her back to me as Malachi retrieved the bottled water from the fridge. She opened her water, taking a long drink. I rubbed her hand gently with the pad of my thumb. I think her nerves were calming since Malachi was carefree, but she still had three people to meet.

"It smells great in here, Malachi! Thanks for hosting dinner."

"*Anytime.* Our home is your home. You know that baby Brother."

I smiled. I was so grateful for my relationship with Malachi. I looked up to him. He always inspires me. I appreciate and love him, and I'm proud of him.

The beauty in all of that was *everything I felt*; I knew he felt the same way for me, too. We always told each other we loved each other. We always hugged each other. Our brotherhood is truly amazing. If God blessed me with sons, I wanted nothing more than for them to be as close as Malachi and me.

"Yes, brother, I know. And likewise."

"I know this well." Mal returned.

A moment later, the side door swung open. Ella and Gabe entered the kitchen from the garage, with Gabby following closely behind them.

"Hey, Uncle Micah!" Gabby exclaimed, darting her way to me and falling into my embrace.

"Hey, Gabby girl."

"Ms. Destiney! I'm so excited to finally meet you!" Gabby left my arms, falling straight into Destiney's, hugging her like they were old friends.

"It's very nice to meet you too Gabby," Destiney replied.

"So that's our daughter Gabby. No introduction needed." Mal shook his head, chuckling. Gabby had enough personality for all of us.

Malachi held Ella in his arms and kissed her lips slow and nasty. I stifled a laugh when I caught Destiney trying to play off her look of surprise. Her eyes had grown wide as saucers. I meant to warn her about those two, but it was too late for all that now. That would have taken all the fun out of it, anyway. Destiney would learn quickly just how incredibly affectionate Malachi and Ella were. They didn't give a damn where they were and who was around.

My parents are the same way. After nearly forty years of marriage, my father still called Mommy his bride and always kissed her on the forehead or the hand. Destiney was quite affectionate, just like I am. She'll fit right in once she gets over her shyness. We were incredibly affectionate with one another.

Finally breaking the kiss, Mal said, "This is my wife, Ella. The queen of this castle."

After pecking Mal several times, Ella stepped over to Destiney, hugging her warmly.

"Destiney, *in the flesh*! Well, aren't you beautiful! Thank you for coming to our home and sharing a meal with us."

"Thank you so much. And for the invitation. You're beautiful, too, and so is your home."

"Thank you!" Ella returned.

"This is our son Gabe," Malachi said. "He's pretty chill. Sometimes we forget he's there."

"Hello, Ms. Destiney," Gabe said, hugging her as well. Gabe had been standing there observing, per usual. He was a man of few words, the polar opposite of his sister Gabby.

"Destiney, would you mind helping me get everything together so we can get dinner on the table?" Ella turned on the kitchen sink to wash her hands. "I don't know about you, but I'm starving."

"Of course I can," Destiney answered as she went to wash her hands too.

"Do you need my help too, momma?" Gabby asked Ella.

"I think Destiney and I have it. Thank you." She kissed her on the cheek and sent her on her way. "All right, everyone. Give us about fifteen minutes, and we'll be ready to eat." Ella said.

Gabe and Gabby disappeared from the kitchen as I followed Malachi to their back patio.

I took a seat, and Mal sat right beside me.

"She's a beauty, Micah."

"That she is. I tell her so all day long. But she's so much more. *Destiney is incredible*. I'm already *so* in love with her. Shit is intense, and it's only been about six months. She's the one. I want to marry her."

Mal's eyebrows were high on his head. "Do you now?"

"*Dead ass*. I'll marry her tomorrow if she'll have me. I had already met her father and her sister. They're great people. Gonna get her over to meet Mommy and Daddy this weekend, but those are just formalities. I know they'll adore her."

Malachi nodded. If anyone understood, he did. Not only did he and Ella marry young, but they also married quickly.

"There's a strong connection between the two of you. I see the way you're looking at her."

"Brother. It's something I can't even explain."

Mal released a deep chuckle. "Been there. You know I get it. Baby brother," Mal sported a wide grin, "If you're already talking marriage, it sounds like you've got your nose open."

"Wide open." I returned with resolve.

Mal roared with boisterous laughter.

"Handle it, man."

ten

DESTINEY

I knew Micah was close to his brother, but this was a completely different level. It was beautiful to witness just how close they were. I'd been observing their closeness and banter this entire evening.

I can't say I've ever seen such a thing. Daijah and I were close. The best of friends. I suppose I thought sisters had a different type of bond than brothers. I'm not sure where I even got that idea. They called each other "Brother" and "Baby Brother". These men were in their thirties. I prayed that they would be close like this if I had sons.

Malachi and Micah were so alike, yet different at the same time.

They looked alike. They had the same deep voice and eerily similar mannerisms. They really could have been twins. They were twins damn near. They are just eleven months apart.

They had the same milk chocolate complexion and the same warm brown eyes.

Malachi was a bit stockier, maybe just an inch shorter. Just as handsome and

charming. Malachi was bald with a goatee. Micah was bald with a full beard.

We sat down to eat at their dining room table. Micah was right beside me, Ella was directly across from me, and Malachi was right beside her. Gabe and Gabby sat on each end. Everything at the table looked and smelled delicious. It was so considerate of them to have so many vegetarian dishes. Most times I went to dinner at someone's house, I'd end up eating bread, salad, or chips. I filled my plate with yellow rice, red potatoes, and smothered cabbage. There was also tri-tip and ribs that Malachi barbecued. Once Malachi blessed the food, we all dug in.

I started with a forkful of yellow rice and cabbage, and my palate exploded. *Everything was so flavorful*, and the rice was fluffy and cooked to perfection. I ate a few potatoes, chewing in delight with my eyes closed.

"Good?" Micah asked me. My eyes shot open to his silly grin, and everyone looked back at me. I immediately felt my cheeks growing warm. I couldn't believe he asked me that in front of everyone. I gave him a look, and then I heard Malachi lightly chuckle as he said, "You good baby sis. We can all concede that this shit is bomb. Ella was so happy to cook for you when she learned you're vegetarian. My baby can cook, but she is flexing tonight." Ella smiled brightly, showing dimples I hadn't noticed before.

"My compliments to the chef." I nodded in agreement.

"I'm so glad. It was a challenge for me to nail great flavors using plant-based ingredients, but I'm pleased I was successful. And girl, I'm going to need some ideas! I've been trying to get them to eat a little cleaner or cut back on the meat."

"My wife wanted tonight's meal to be plant-based, but I wanted me some ribs," Malachi said, taking a bite of the ribs in his hand. "Maybe someday. Today ain't it. *Sorry*." He took another bite.

I couldn't help the laugh that escaped; Micah and Ella laughed right along with me.

***

We'd all finished eating, and I was helping Ella clean the kitchen. Gabe and Gabby had headed upstairs. After the men helped us bring the food in from the dining room, they talked about catching some of the basketball game.

"You good, sweetheart?" Micah stood close to me as I was preparing the sink for dishes.

Looking up at him, I nodded my head. "Yes baby."

He kissed my cheek softly. "Alright. I'm going to the restroom, and then I'll be in the living room with Mal if you need me."

"Okay."

I started washing the dishes, and in my peripheral, Malachi brought Ella to him and said something in her ear. After she giggled, he kissed her lips for a good while. This was the third time they'd indulged since I'd been here. When they were in the middle of their second lip lock, Micah told me they were excessively affectionate and always had been from the start. I hadn't realized he meant it like this, but I was all for it. I loved that for them and found it incredibly sweet. Once I was comfortable enough, I knew Micah and I would fall in the PDA line. Maybe not to the same degree, though.

"You really don't have to do that Destiney," Ella said as she joined me at the sink. "It's your first time in our home. I'm a terrible host to have you do the dishes."

"Oh, no worries. It's the *least* I can do. Please allow me to help. Besides, I ate so much more than I should have! If I sit down, I'll fall asleep!" We both laughed.

"How about if you wash, I'll dry?" she offered.

"Sure."

"Alright."

"Thanks again," I told Ella. "Everything was delicious." It really was, and I really enjoyed myself. Malachi and Ella had a beautiful home. Though it was grand and expansive, it was cozy and inviting, and they made me feel so welcome.

"My pleasure. I have some cheesecake if you have any room for dessert."

I shook my head rapidly. "As great as that sounds, I am stuffed. But thank you."

"Same. I had too many potatoes." Ella chuckled. "Next time, let's save some room," she said sweetly.

"You've got a deal." I returned.

"So, Destiney. I have to say that you must be someone incredibly special to Micah. He hasn't brought a woman around for a few years."

I couldn't hold back my smile. "Micah is special to me, too."

"I see it all over the both of you. After hearing so much about you, it's great to put a face with the name. You're so sweet and gorgeous. I love your locs."

My smile had grown. "Thank you, Ella."

"Aww! You're blushing! You two are serious. I can see why my brother-in-love is so crazy for you."

"Yeah. I'm feeling like he's it for me."

"I love that. When you know, you know. Things were quick with Chi and me. It was just fifteen months from the day we met to the day we married. We got engaged on our first dating anniversary and married three months later."

"Wow, and so young. That's beautiful."

"Thank you. Can I also say that I look forward to finally having even teams? Girl, Gabby and I are outnumbered." She laughed again, and I laughed too.

I loved her infectious laugh and her low-key personality. Ella was beautiful. Taller than me, I'd say 5'6 or so. Slender with caramel skin, dark brown eyes, and black hair that sat right at her shoulders. It framed her heart-shaped face perfectly. No doubt she's been drinking her water and getting her beauty rest. Or maybe Sis just had some good genes. Her skin was vibrant and clear; in my humble opinion, she didn't need the minimal makeup she wore. Ella was classy, an eloquent speaker, sincerely confident, and kind. From where I sat, Malachi and Ella had something amazing, even all these years later, and I was glad to witness it. Live and in living color.

Gabe and Gabby were the perfect blend right between them. Gabe was physically built, just like Malachi and Micah. Tall and muscular. But he and Gabby had Ella's entire face. Gabby was gorgeous, just like Ella, and had her mom's dimples to match. I loved her natural hair she had in a twist out flowing freely just like her free spirit. Gabby was a knockout already at just twelve years old. But her girly innocence is what gave her charm.

"Hey, let's get together next week while Micah is in Glendale. The three of us ladies. Maybe brunch or something. Would that be cool with you?" Ella asked.

I beamed. "*Absolutely!* I would love to."

I was so excited to get to know Ella and Gabby and get closer. I liked both of them so much already.

eleven

DESTINEY

"Can I get you anything else, sweet darling?" Mr. Walker asked, taking away my empty plate. I love Micah's voice, and Mr. Walker's was quite similar. It was just as deep, with an extra layer of texture. Maybe gravelly is the word. If this were indicative of the way Micah would sound in the future, I could only imagine what pillow talk would do to me.

"I am stuffed, Mr. Walker," I said, shaking my head. "But thank you so very much." I'd just finished a generous piece of peach cobbler. The piece Mr. Walker gave me was so big that it was more like two pieces. I turned to Micah's mother, saying, "Everything was delicious." And man, was it! This woman could cook! Like *really* cook. Micah said his mom was a great cook, but he was being modest. He didn't allude to her being on this gourmet chef level. He mentioned on several occasions that she could bake a delectable dessert. And *oh my*!

Her peach cobbler was quite literally perfection. The peaches were cooked perfectly, and the sweetness was just right. The crust was also perfectly moist and flaky.

Perfection. I now knew precisely why Micah kept his ass in that gym.

"I'm so glad you could join us. You are so very welcome. Really." Mrs. Walker grabbed my hand and squeezed it gently.

"I'd love to help get everything cleaned up. Please." I stood, attempting to help collect some of the remaining dishes from the table.

"Nonsense! The men are on kitchen duty." Mrs. Walker laughed heartily. "I cooked up a storm, and you're our guest of honor." I sat back in my chair as Micah and Mr. Walker cleared dishes and returned the food to the kitchen.

"You heard the lady. Do not touch a thing," Micah said as he kissed me sweetly. It was just at the corner of my mouth. I turned my head in his direction, and he quickly stole another one right from my lips. My face grew warm immediately, but I couldn't hide my smile.

I heard Micah's light titter as he scurried back toward the kitchen with his hands full. Before disappearing around the corner, he looked back, giving me a mischievous grin.

He didn't need to steal it. I'd give him as many kisses as he wanted, anytime he wanted them.

But Micah knew me well and knew I'd be hesitant about kissing him in front of his parents.

And I was.

I felt a little shy, especially now, with his mother sitting across from me. It was just a little kiss, but... I was feeling bashful anyway, looking everywhere but at her, even though we were the only two people in the room. I couldn't even look up at her, let alone make eye contact. It was a fact that I was *absolutely* the only one making this a big deal.

I really should be used to this by now.

Unsurprisingly, the seasoned pair of Walkers was just as affectionate as the others.

And these Walker men looked a lot like their father. *Very* similar. Chips off the old block. Apples that didn't fall far.

Mr. Walker is a silver fox if I've ever seen one. He was bald too with a neat salt-and-pepper beard. Mostly salt. Micah's beard was fuller. Mr. Walker was about a shade darker than the brothers. Micah had him by a few inches. I'd say he was six foot even. Broad. Strapping. Looking great in his early sixties.

But anyway, this affection stuff was a thing around here. Naturally, *Mr. Malcom Walker* had his way of showing it. He was still sniffing behind his wife as if they were thirty years younger, least of all married more than thirty years. It was so damn sweet the way he kept Mrs. Walker's hand in his.

Multiple times this evening, I observed him bringing his wife's hand to his lips to kiss. He used gracious words. He spoke kindly to her, complimenting how delicious everything was, almost as if he was tasting her food for the first time. He expressed extreme gratitude for the lovely meal she'd prepared.

Lovely it was. An award-winning presentation with fine China to match.

These Walker men were the type who took great care of their women, showering them with love and affection. It was evident. Micah had been taking such great care of me, emotionally and physically. I saw the way Malachi handled Ella and now saw the way his father catered to his mother.

And as a side note, I love how Micah talks to his mother. The softness he shows her, the adoration he shows her, the affectionate way he speaks with her—all of this directly translates to how he handles me.

I could see precisely where the Walker brothers got all this from. They truly learned from the best.

Conversely, I thought of my upbringing. Dad did a great job providing for Daijah and me. In theory, he was an excellent example of what a provider and protector looked like from a father-daughter perspective. But since we lost Mom when Daijah and I were so young, and Daddy didn't date, we didn't have a firsthand example of him catering to a woman in this way.

This was a crash course if I've ever seen one.

"Micah tells me you enjoy a cup of tea," Mrs. Walker said, pulling me from my thoughts. I looked up to find her smiling warmly at me, and I was grateful for the distraction.

I gave her a smile of my own. "I sure do."

"How about we have a cup and chat while they finish up in there?"

"I would love to."

"Great. Head into the living room. I'll be right behind you, honey."

"Yes ma'am," I returned, doing just as I was told. I went to the next room and sat on the comfy sofa. Micah's parents still lived in his childhood home, and there was something so special about that. I loved their cozy house. It wasn't vast or extravagant. But his parents' house reminded me of my childhood home. It was inviting, with a nostalgic charm about it. I knew it was full of great memories, which gave me such a warm feeling. Their living room was modest, with lots of family pictures, new and old.

The focal point for me was the expansive bookshelf. Micah told me his mom was an avid reader, but this was beyond anything I had imagined.

This was something that could have come straight from Pinterest. The entire wall was covered in what had to be hundreds of books, with shelves from floor to ceiling. My eyes roamed row after row. I loved everything I saw, and many titles stood out to me. What was most intriguing were the classic urban fiction titles we all saw an aunt or older cousin reading. *Waiting to Exhale, God don't like Ugly, The Coldest Winter Ever, Milk in my Coffee.* Then I saw historical fiction titles like, *The Color Purple, Beloved, The Street, Their Eyes were watching God, I know why the Caged Bird Sings.* Biographies, memoirs.

I saw various titles by Langston Hughes, James Baldwin, Eric Jerome Dickey, Carl Webber, E. Lynn Harris, Octavia Butler, Toni Morrison, and Kimberla Lawson Roby, among many others. I even peeped a few Chicken Soup for the Soul titles—I haven't seen a Chicken Soup for the Soul book in years.

"Here we are love." I turned toward Mrs. Walker's voice as she entered the living room with a tray carrying two cups of tea. She sat them gently on the coffee table in front of us. "I added a little sugar, but please tell me if you need more."

"I'm sure it's perfect. Thank you, Mrs. Walker." I pulled my saucer closer to me, inhaling the aroma. "Green tea and… lemon. Yum. This will be great."

Mrs. Walker's eyes grew wide with high eyebrows. "Wow! You haven't even taken a sip. That's impressive."

I shrugged lightly, chuckling. "Those notes stand out. Some tea blends are so complicated that I may only be able to pick out one layer. If that. My father is the *best* at it. He's a *tea enthusiast extraordinaire*. I get my love of tea from him." I smiled wide. "I've learned so much from him."

She nodded. "So I've heard. He seems to be a great man. Raising you so well… and your sister. Your mom would be so proud of the beautiful woman you have grown into."

I smiled. "Thank you. I miss her a lot these days. Especially…" I halted my words, unsure of how much I wanted to share. Also attempting to curb my emotions. I had been such a ball of feelings lately, crying at the drop of a hat. I didn't want to do that right now. That would be embarrassing. I looked across at Mrs. Walker, who was looking at me expectantly, her warm smile reassuring me to continue. Not wanting to leave her hanging, I said, "Just with everything going on, I guess," Shrugging again.

"Like falling in love."

I tried to keep my smile at bay, but it was useless. I cracked an enormous grin that spread across my entire face within seconds. She called it. And it wasn't a question.

Mrs. Walker laughed heartily, then took a sip of her tea. "My goodness. Look at you! That smile is all I needed to see."

I looked away again, embarrassed as usual, and Mrs. Walker continued, "I know the feeling, and it's nothing to be shy about. These Walker men are truly a rare breed." She paused momentarily. Then, "Glad you snagged yourself one," she winked at me, and my heart squeezed, "My Micah bear loves you, Destiney. And I love you for him, honey."

Beaming, I declared, "I love him too. So much. I don't even know when it happened, but it was easy to do. He's so easy to love," I sighed. "Micah is amazing. I've never been in love before. But this feeling is strong and all I can think about." By the way, that *Micah Bear* nickname was absolutely adorable.

She nodded, laughing lightly, "You're a woman in love. It's not something easily explained." She took another sip, and I took one too. It was a great cup. Herbal teas were typically my first choice, made from dried herbs, spices, flowers, or fruits. *But you could never go wrong with Green*. Best of all, green tea is so good for you. "Listen…you've done a beautiful something with my son's heart. I immediately noticed the change in Micah. In the best way. I'm over the moon for both of you. It really is a beautiful thing." She lifted her teacup. "Let's toast to new love."

"To new love!" I gently tapped my cup with hers, took a generous sip afterward, and thanked God for sending me my sweet Micah for the millionth time.

***

"So."

I peered to my left, meeting Micah's awaiting gaze. He wore the cutest smirk, so I gave him a lazy grin. We were headed to my house so he could drop me off. Unfortunately, I didn't want our time to end, but I needed to go home. It was getting late, and I had to be at the site in Roseville bright and early. We were about halfway finished, but the projections were concerning, so the plan was to make up some time. The crew would need to be on-site for an extended schedule for the next three days minimum. When the Artistic Director informed us that we were at risk of falling behind, I wasn't even surprised.

Becky's ass was to blame.

I'd had the most amazing time with my love and his adorable parents the past few hours. Mrs. Josette Walker is *gorgeous*, first of all. She had a classic beauty. Something akin to Claire Huxtable. Warm brown skin and black hair with scattered grey strands. Very few wrinkles. The years had been kind to her; clearly, she had been loved well.

It's a fact that well-loved women show up differently.

Mr. Walker called her his bride when speaking *of her*. When he was talking *to her*, he called her Joey. That was so cute that I could hardly stand it.

Mrs. Walker and I spent time chatting and getting better acquainted, and by the time we left, my heart was so full.

I wasn't even sure how I could say this so soon, but I really did adore that woman. I loved her kindness. I loved her hospitality. But her heart… it was so pure and open and genuine. I felt an outpouring of love and a gravitation towards her that seemed to come naturally. And somehow, simultaneously, it was as if she cared just as much about me, too.

Maybe it was maternal. I hadn't had my mother in the physical for close to twenty years. Maybe Mrs. Walker filled a void I didn't realize I had.

I couldn't call it… but whatever it was, it further confirmed that Micah was my one.

We continued cruising, and a tiny grin settled on my face, thinking back to the pinnacle of the night. Once the men finished in the kitchen, they joined Mrs. Walker and me in the living room, and the four of us laughed over the cutest baby pictures of Micah. I couldn't help myself as I cracked up at photo after photo. Micah was a good sport about it. Then there was one that had me so hysterical that I was laughing until my sides hurt.

Micah had to be about eleven or so and long and lanky with thick glasses and braces. He seriously looked like Urkel's twin! The only thing missing were suspenders.

"Mommy! You trying to scare her away or something?"

Mr. Walker and I were in a laughing fit.

"Oh, hush Micah bear. She already loves you! No way a few old pictures will change that." Mrs. Walker was right. I loved me

some him. But it was still funny. Micah gave me a smirk as I carried on laughing.

"I got something for you. I'll be having a talk with Mr. Evans; you already informed me you had an awkward phase," Micah said playfully.

"You wouldn't!" I was still laughing. *"Don't be like that baby."*

Mrs. Walker proudly showed me pictures from precious moments over the years. It was the sweetest thing seeing Micah and his brother Malachi when they were small. They were *adorable* little boys, beaming proudly at spelling bees, honor roll assemblies, baseball games, Christmas plays at school and Easter Sunday plays at the church. The Walkers were such proud parents. Rightfully so. They did a phenomenal job raising their sons, who now lead successful lives of their own.

Anyway, as we rode in silence, I thought about something else: I realized precisely why it was so easy falling for Micah. He was so much like his mother, and he was *incredibly* close to her. Apart from that, he was a lot like his father, and they had a great relationship as well. I loved seeing their dynamic. Micah had the absolute best of them both and had grown into this incredibly amazing man. A man who somehow, some way, for some earthly reason, chose to love me. That shit was bananas.

"Destiney baby."

"Hmm." I gave a languid moan with slow, fluttering eyelids.

Micah released a boisterous chuckle, "Look at you. Seconds away from a food coma." He drew out his laugh.

"Ain't my fault your mom kept stuffing me with her food. How could I say no to her. And it was *soooo gooood*

105

Micah. Oh. My. Goshhhh." My eyes are shut now. The *itis* kicked in a long time ago.

Of course, it was no help that I was lounging comfortably in the plush passenger seat of Micah's Mercedes Benz. Being rocked to sleep damn near by the smooth ride. The temperature just right. Soft R&B whispering in the background. Micah called it. My ass was ready to knock out.

"Indeed. Mommy loves to cook. She's the best."

My response wasn't momentary, I was sleepy. "And… that peach cobbler…like…what the hell…never have I ever." I'd keep talking to Micah, we were less than twenty minutes from my house. Too short of a drive to sleep. We passed Micah's home on the way out. Mr. and Mrs. Walker lived halfway between Micah and Malachi's house, and I loved that they all lived near each other. "I loooove your mom." I really did. "She's soooo amazing." She really was.

"That she is. And she is already so fond of you baby. I believe she was before she officially met you."

"Yeah?"

"Indeed. Gabby girl informed her you had been over to meet them, sharing with her how much she enjoyed your company. So, Mommy was patiently waiting her turn."

"Aww. I'm glad it finally happened."

"It's a fair statement to surmise Daddy loves you too," Micah paused for a beat. Then, "He gave you a corner from the peach cobbler. In my family, the corners are *everyone's* favorite. You've already won him over."

A closed mouth smile slowly made its way across my face; my eyes still shut, "Aww. That makes me feel good… your dad is so awesome… and I love the corners too," After a brief pause, I said, "Theres only four corners. If everyone likes them how does that work out?"

"We be scrapping for them corners."

"Wow." My chuckle was low but vibrated deep in my belly.

"You still with me love?" Micah asked after we rode in silence for a little bit, lulled by Jodeci's smooth harmonies. The volume was so low I had to listen intently to make out the lyrics. "Come and talk to me." The epitome of a 90's slow jam classic. Micah reached over the console to take my hand in his.

"Yes baby," I absently rubbed my fingers with his. My eyes were still closed. I settled a little lower into the seat.

"I'm so glad they were able to meet you tonight. Finally, I knew they would adore you. Just like I do."

"I loved meeting them, too. They are wonderful. Really wonderful. You are blessed Micah."

"Thank you love. Indeed."

We cruised in comfortable silence. "Truth moment." Sitting up, I opened my eyes, glancing around. We were passing the Florin Road exit, less than ten minutes away from my house. I wanted to share something I had been harboring for the past few hours.

"Please do."

"I'm intimidated."

"Intimidated," Micah parroted moving his hand to my inner thigh rubbing softly. "Really?"

I waited for a beat, "Not in the way you're thinking."

"How do you mean?"

"It's trivial."

"Try me."

"Like. Okay…Your mom can cook. *Cook*. Ella can cook. Even Gabby can do a little something, something."

Micah remained silent as we cruised down the freeway.

"Micah," I called peering to my left to find him focused straight ahead.

"Yeah baby?"

"Oh my gosh. You heard me, right?"

"Yeah. Just waiting for the punchline."

"Micah." I tittered lightly, shaking my head. "You can be so silly sometimes. There isn't one."

He released that silly chuckle of his, then, "Okay. So…" He cleared his throat as he continued gently rubbing back and forth from my lower to upper thigh. What he was really doing was trying to calm my nerves. He was so aware, and he knew me so well. I didn't have to tell him. He likely realized I had been carrying this for a while.

Since Micah was such a sensitive being, he was hyper-aware of my feelings and constantly checking in on my mental. He had a way of handling me whenever I was in my head about something. I appreciated this so much and I loved him even more for it.

Truth be told, I loved everything he did to me and for me. Period.

The way he handled me in general.

In the meantime, I was starting to get excited because he was inching even closer to my pussy. I loved Micah's massive hands, and let me say, *his hands could cover a lot of real estate.* Micah was a man's man, with manly hands and meaty fingers. Yet somehow, he was always gentle whenever his hands were on me.

"I'm glad you told me baby." He pulled me from my thoughts with his comforting tone, "That isn't trivial. I get it, and I understand. I mean, Mommy and Ella throw it down." I looked over at him to find him already looking at me. After a second, he looked forward at the open freeway ahead. "So, here's the thing; I love my sis, but Ella couldn't cook like she can now when Mal first started bringing her around." My eyes grew wide, and my lips parted. "For real. After they graduated college and moved back, Mommy taught her. Ella is dope though because everything Mommy taught her; Ella made her own with a personal spin. Mommy can teach you. She wouldn't mind at all. It honestly comes with the territory. Spend some time with Mommy, you'll learn. Besides... I plan on keeping you around so... you'll be just fine." He captured my hand and brought it to his lips kissing it softly. He littered wet kisses all over my hand. "Also." Micah paused, waiting for me to look in his direction. Then, "Cook for me. All the time. I'll eat whatever you fix me. The more you cook the better you'll get. Just keep doing it baby. It's the best way to be great at something. Cooking is an art after all." He winked at me, and it was the most adorable thing.

Wow.

"That sound like a plan?" I nodded at a loss for words. "Everything good now?" He pressed showing that grin I loved. I nodded again, still unsure of what to say. Micah literally made me feel a hundred times better. I was anxious as hell, and Micah did what he did best.

Spoke life into me.

An issue that seemed so big in my world was really no biggie at all once he gave me his take on it.

That was Micah. Always calm. Sensible. Levelheaded.

He had a gift. Micah could seriously talk anyone off a ledge. Maybe his emotional balance will rub off on me at some point.

"You sure she wouldn't mind?" I asked finally. "I don't want to impose or barge my way..."

"Oh, she would enjoy that! Cooking and teaching are her happy places. And Mommy is *crazy* about you."

"Is she?" I smiled again. I adored Mrs. Walker. I really, really did. She was a dream, and I was convinced there was no one else in the world quite like her. It was no wonder Micah was so close to her. Not in a momma's boy kind of way either. He adores her. And I loved that.

"Yeah baby. She loves you so much already. You'll see more of her now that you've met. Don't be surprised if she asks to see you. *Without me*." We both cracked up at that.

"That's so sweet."

"But who wouldn't love you? *My woman is amazing.* You should meet her. No doubt in my mind you'd fuck with her too."

Cracking up, I said, "You're something else." I squeezed his very toned left bicep.

"But you love me."

"That I do. With my whole heart Micah."

"Yeah? The *whole* thing?"

"The entire thing." I declared.

"I love you too Destiney baby."

We were sitting in front of my house now, turned in our seats completely facing one another.

"And likewise. You have my heart. I love you. *So.* My sweet Destiney baby. I'll give you whatever you need. Anything you want."

Damn.

Meanwhile he was still rubbing my thigh, and my panties were soaked. As usual. I changed panties multiple times a day now that we were hanging out.

"I have everything I need baby. You take good care of me."

"You already have gas for the week? I need to take your car around to fill her up?"

"Already filled up. I'm all set." I did not enjoy getting gas on a Monday morning with all the other procrastinators. Micah either and thanks to him, I acquired a habit of getting gas for the week before the weekend was out.

"Alright." Micah hadn't stopped rubbing my thigh. His hand was warm. They were always warm, and it felt so good. He'd been venturing higher, and things had already begun to wake up down there. I really needed to get in this bed, but suddenly, I wasn't so tired anymore. Before I could get lost in the moment any further, Micah got out of the car. I reached behind me to grab my purse as he walked around to my side. Opening my door, he was gentle as he pulled me to him, closing the car door behind me. Micah gracefully leaned me against his car and pressed his lips to mine as we quietly shared a few sweet kisses. Each kiss lasting longer than the one before. I wrapped my arms around him, and his arms came around me deepening our connection. He fed me his tongue and we hungrily kissed each other, sensual and unhurried. We kissed for a good while.

"Get inside baby." Micah managed to whisper, breaking our kiss for probably half a millisecond. His voice had fallen to that deeper register it would go to whenever things were hot and heavy between us. I fucking loved that shit. He told me to go inside, but he still hadn't let me go. Not that I wanted him to. I could feel his hardness as he pressed into me. My panties were already done for. We kept kissing.

"I don't like to be away from you baby." I pretty much whined into his mouth.

"You don't ever have to be away from me."

We were still kissing.

"Mmm…What do you propose?"

111

After several long seconds, "…I'm staying here tonight."

I shook my head gently but never disconnected our lips. Once I eventually broke away, I looked up at him. He met my gaze with low lids. I knew mine were just as low. "Baby. I have an early day that will be just as long tomorrow. If you stay here, we both know I won't be going to sleep anytime soon."

He released a boisterous laugh. "That so?" When he calmed down, "Tell me when I can see you again."

"When we break for lunch, I'll be able to chill with you. If you can get away, you're welcome on site."

Micah nodded. "Bet. Come by tomorrow evening beauty. I need you back in my arms expeditiously. Remember, my flight is late Tuesday morning."

I nodded, smiling. "I'd love to."

He nodded too. "Indeed." He kissed my forehead, lingered there, and then moved aside, leading me up the steps to my front door.

"About to hop in the shower, but text me when you get home?"

"Baby." Micah hung his head. "You just gave me a visual. Do not tell me you're getting in the shower if you want me to leave."

I laughed. "I'm sorry baby." We shared another sweet kiss, no tongue, which was a better idea. If Micah had gotten started, then I certainly would have gotten started, and we would have needed to keep it going.

"I'll let you know when I get home, my love." He murmured against my lips.

"Drive safe baby."

I watched him drive off before I closed the door behind me.

I was *this* close to asking him to stay overnight with me. I don't know about Micah, but I wanted to go all the way. *Been* wanted to. For a while now. In true Micah fashion, he's been waiting on me, so I decided to bring this up for discussion when he returned from Glendale.

***

Mrs. Walker was so wonderful. Just the sweetest.

She joined Ella, Gabby, and me for brunch at Friends with Benedicts in Folsom. Folsom was a town about thirty minutes east of us. Ella picked me up, and the four of us rode out together.

I'd never been, and Ella highly recommended the place. It certainly lived up to the hype. I couldn't wait to take India and Daijah there. And maybe I was getting ahead of myself, but I couldn't wait to introduce them all.

Anyway, we had such a great time. We ate on the patio, enjoying the lovely early fall weather. Fall is my absolute favorite.

The food was phenomenal. We talked and got better acquainted. We drank mimosas and laughed until we cried.

And as it would turn out, Micah was right.

The very next week, Mrs. Walker asked me back, wanting to make plans for the following weekend.

While Micah was in Glendale, he sent me a screenshot of the exchange between him and her. It was the cutest thing.

Mommy Bear: Bring me my sweet girl next Saturday I'll need her help preparing Sunday dinner

Sure. What time would you like her?

Mommy Bear: About four

Indeed

Mommy Bear: Find something to occupy your time.
She'll be busy with her
Mommy in love, and we have lots to do
Do not go trying to steal my wife Mommy
Mommy Bear: Too late. I have decided I am keeping her

It was so funny too because right after the screen shot, Micah texted me saying, ***Told you. I just knew you'd get invited without me***

I laughed too. Then smiled from ear to ear.

I missed the hell out of Micah while he was in Glendale and spending time with the ladies that meant so much to him helped me feel better.

I couldn't wait for my man to get home though.

twelve

MICAH

"I have good news and bad news."

As expected, Ellington's brows furrowed, then rose in alarm. I couldn't help myself and chuckled blowing my cover. "Don't worry, your job is safe."

I arrived in Glendale earlier this afternoon and I was onsite in our corporate office working on a few things before I had to get to some meetings. I decided to call Ellington in for a quick zoom meeting to give him an update. I figured this news would be best delivered in person, but now that it was officially official, I couldn't contain myself, deciding to tell him immediately.

A look of relief washed over Ellington's expression. He chuckled too. "Well, I'll take the bad news first boss. Then there's still something to look forward to."

"Fair enough." I nodded, chuckling. "The bad news is you are no longer reporting to me effective Monday."

"Oh. Uh… you moving on?"

"I am not. But you are."

His brows were back at his hairline. "How's that?"

"I'd like to offer you the System Manager of Program Development position, and you'll report directly to Charlie Simpson, the System Program Director." Ellington's eyes grew in surprise. "If you accept, the position will include a sixteen percent salary increase and a twenty-thousand-dollar sign-on bonus. You can counter. But I insured you received a generous increase with room to grow in the position."

His eyes had somehow grown even bigger.

"Wow! This is… I mean… I don't know what to say boss." He put his hands on his head. "I had no idea there was even an opening for that position. Actually," He laughed again, "I've never heard of that position."

"Well, there wasn't one. Not initially, anyway. I've been talking to our CEO about expanding the enterprise, and we will need a few more feet on the ground to make that happen. We discussed creating a few additional roles and responsibilities, which is how this position came about. When Larry asked if I had anyone in mind, I recommended you immediately. I know you'll be instrumental in moving us forward. You've already shown yourself worthy."

"Wow. I'm so thankful you mentioned me. I… I'm so appreciative of everything."

"It was all you and your hard work. It was an easy decision. You're my first choice. So, I take it you'll accept?"

He laughed, "Yes, I will!"

"I'm so pleased. Well, enjoy the rest of your week. I'm still available if you need anything while I'm in Glendale. I'll be back at the office on Monday, and we'll get you transitioned."

"*Great!* Boss, I sure wish I could shake your hand. Hug you, something. Thank you doesn't seem good enough."

"It's plenty. You're very welcome, E. Keep up the great work."

"Yes sir. Wait, What's the good news?"

"We'll be able to get together outside of work since I'm no longer your direct superior. You and the wife can come by and chill with my fiancé and me. She'd love to meet your wife." Ellington really was like a younger brother. I'd told

Destiney about Ellington. I told E about her, too. They'd even invited us to his daughter's first birthday party, but I couldn't accept it. Fraternization. All that. I didn't want to put either of our careers in jeopardy.

He smiled wide. *"Fiancé?"*

I laughed. "Almost. She's pretty special, and that's the plan."

***

After meeting with Ellington, I glanced at the clock. I had another half hour before I needed to head down the hall to the conference room for a meeting. That meeting would take us through to lunch. After that, we had a presentation and a couple of fireside chats, which would take us through the end of day one.

When I arrived in Glendale late this morning, I checked into my hotel and settled in just a bit before heading to the office.

I checked my email and learned I'll have to go to Chicago in early November. Our headquarters were in Chicago. I'd be there for eight days. They rotate locations, and last year, that trip was held at the corporate office in San Francisco.

I sighed.

San Francisco would have been *so much better*.

In my current role, I have to travel semi-frequently for work. At one point, none of that bothered me *too* much. I don't *love* sleeping in hotels. Or eating take-out for every meal. But it wasn't *all* that bad.

Back when I only had to think about myself. Literally. No plants to water. No pets to feed.

Now that I have Destiney, I immediately thought about having to be away from her again.

And I didn't like it.

So, I'd see if Destiney can join me on that trip since I have the exact dates.

I wanted her with me.

I smiled, thinking back on our earlier conversation while I was still at the hotel.

Just like clockwork, she called me on Facetime. I was expecting her to call me too.

"Hey Beautiful."

"Micah..." Her brilliant eyes were wide. Her voice cautionary.

"Yeah?"

"There's a ring on my finger." She held her hand up, and I saw the gold band flashing on her dainty finger.

"Yes. There is." I told her confidently.

"Pretty sure it wasn't there when I went to sleep..."

"I put it there. Before I left you this morning."

Destiney spent the night with me. I had to get to the airport early before she had to get up. So last night, I gave her a key and told her she could leave when she was ready.

Anyway, this morning, I got up and took a quick shower. After I was dressed, I got everything downstairs and in the trunk. I came back up a final time to kiss my sleeping beauty and then slipped a thin gold band on her left ring finger. She never woke up. Hardly stirred even.

*"It's not one of **those**. That's coming though. That's a placeholder. Like a pre-engagement ring. Since I have to be away from you, I need to mark my territory."*

Clarity settled over her. "Micah. My goodness. You just..." She chuckled, shaking her head. *"You just don't cease to amaze me."*

She smiled so wide it reached her pretty eyes. "It's **so** cute. I love it. Thank you."

"You're welcome. It's a classic band for a classic beauty. And you can wear it even when you're working. It won't interfere. I just want something there." It was no biggie. The ring was fairly inexpensive. Fourteen karat gold. A thin band, perfect for her petite finger. Durable and would serve its purpose.

I was serious. I needed people to know my beauty was spoken for.

"Micah, it's perfect. It's exactly what I would have chosen for myself."

Destiney told me that due to the nature of their work, many people in the art space had alternative-style wedding rings. Some had silicone or ceramic rings. Some had tattooed rings. Some didn't wear anything on their finger; instead, they wore their ring on a chain hanging around their neck.

I looked around, researching, and decided this was perfect for my baby.

There isn't much classier than a simple gold wedding band. Only a select group of women can pull it off. It takes a level of class, confidence and self-assurance.

I certainly planned to purchase a beautiful ring for her.

In the very near future. Something she could wear now and then, on special occasions at least. When she wouldn't be handling chemicals and paints.

"I want to give you everything baby. Every little thing your heart desires." I told her. I knew she probably needed to hang up and get ready to head to work.

"Aww. You're all I need baby." She said. Destiney was reasonable. She didn't ask for much at all. But I was going to keep reminding her. I was here to make all her dreams come true.

Anything in my control. Anything in my power.

"You're all I need too baby. But don't you forget what I said love. Whatever you want is yours. And I want forever with you." I've told her that many times.

"I know baby. I love you, Micah. So much. I want forever with you too. My heart is yours, and I'm not going anywhere."

"I love you, beautiful Destiney." After a beat, "Oh sweetheart, I wish I was with you right now."

"Me too baby."

"I'll be back in your arms in three days," I told her.

"Can't wait baby."

After a beat, "I want to take my beauty out when I return Friday. Get some food and a drink or two. Can you swing that?"

"Yes, I can." She said sweetly.

"Indeed."

"Where are we going baby?"

"Hmm. It's going to be another lovely fall evening. Revival on J. That cool?"

"Oooh, you fancy. Hell yeah!"

We laughed.

"Well, I'll let you go beautiful. I'll text you later, but we'll talk this afternoon alright."

She nodded. "I love you, Micah."

"I love you, Destiney baby."

I was so in love with her. I missed her so much and had just been with her several hours before.

Many women fail to realize that if a man loved a woman, *truly* loved her, and wanted to do right by her, there is almost *nothing* he wouldn't do for her.

Especially if he was trying to wife her.

Jodeci said it best, "*whatever you want, whatever you need, my heart belongs to you. Whatever you need... there's nothing I won't do...*"

That was my current situation. And I didn't give a fuck.

***

"Somewhere along the way, folks started to lose sight of something." Malachi had my undivided attention. He sat silently for a few more beats. Then, "You want me to tell you what it is?" he asked me.

"Yeah!" I shot back.

He chuckled.

"I was just pausing for effect."

I shook my head and ran my hand down my face.

Mal and I were on the phone, chopping it up. After a long day, I'd finally returned to the room and showered. I had some dinner, and I spoke with Destiney briefly. She was back at her place, though I told her she was welcome to stay at mine. *Ours.* I didn't need to be there for her to stay there. I trusted her. But Destiney said India needed to get away from home, so she returned that way India could spend the next day or so with her. I'd had the chance to meet India, and she seemed cool. She reminded me a lot of Destiney, as a matter of fact.

"Well?" My voice was slightly annoyed.

"You only have to get it right one time," Malachi said. "It's really that simple. Ella is my forever, and I handle her as such. I took vows. Cultivating our friendship, prioritizing our relationship, and keeping our marriage at the forefront of my mind. I consider how everything I do will affect her and our children. The grass is green where you water it. It should take the pressure off. You found your wife, marry her. When you do, do *everything* you can to show up for each other daily."

"I see. You're making sense, brother." I replied. I understood the revelation. I'd seen it with Malachi, Ella, my parents, grandparents, even colleagues.

"And one more thing, baby brother. For now, anyway."

"What's that?" I asked.

"In my humble opinion, married sex is the best sex."

I said nothing as I regarded his statement. "You for real?" I lightly chuckled even though this conversation was not meant to be a humorous one. I always valued the marital advice Malachi shared with me. I was confident he wouldn't steer me wrong, and he was so open and generous with me. I didn't take it for granted.

"Nothing better," he continued, "Now, two types of people would argue with me. For the record, I don't give a fuck, and I'm saying it with my chest. But for the sake of this conversation, I'll tell you *exactly* who they are; a single person out here fucking 'round to fill some void and a married person who isn't prioritizing the shit that matters."

"I see." Just like before, he stunned me with revelations that weren't deep or complicated.

These sentiments had somehow been lost among so many people, and the institution of marriage suffered in the process. Everyone wasn't interested in marriage. I understood that. But *I* certainly was. Destiney was too, and she was the woman I wanted. Considering that, I regarded Mal's words.

"You think you'll get that good shit right now, *marry her* and see what I'm talking about. It's like fine wine. The intimacy deepens because you share it with your better half, the person with whom you experience everything. *Each time* you come together intimately you are aiming to please one another." He paused, "Sex is something the hookup culture has ruined. You don't even have to make it about religion. But once you know, you know."

We shot the shit a bit longer. Later, while I waited for Destiney to call me, I lay on my back, the TV watching me.

Before we hung up, I ended up telling Malachi we weren't quite giving each other the good shit.

But we were damn close.

"How's your wife doing anyway?"

"She's good. Missing her like crazy out here. By the way, we're still holding out."

"Good for you, baby brother. No need to rush. I'm getting enough for us both."

"Mal really?" He thought that shit was so damn funny. *"You play way too much man."* Mal was still rolling. *"Anyway, the tension between us is intense. Been messing around. May not be able to hold out much longer."*

*"No doubt. Listen man, if you can imagine... the moment will be **that** much sweeter. This shit is a marathon. A slow burn. Enjoy the ride and the time you're spending with your wife. Wait for the right moment. You'll know when it's time."*

I smiled at his term of endearment. Whenever Malachi spoke *of* Destiney, he referred to her as my wife. When he was talking *to* Destiney, he called her baby sis.

I didn't have to ask him why because I already knew.

My brother was manifesting that shit.

Malachi was so satisfied and fulfilled in his marriage that he wanted anyone who desired marriage to experience it.

Malachi was a *very married man* and proud of it. He promoted married life and believed in the infinite opportunities that *we could all get some*. Even for a seemingly lost ass cause like Raymond.

I thought over everything Mal said, and I couldn't agree more.

I felt like the time was near. Very near. And there was no doubt in my mind that it would be beautiful. I love Destiney *so much*. Madly. And loving her as much as I do would absolutely translate when we finally do.

I could imagine that sex within covenant is nothing short of amazing.

It seems there is something beautiful about being intimate with someone and knowing they will never give it to anyone else. To me.

Knowing they'll stay with you because they're committed to you.

Knowing they will come to you and no one else whenever they have the desire to be sexually fulfilled.

They want *you* to satisfy *all* their needs. They know you. They honor you. They want to please you, and you get to try again. And again, and again. And likewise. They get the same from you.

I wanted that. With Destiney. I can learn what she likes and how I can please her. She can learn from me.

I planned to make it abundantly clear to Destiney that should we take this next step, *no one* else can have her. Once I've had her, I don't want another man to have her ever again.

thirteen

DESTINEY

Fall was in full swing.

It was still relatively warm, which was typical for Sacramento. Fall temperatures didn't cool down completely until later in the fall season most of the time. Some fall days would still be in the upper eighties.

Aesthetically, there was no question. The leaves had turned. Pumpkin-spiced flavored cereal was back on the shelves. That was always the most telling. I absolutely love Pumpkin-spice Cheerios. And kids were back to school.

I wrapped up the project in Roseville. *Thank God.* It would be quite a while before I agreed to do something else like that.

I signed contracts for two shopping plazas in West Sacramento. I was excited because I hadn't done window lettering in a while.

Today, I worked at a cute coffee shop doing window art. They also had a chalk wall with their menu and prices, where I drew some fun fall designs. Leaves, acorns, squirrels, coffee mugs, teapots, and so on. It turned out adorable, I dare say.

The owners were a thirty-something earthy black couple who moved here from Philly. They had a great vibe and were a joy to work with. They'd only been in business for two years, but this was clearly their passion. They were vegan and used natural ingredients, serving vegan and non-vegan options.

I told them I was vegetarian, but I respect vegans tremendously. I don't think I could be one. I didn't tell them, but I love *real* cheese and *real* ice cream too much to be vegan.

Anyway, they were so kind to me. Though they were a coffee shop, they had an impressive selection of teas. Of course, once I learned that, we talked for a while. About tea and life in general. A generous offer was extended to me for as many lattes as I wanted while I worked. I didn't go too far with that. Before I was done for the day, I gave the wife of the pair my phone number. They were expecting their first baby in early January, and she wanted to get something painted in their nursery. It would be my pleasure to work with them again.

And I absolutely love cute coffee shops.

I always dreamed that I owned a bookstore with a coffee shop in another lifetime. Anything's possible. My next stop in the plaza was a consignment shop a few doors down, and I'd be there bright and early tomorrow.

Speaking of January, that will be a busy month. Daijah set a date. She and Julian would be married on the third Saturday in January. She didn't want anything extravagant, just a simple winter wedding. That seems so romantic. Roni and Vic will be her bridesmaids, and I'll be her maid of honor.

Soon, we'll be planning her big day. I was so excited for her.

Micah's birthday was also in January, and he'll be turning thirty-five. Malachi's is in February, and he'll be thirty-six. Micah told me that since they're eleven months apart, they are the same age for exactly twenty-four days, and during that time, they call each other "twin." Once Malachi has his birthday, they go back to calling each other brother.

That was so cute. And I needed to think about what I would do for my man's birthday. He does so much for me.

When Micah got home about two weeks ago, I was so happy. I missed him so much. You would have thought he was gone much longer than four days.

I was spoiled. I knew that. And I was so attached to him. Seeing Micah as much as I had, then not being able to see him at all, was like ripping the ground from under me.

When he came home, we went to Revival in Downtown Sacramento.

Revival was a rooftop bar on the third-floor pool deck of an upscale hotel. Steps away from the Sacramento Kings arena. The ambiance is beautiful. It was dark out, so the pool was illuminated. The lights gave a chill vibe. The Downtown Sacramento skyline made for the perfect backdrop. The decor was *lovely*. There was an expansive patio with indoor and outdoor seating options. A DJ too.

Anyway, Micah and I hung out for a couple of hours. Enjoying each other. It was so chill. We ordered a drink and some fries while we waited for our food. And the food was so good.

Anyway, this was the first time we'd had fries together, and it was so funny because Micah was teasing me about how I was eating my fries even though *he* was the one doing it all wrong.

Micah covered his basket of fries generously with ketchup. I made a face, and when he capped the ketchup, he caught my eyes as he leaned over to put it back.

I'll admit I had an expression that was part grimace and part disgust. He laughed, likely because he'd never seen that expression before.

I am incredibly expressive. Once, Micah told me I was one of the most expressive people he knew. But this one was new to him, I'm sure.

He studied me briefly, and I pretended not to notice. Then he looked down at his fries and then looked back up again.

Finally, Micah said, "Oh, I get it. You're a dipper." He cracked up. "Good thing we aren't sharing these. **I am not** a dipper."

"Clearly." I picked up the ketchup bottle, then moved one of the saucers on our table and squirted a small amount of ketchup neatly into the corner of the plate. I wasn't paying him any mind as I grabbed a fry, dipped it, and took a bite. Then another. After eating a few more the same way, I finally looked up and caught **him** staring.

"What?" I asked mid-chew.

Micah shook his head. "You are the neatest French fry eater I have ever seen."

"Neat?" My brows were knitted.

Micah chuckled lightly. "Very neat."

"Why? Because I didn't squeeze half the ketchup bottle all over them?" I asked pointedly. "That is a lot of ketchup," I said. "More ketchup than fries." I made a face.

Micah guffawed at that. "It's not **that** much. Come on." He grabbed one, shoving it into his mouth. After another, he said, "ketchup is **made** for fries. Like peanut butter was made for jelly."

I shook my head. "Not that much. You ruined them. They're probably soggy now. Eww."

"They're perfect like this."

I shook my head again. "No way."

Micah continued eating his fries and said, "You're doing it all wrong anyway."

"What are you talking about?"

"The way you're dipping them. You can't get any ketchup on there doing it like that. It should be more like a scoop. And you only dip each fry once? What about the long ones?"

It was my turn to laugh. "Micah. Seriously? Why are you overanalyzing the way I eat my French fries?"

Micah was rolling at this point.

"Don't worry about what's going on over here. And for your information; there **is** such thing as too much ketchup. I can't eat them like that. One dip is all I need."

Micah was still cracking up.

"Micah." I playfully whined. "Stop laughing at me."

"Okay, okay. I'm just messing with you baby." He grabbed my hand across the table and squeezed it. "One last question though: you couldn't even squirt the ketchup in the basket with the fries? It had to be on a separate plate?"

"Oh my gosh," I said deadpan, rolling my eyes, and he was cracking up again.

"Okay baby. I'm done. I promise." Micah squeezed my hand gently. "You are so cute. I love learning all these quirky things about you." Micah said genuinely.

I did too. I loved everything about Micah.

Even the disgusting way he ate his French fries.

"I am absolutely crazy about you. Insane. I care about you so much. Even though you're a neat freak French fry eater."

I playfully rolled my eyes. "I care about you too baby. So very much. Even though you managed to ruin a perfect basket of French fries." I shrugged my shoulders. "Guess everything about you couldn't be perfect."

I tried to keep a straight face but lost my resolve just moments later, trying to stifle my laugh.

Micah shook his head. "You couldn't even keep a straight face. Maybe next time baby."

Some nights later something else happened. Well two things happened. Nothing major, but significant.

Micah and I were headed out to watch a movie and hang out. Once we reached the bottom of the stairs, instead of heading left toward the garage, Micah stood in the entryway that connected to the living room.

He stood there silently for a few minutes.

"Are you alright baby?" I asked, standing beside him. He seemed to be in deep thought about something.

"Yeah." He took my hand. "Do you like this space?" He gestured around us. "I want you to feel at home and comfortable. If here isn't that we can look for another place."

My jaw dropped. "You just had this house built," I said in disbelief.

"Your comfort and happiness are my priority. I don't care. It's only a house. *You* make it a home. When I said I'd do anything for you, I meant that. Once we're married, we can move or have another house built. Whatever you want."

"Micah, I *love* this house. And I want to be with you, anywhere you are. That is home to me." After a beat, "This space could use a lot more color, though."

We both laughed.

"I saved that for you." Micah kissed my forehead. "In fact. You see that wall over there." He gestured toward a partition wall in the living room. It didn't even go to the ceiling but was super wide and very high. It was bare aside from the fireplace, which opened on both sides.

"Yeah. What about it?"

"I want you to paint something on it. Just blast that shit."

My eyes grew wide. "*Say whaaa?*"

He turned to face me. "I want you to paint something there."

My mouth formed into an *O* as I made my way over. I touched the wall. I looked up and down again. Then looked back at Micah and he chuckled.

"What are you doin?"

"Are you *sure*?" I asked.

"Positive. Why?"

I shrugged. "What did you have in mind?"

"You decide. You have full creative control. Whatever you're feeling, go with it. Don't worry about colors. I'll replace the furniture if I need to." He pulled out his wallet and gave me his Amex platinum. My eyes grew wide as he said, "Get whatever you need. As a matter of fact, keep the card. Use *that* from now on. *For everything.*"

***

"You good baby?" Micah asked me as he absently rubbed my thighs. I was on his lap, leaning into his neck.

"All good." I returned.

A few days later, we were at Malachi and Ella's. Micah and I had been here for the past few hours.

It was just the four of us. Gabe and Gabby were with Ella's parents for the weekend.

Currently we were sitting out on their back patio enjoying each other. I loved their patio; it was equally astonishing as their home was. An expansive awning covered it. There was a huge built-in barbeque pit with a cooking area and sink as well as a bar and prep area. The bonfire was lit, and a 90's playlist was going.

The itis was setting in for all of us, and Micah's lap felt pretty good right about now.

Malachi grilled salmon and corn on the cob, and Ella made a delicious broccolini and rice noodle stir fry ", especially for me," her words, not mine. Of course, there was plenty for everyone. I ate so much of it; I should be ashamed. Not only was it tasty, but it was colorful and cooked to perfection. The best stir-fry has the perfect crunch, and Ella understood the assignment. I loved the abundance of veggies, fresh ginger, and fresh garlic. She was chillin today, but this was my third time over here for dinner and all I know is Ella could cook her ass off.

"Here's your blanket Des." I snapped from my daze as Ella covered me with a throw blanket.

"Thank you, Ella." Micah and I both returned.

It was starting to cool off just a bit, and she offered to grab one for me when she went inside to get one for herself. I was still on Micah's lap, and he had been caressing me all over my lower back and my thighs.

Slow jams from the 90s had it so romantic out here.

We were in our own world, sitting across from Mal and Ella. We were all enjoying the moment, so there wasn't much talking. Surprisingly, when they'd gone into the house to get the food inside, they were only gone for a few minutes. Knowing how they got down, I didn't think they'd be back anytime soon. I hadn't even heard Ella come back until she covered me with the blanket.

I looked over at Ella when I suddenly heard a bunch of giggling. She was sitting on Mal's lap, and he had his face in her neck, telling her something. She continued giggling, and there were a bunch of movements underneath their blanket.

"Don't mind us baby sis. I'm extremely affectionate with my Queen. Micah and I come from the same stock, so as soon as he done acting scary, he gone fall right in line." Malachi said.

"Ain't nobody scary." Micah volleyed. With that, Micah took my face in his hands and kissed me passionately for several minutes. It was one of the most intense kisses we'd shared *by far*.

We kissed with so much fervor that Mal was whistling, Ella was squealing, my pussy started thumping, and my panties were soaked. I wished we were alone because we could have seriously taken it there.

"I see you baby brother!" Mal said when we finally broke apart. "Glad you got wit it."

I looked at Ella, and she wore a grin with her eyebrows high on her head.

I felt a little embarrassed, so I put my head down.

"Are you alright my love?" Micah asked me as he rubbed my back.

"Yes I'm fine."

"You good baby sis?" Mal pressed.

"Leave them alone baby. She's probably feeling bashful after kissing like that in front of us." Ella said. "Come on Des, let's go find some wine and have girl chat."

After pecking Micah on the lips, I followed her inside. We stopped in the kitchen, and she perused their extensive wine collection.

Once I slid the glass door closed, Ella giggled, "Des, that was making *me* hot! These men of ours are something else." She abruptly turned to face me. "Oh my gosh. I hope you aren't uncomfortable."

"I was a little bit, but I'm fine." I shrugged.

"Okay good. I think you know by now that this is a haven. You can be openly affectionate. You can enjoy him loving on you with no qualms, and you're safe here to show your man as much love as you want. Chi usually wouldn't make a spectacle out of it, but I think he was just giving Micah a hard time.

"Yeah, I figure that's why he asked if I was okay."

"*Yes*. Chi is protective of his *baby sis*. It's adorable, actually. I feel the same way. I never had a sister, but I love having one in you." Ella smiled, hugging me.

"Me too. I'm so glad we met."

Ella opened a bottle of rose and poured us both a hefty glass. Handing mine over, she said, "Let's toast."

Smiling, I asked, "To what?"

"Hmm… to our sexy men who adore their women and their reckless love for us."

"I'll toast to that."

I took a generous gulp, and I knew I'd be horny as hell by the time we left. I discovered that drinking wine at Micah's did that to me.

I decided I would ask him about lovemaking.

Tonight.

When we got home.

Ella and I made our way to the living room. After grabbing the remote, Ella sat down next to me. "Let's see what's on Netflix."

I loved hanging out with Ella. She was so much fun to be around. We talked so much, and we laughed even more.

***

Ella and Gabby came out to *Chalk it up! Sacramento*, which was a huge turnout. Our squares looked terrific.

We drew a monarch butterfly perched on a sunflower. It was beautiful. India and I always had such a dope collaboration.

And Gabby was so inspired by all of the artwork she saw. I loved that. She'd been asking me millions of questions about art, and she'd followed a bunch of artists on the gram.

Once I saw her interest piqued, I bought her a sketchbook and colored pencils. I couldn't help myself. And Gabby was so appreciative.

Also, Ella and Gabby met Daijah and India.

Micah came out too and I was all smiles. Like a kid on Christmas.

fourteen

MICAH

"We don't have to sweetheart." I managed, grabbing both of her soft hands in mine.

Destiney stepped closer, eliminating the small space between us.

"You don't want to, do you?" I heard the slight air of disappointment as she peered at me with doe eyes.

I chuckled. "Does it look like I don't want to?" I was so damn hard that it was painful.

She chuckled softly. "I'm completely naked right in front of you, and I don't know when I'll ever work up the nerve to ask you again." She shook her head. "Please baby. Why won't you have me." It wasn't a question. She moved even closer, our bodies skin to skin, and my hard dick pressed between us.

"That's the thing. I want you so much. You have *no idea* how much." I ran my hand down my face. "But I want to marry you first. I respect you. I told you I'm not going anywhere."

Destiney searched my eyes. She placed her hand on my cheek and rubbed her thumb over my bottom lip. "I'm not going anywhere either."

Lifting her hand to my lips, I kissed her fingertips, studying her gaze for a moment. I was sure there would be a full moon tonight. Her sexuality was on full display. This had never been the case.

Where she was usually reserved, bashful, and slightly guarded, today she was hungry, eager, and open to explore. Finally, I said, "I only want this if you're sure. We can wait."

"I want this." She returned, resolute and without pause.

Still holding her hand, I lead her to my bed. "Lay down baby."

Climbing in on top of her, I positioned both of my hands on either side of her, slowly kissing up her neck, her chin, her cheeks, and her forehead. Her skin was soft and smooth. I gently kissed her lips, and she kissed me back. We kissed for several minutes deeply and passionately, our tongues dancing to their own rhythm. She spread her legs wider as I settled between them. I could smell her arousal stewing; meanwhile, I was still conflicted about taking this next step.

I took in the view of her naked body. She was a sight to behold.

"Beautiful Destiney. I love you baby."

"I really love you too Micah. So much." She returned sweetly. Her eyes were trained on me, her voice laced with desire. She smiled at me. I swear her smile was one of the many things that made my heartbeat for her so.
I held her gaze for a moment, contemplating. "So, you'll be my wife? Once I've had you, I don't want another man to have you ever again."

She grinned real big, "Not you proposing right now!"

"Deadass! I'm making sure we don't start something we can't finish. You can trust that I'm a man of my word; I want you to be my wife. Especially if we-"

"Yes, I will. Deadass." I couldn't even finish. She placed her arms around my neck, pulled me lower, and kissed me.

137

The palpable yearning of her body emanated as she held onto me. I kissed her lips again, possessing the same fiery passion she had. We kissed for a good while. Kissing her was one of my favorite things to do. To that end, I was still contemplating. I cared for her so much, and being direct was the best way to proceed. I also needed her to be as comfortable as possible.

I sat back on my haunches. "Should we use a condom?" She looked away, likely embarrassed, and knowing her as the demure woman she was, I had a feeling it would happen. "Whatever you want to do is fine with me." I wanted her to make an informed decision. I was also stalling, if I was being honest. Deep down, I was hoping she'd change her mind. We could stop this as soon as she called it, even until the last second. She remained silent for a beat, processing everything.

"Can we?" She returned, now looking up at me. "Thank you for checking."

I gave a reassuring nod, "Absolutely."

I leaned over, reaching into my side table to retrieve a gold-foiled wrapper. Before strapping up, I kissed her shoulders and her neck. I wanted to make this a special moment for her. She told me it had been a number of years since she was intimate, so I knew I needed to take my time with her.

Unfortunately, a little pain was inevitable, but I would be gentle.

After sliding on the condom, I resumed kissing her all over. I tasted her to get her wet for me. I knew that would help when the time came.

"Baby," I said when I returned to my position on top of her.

"Yes baby?"

"Are you ready?"

"Yes." She replied without hesitation.

I began pressing into her slowly, giving her a moment to adjust to my girth. I didn't expect she'd be able to take all of me. Not this time.

Destiney was so damn tight. She felt like a virgin.

I'd penetrated her entry with just the tip when I felt a squirm beneath me.

I held her close whispering in her ear, "Relax baby, we'll take our time." Kissing behind her ear, I said, "I would never hurt you." She was so wet for me, but I needed to focus. I was on a mission to please every inch of her body the tender way she needed me too.

"Are you alright, my love?" I hardly moved as I gingerly whispered in her ear again, kissing up her neck and the side of her face. "You're driving this thing. Tell me what you need... whatever you want from me." I assured her, and I meant that shit. Destiney could have anything she wanted from me. I was deliberate in each move I made; as tight as she was, I wouldn't last long if I wasn't careful. I certainly didn't want to get carried away and cause unnecessary pain. She placed each of her hands on my biceps.

She ran her hands across my chest and said, "You're so big baby, but it feels so good." She spoke softly, looking everywhere but at me, and I knew she was feeling shy.

"Yeah?" I pulled out completely and entered her again, even slower this time, going just a little deeper; I gave her a minute to adjust to me again. "I want your eyes, Beauty." I kissed her lips, and as she peered up at me. I searched her languid expression for any sign of discomfort.

Kissing her forehead, I said, "You feel so good too. So tight around my dick." I was convinced long strokes would feel incredible, but now wasn't the time for that.

For the moment I would work on getting the two of us acclimated.

I gave her a little more, and she gradually opened up for me, getting wetter and more responsive. I continued to pace myself. "You feel amazing, sweetheart." I lifted her hips and slowly slid my hardness deeper into her slick pussy.

"My goodness, you feel amazing too baby." She said, our eyes still locked. After a few seconds, she began to look away again.

"Eyes baby." Regaining a burning gaze, we exchanged unspoken devotion and understanding, intensifying our connection. My passion and fervor for her directly impacted the intensity I felt. The conversation we were having with our eyes brought us greater intimacy. There were no words. Words couldn't explain it.

I was so fond of her.

I cherished her for so many reasons. I wanted her to be gratified far beyond anything carnal, and I would execute that. For now, my mission was to bring her as many orgasms as she could handle before I even considered my own climax.

Our slow lovemaking was bringing her to the edge; her sporadic whimpers and moans made it obvious, but I could still sense trepidation. I gave her more of me and maintained slow, deliberate strokes. She received me, gripping me like a glove.

"You ready to cum baby?" I asked in her ear. I kissed her forehead, knowing how much she loved that. "Let it go for me, and I'll make you cum again and again." I continued my slow, deliberate strokes. She continued to open gradually, and I entered her even deeper. Positioning myself close to her body, I could feel her breath on mine. I connected our lips again. Taking her lips into my mouth, deepening the kiss, and she sucked my bottom one passionately. Her soft hands were rubbing me with need. All over my back and all over my shoulders.

I roamed her body, letting my hands and tongue lead the way. I licked over her erect nipples, giving each one equal attention. I cupped her full breasts in my hands, running my thumb over her distended nipples. She responded by arching her back, and I discovered this had to be another one of her spots. I spent more time there.

"I'm about to… Micah…I'm…" She lifted her hips to meet my strokes, and I almost lost sight of my task. Regaining control I said, "Mmmhmm…go head baby, I got you."

***

I opened my eyes immediately when I felt Destiney's side of the bed cold and empty. I turned to the other side, grabbing my cell from the nightstand. It was hardly nine a.m. My restroom door was ajar, and I knew Destiney wasn't in there since the light was off. I pulled some joggers on and headed downstairs. When I didn't find her in the kitchen, I looked out of the kitchen window facing my backyard.

Not there either.

I headed to the office, where I knew she had to be.

I knew my baby, and I got the feeling she was trying to avoid me. How she would do that while she was in my house was a mystery, but still. I didn't want to make her any more uncomfortable than she already was.

Just the same, this needed to be addressed. *Expeditiously.* As TI would say.

There wasn't a damn thing Destiney needed to feel embarrassed about.

The sweet love she gave me last night… I was already thinking about indulging in her again. But I needed to pace myself.

I opened the door, and she was perched at the desk with her oversized sketchbook; she was working on something colorful. And *dope*.

But it seemed like a cop-out.

"Good morning, sunshine." I supplied.

"Good morning." She tossed over her shoulder.

"Are you alright?"

"Yes."

"Couldn't sleep in? You felt some inspiration this morning?"

She chuckled lightly, but it held no mirth. "Yeah. Seems that way."

"Hmm." I gave her a few beats. "Destiney baby?"

"Yes." She tried with all her might to say it casually. I saw right through it.

"Positive?"

She said nothing. She wouldn't look at me either.

"Destiney baby." I pressed. Ever so gently. I leaned into the doorway. "Can I have those pretty eyes? *Pretty please*."

Slowly, she gave them to me.

Yeah.

She squirmed under my gaze, and I *knew* I was right.

"Baby?"

"Yes."

"Please come here."

Destiney capped her pen, placed it on the desk, and then rose to her feet. I gave her a reassuring smile as she padded toward me.

Taking her hands in mine, I held her gaze. She still seemed trepidatious.

"Do you regret what we've done baby? Please be honest."

"No." She shook her head gently. "I don't regret it at all. Any of it."

I nodded. "Indeed. I'm so glad you don't baby. And neither do I." I took a moment, then, "But I get the impression you're in that pretty head of yours." I caressed her fingers in mine, taking my time with this. I realized a while ago that this was the best way to handle her. "Like… maybe you're feeling bashful with me? Now that we've made love." She looked away briefly, but I gently used her chin to turn her face back toward me. "Would I be correct? I need your honesty."

Destiney nodded. I always preferred that she used words with me, but this would do.

I nodded too. "Indeed." I gave her another beat. "Baby." She looked at me expectantly. "How can I help you with that?"

She smiled warmly around a light titter. "Micah… I… gosh. This is *sooo* embarrassing."

"What are you embarrassed about?" I needed her to understand there wasn't *anything* she needed to feel embarrassed about. Had her warm body still been beside me when I woke up, I would be inside of her right now. It was clear she wasn't quite there yet. I could rock with her till she was.

She shrugged her shoulders, releasing a heavy sigh. "I don't know. I guess… because you saw me. You heard me. I've never done those things with anyone else. I feel exposed. I *swear* it isn't you. You were perfect. You knew exactly what you were doing. You are *incredibly good* at what you were

143

doing. It's a personal problem." She laughed again. It was adorable.

"I see. So. Can I tell you something, Destiney baby?"

She nodded again.

"I loved everything I saw. Everything you blessed my eyes with. Every. Single. Thing. Your body is beautiful. You shared the most intimate moments and parts of yourself with me, and I do not take any of that for granted. At all. And I love the way you sound. Your voice. Your words. It was like the sweetest music in my ear."

I brought her hands to my lips, kissing them softly.

"I'll also mention that I have much more to look forward to. I'm patiently waiting for that sexy monster to make *her* introduction." Destiney's brows dipped, and I bit back my laugh. Trying my damndest to keep a straight face.

"Monster?"

I nodded. "Yep. You get good and comfortable. She's going to come out, and I can't wait to meet her."

"What do you mean?"

I smiled really big. "I've read that artists make the best lovers. I'm *convinced* you would love fiery. Fiercely. With an insurmountable passion. There's a depth to you. Your attention to detail. As sensitive as you are, you're hypersensitive and keenly aware of those around you. And their feelings." I was still kissing her fingers. "Your heart is big and open, and you give freely of yourself… aiming to please… you're emotional, and your soul is wide open to give and receive. And I don't mean freaky. *Not that I would mind.* But the level you're capable of going is far beyond that."

Destiney's mind was blown. I could tell. She swallowed hard and croaked out, "You sound so sure."

"I am *one thousand* percent sure."

"*Damn.* Alright then."

fifteen

MICAH

"Your dad is so low-key! Does he ever get angry?" Destiney asked me.

"Very rarely. That's Daddy. Low key like that pretty much all the time."

The moment could not be more perfect. The lights in my bedroom were dim. My playlist was going. We were lying in my bed talking, clad in nothing but undergarments. I was in my drawers, and Destiney was braless in a pair of black lace panties. She told me they were called hipsters. I asked her once, revealing they were my favorite style to see her in.

She had gotten to the point where she was comfortable enough to walk around in her bra and panties. Or only her panties… beyond just a few steps from the bed to the bathroom. A close second would be cheeky panties- she told me that too. One day, she walked by me in a pair; I noticed the difference and asked her. She's so cute because my revelation made her bashful. That didn't surprise me, and it was adorable. Anyway, and this is random, but I enjoyed the variety. Men generally wore boxers or briefs, but women had such a litany of options. My mind was blown because aside from granny panties and thongs, I was completely unaware of all the others. Apparently, they each served a specific purpose. Whatever floated her boat worked just fine for me.

I loved to see her in anything… *and* nothing.

145

"Yeah. That's where you get it from." Destiney said, pulling me from my thoughts. "Raising three knuckleheads was sure to ruffle his feathers at some point I bet."

I laughed. "Yeah. I mean, there were plenty of those, but he was never enraged like the Hulk or some shit." We chilled in comfortable silence for a beat or two. I was on my back, and Destiney was lying on her belly, her head resting on her arms, facing me. It was after midnight now, and we had been talking for hours, as usual. I loved talking to her. We could talk for hours. The subject was never a factor. And I was absolutely enjoying the view. Her soft, slightly toned body was a sight to behold. It was late, and her big, beautiful eyes were beginning to get lower. I loved her bedroom eyes. Destiney is such a lovely girl. She was simply stunning, and I was drawn to her like a gorgeous painting.

We spent the entire day together, and I enjoyed every second. Today was Saturday, and we both had the day wide open for once. Since Destiney was involved in so much community work, her weekends were always booked. Oftentimes, for weeks out. My weekends were a hit or miss. I would either be coaching or officiating most Saturday mornings and Sunday afternoons. But this weekend was all about her and us. No work, no distractions.

Yesterday evening, I picked her up, and she spent the night with me. This morning, as soon as she woke up, she let me make love to her. Then we made breakfast, and we made love again after we ate. That put us back to sleep. When we woke up in the late afternoon, we had lunch delivered- from two places. We had been eating on it all day. My playlists had been going for hours. So long they'd asked at least a dozen times if I was still listening. We didn't need to fix any dinner because we were still full off the lunch we had pigged out on.

I remember Destiney saying earlier that *I would starve at her house*. And that *I had a clean-ass fridge*. I was cracking up at her. She's so funny. I don't think she knows how silly she is sometimes.

"Yes, it's neat, but that's not what I mean. You have fresh vegetables. Fresh fruits. Water. Organic this, free-range that. Daijah and I are in our twenties, 'and we eat like it,' as my dad always says. You eat healthier than I do. In fact, it was a very common misconception that I must eat healthy since I'm vegetarian—jokes on them. I probably eat worse than people would even believe. I love carbs, first of all. And I do eat vegetables, but certainly not enough raw ones. I cook the hell out of my veggies."

I realized that subconsciously. I've cut back on the meat. When I cook for us, which is pretty often, I don't fix meat. When we go out, I may get some. I may not. Depends.

Our conversation had transitioned again, and now we were trading stories from our teenage years. I'd given her a run of the mill on all the foolery Malachi, Raymond, and I had found ourselves in. She'd shared stories of her own about her and Daijah, and we'd been cracking up.

Destiney perked up suddenly, "What's the most upset he's ever been? Give me a good one! I just know it had something to do with Ray."

Destiney was right. Anytime there was trouble, my dear cousin Raymond was at the center of it. Malachi and I were good kids. Thankfully, we were not corruptible because Ray would have fucked us up with his shenanigans and foolishness.

I thought it over for a minute. Truth be told, I was not always directly involved in the juicier stories. I'd just hear about it whenever Daddy got on Raymond and Malachi about it. According to Ray, I was too young to hang out with them even though Mal and I were only eleven months apart. I guess at that age, it made a big enough difference. Especially once they were teenagers.

Something came to mind, and a deep rumble rose from my belly. I cracked up for a while. *A good while.*

"What?! What?! Tell me!" I was still cracking up, and Destiney began to laugh, too, even though she had no idea what I was laughing at.

I shook my head. When I finally calmed down, I said, "Okay… so, the church we grew up at, Mommy and Daddy still go there. Well, the pastor has two daughters. One was Raymond's age, and one was Malachi's age. Ray was always chasing the younger one. Since we were kids, she eventually started to like him back, and by then, Ray was fourteen, Mal was thirteen, and I was twelve. But, with her being a PK (pastor's kid), she wasn't allowed to have a boyfriend. You know, they couldn't talk on the phone or hang out. They just saw each other at church, and that was pretty much it." Destiney eagerly nodded. "The pastor's wife was not fond of Ray. I never knew why, but I guess I can't blame her. Ray is out there. She'd tried to push her older daughter onto Mal for years, but he wasn't checking for her. Anyway, the pastor's wife was convinced Ray was damn near grown, and we *had* to be lying about his age. She knew he wasn't grown. But Ray was tall, stupid tall, so he looked older because of his height. Mal and I were tall too but not as tall as Ray. Ray was super tall when we were still kids. Like, he was tall as hell at thirteen and never really got much taller. Mal and I gradually grew into our statures. Plus, we all had a deep ass voice, even back then. Honestly, I think she just wanted an excuse not to like him.

"Yeah."

"Okay, so Ray and the PK would sneak around a lot. Ray was always trying to devise these crazy ideas to get alone with her, and Mal would cover for him sometimes. Ray was wild, though. And he was like dead set on having sex with this girl. And eventually, it happened. He went to her house, and she snuck him in through her bedroom window. But get this. Her cousin was spending the night, and that nigga had a menage at the pastor's house."

"What?!" Destiney shrieked.

"Yup! Ray the real MVP for that one. I wonder if it was planned like that." I cracked up all over again.

"And they got caught?"

"No, they didn't. Ray slipped in and out without getting caught. Some time went by before it all came out. I think maybe a month or two."

"How did it get out?"

"The cousin wrote all about their menage in her journal. Her mom found it, who is the sister of the pastor's wife, and since she hated Ray so much, they took it to the pastor."

"Damnnnn."

"Yup. They demanded to have a conference with Mommy and Daddy. Then, the pastor spent the better part of the next few months preaching to our family indirectly about Ray's indiscretions. Since Ray had to sneak out to do the deed, Daddy was furious at Mal and me because he was convinced we knew about it. *I swear I didn't know shit.* Mal knew but never admitted to it."

"Yeah, I can imagine he was angry then."

"Oh yeah. It takes a lot to disappoint Daddy *that* much. And in this case, I was actually innocent. We were grounded for weeks. Couldn't go anywhere. No phone. No T.V."

"Shiiit. Ray would have been home free if it weren't for ole girl writing about it in her journal." Destiney chuckled, and I joined her.

"Right. Ray was a savage, though, having a menage at fourteen!"

"You ever snuck into a girl's window?"

"Naw. I was way too scared." I looked over at her. "You ever snuck a boy into your bedroom window?"

"No. Never." After a beat, "Snuck one through the front door."

My eyes grew wide as saucers. "For real?"

She nodded. "Yup. Daijah was dating a guy, and he came by with his cousin one night. They parked down the street and waited for my dad to go to sleep. He took forever, but once the coast was clear, we snuck them through the front door."

"Let me find out!" I laughed again.

"Nothing happened. We just made out. Definitely wasn't a menage!" Destiney laughed. After we calmed down, "You ever had a menage Micah?"

"I haven't. You?"

Destiney shook her head, "I haven't either."

"It's not something I'm into. I don't like to share. I want my woman all to myself."

"I feel the same way. I wouldn't want to share either."

Shifting gears, I asked, "So tell me, what's something you've always wanted?" She peered back at me with those low lids. Her beautiful face was mysteriously absent for a split second. But I saw it.

My brows knitted together in alarm. "You, okay?"

"Yeah... that question has me thinking of some things. That's all."

"What things baby?"

"You may not necessarily mean tangible stuff with that question... but my mind went there because you're such a giver. You spoil the shit out of me." She chuckled. "It's so sweet. I don't want for anything with you. I have everything I need. I'm content." She sighed before continuing, "But something I've always wanted... is something I'll never get. Not in this lifetime anyway."

"What is it?"

Destiney looked just past me. "It's... it's to have my mom back. To have her here again. I miss her so much. The older I'm getting, the more I wish she were here. Especially now that I have you. Meeting you, falling in love with you. I would have loved to tell her about you." She began to cry, and I immediately pulled her into my arms.

"Sweetheart, I didn't mean for this to be painful for you. I'm sorry." Things had shifted so quickly, and I felt awful about it. I rubbed her back softly, letting her be. I knew she probably needed to get it all out. We'd spoken of her mother many times, but this was the first time she'd broken down *like this*. Once she gathered her composure, she laid her head on my chest.

"She's with you in spirit always. You can still tell your mom about me..."

I felt her nod, but she said nothing. "Please tell her about me." I continued to hold her. This always broke my heart. I was so close to my mother. I couldn't imagine life without her. "Tell her how much I love you. I'm so into you. How happy you've made me. How ready I am to make you my wife and have babies with you." Then, "For what it's worth, we can share Mommy. You know how she feels about you. She loves you like a daughter. I'm actually convinced she loves *you* more than she loves *me*." Destiney chuckled, and it was music to my ears, and now I felt a little better about this. "You know it's the truth. But I don't mind at all." Destiney settled into my embrace, wrapping her arms around me, and we chilled in silence, surrounded by the slow jams, still whispering in the darkness.

She was quiet for several minutes, and I thought maybe she had fallen asleep. "Thank you for being patient with me... I just had a moment there."

"You can have as many moments as you need, baby."

"Thank you for caring so much about everything that is me. Even the things I'm still working through. I'll be honest… I kind of hide that part of myself away. You're so compassionate. Sincere and intentional." She continued, "No one's done that before. Just my father. No other man has done the things that you do, Micah. I appreciate you more than I can put into words. That's all."

I gently lifted her chin and kissed her forehead softly.

"Thank you for being vulnerable with me. I want to be here for you. I know we can work through things together. Feel free to open up with me, sweetheart. Trust me with your secrets. I'm not going anywhere else with them. I want to tell you all of mine too." I kissed her forehead again. "You're safe with me. *All of you* is safe with me."

She sighed. "My goodness Micah. Can you be any more perfect?"

"I'm *far* from perfect sweetheart," I told her without pause.

"Well, you just never cease to amaze me."

I was beyond amazed by *her*. We'd be here until the wee hours of the morning if I tried to put *that* into words. In the meantime, I settled with, "I just want you happy love. You're the most important person in my life now. Anything you need, you tell me."

"Alright."

"Baby."

"Yeah." When I didn't reply immediately, she looked up at me. Her eyes still held a tinge of red, but she was so beautiful. I'd like to think the change of events brought us even closer.

"I love you."

"I love you too."

"Can I kiss you?"

"Yes." I captured her lips, pecking them with soft kisses. I drew back, asking her, "Should we call this a night? What do you think?"

She silently nodded, and I lightly chuckled. "Way ahead of me huh?"

"I can't hang like you can. I'm always way ahead of you in this department."

I cut off my lamp, stopped my playlist music, and settled in, pulling her close to me. We both fell asleep shortly after.

sixteen

DESTINEY

The fact that Micah knew I called myself trying to hide from him was wild. Comical actually.

My man knows me inside and out. Forwards and backward. It's as sweet as it is ridiculous. In a good way, of course. I find it incredibly thoughtful that he has taken the time to get to know me. I've made an effort to do the same. Studying him like he is my favorite subject. And he is. Enjoying every moment of it.

But I was rolling when I really thought about it. Like, I was also thinking, damn, I didn't realize I was *that* easy to figure out.

And anyway, I really should have just stayed my tired ass in that bed. I was tired too.

Blissfully tired. The way Micah made love to me was like the shit I read about in my romance novels. But better if you can even imagine it.

Honestly, I never thought it would actually happen to me. My goodness.

So, that was several days ago, and since then, Micah had been sexing me silly.

I'm glad we were patient with all of this. Though it was very sexually frustrating at times. And we'd come close. Dangerously close. Many times. We talked about waiting- more than once. And back then, there were times I wondered if I could hold out. I wondered if he was thinking the same.

Shit got creative before we finally got to the pinnacle. We'd done some simultaneous… masturbating. And mutual masturbating. I was getting better at stroking out his climaxes. I was damn proud too.

And Micah was so good to me; he took such good care of me. I didn't even think twice about it.

There were *many* things I was willing to do for him that I wouldn't have even considered for someone else. The way he affirmed me mentally, first of all.

The way Micah catered to my mind and my body. I couldn't even begin to explain it. And the care he took with me and my mental.

The way Micah handled me, the way he spoke to me.

Yeah. For him, I could absolutely be *freak nasty*. It was easy.

For Micah, I'd do it without a second thought.

I'm his woman. He's my man. Pleasing him was something that satisfied me, too.

I wanted to please him the way he had been pleasing me. Sometimes, I just didn't feel equipped. Was I even capable due to my lack of experience?

One night, I shared this with him. And Micah didn't make me feel bad. Instead, he promised to show me.

Micah always told me that he was so pleased with me. Even if he hadn't told me… he made it abundantly clear.

Micah told me he loved the way I tasted. And he was *always* wanting to taste me.

He would make me cum and then get ready to go back down and taste me again. I had to tell him I needed time to recuperate. Just yesterday, as a matter of fact.

"I need a few minutes, baby…after the way you feasted, I'm still feeling sensitive down there. Can we kiss for a while?"

155

"Hmm…" Micah chuckled softly. *His bedroom eyes fixed on me. "Forgive me, I can't get enough of your sweet pussy, my love." Holding me in his arms, he kissed my lips. "Your smell. Your taste. How wet you get for me. The way you sound."* He peppered kisses *all over my cheeks and my lips. "Love kissing you too."*

Yeah.

Everything happened organically. We were intimately familiar. And the fact that we'd gotten intimately familiar *before* we were intimate meant the physical intimacy was guaranteed to be explosive. Intimate isn't always sex. I think many people forget that.

I swear. Once we connected, we were catapulted into another dimension.

And… *fuck.*

His strokes. They were deep and slow.

His moans. They were deep and beautiful. Laced with pleasure and satisfaction.

Micah took his sweet time doing shit to me.

Like, I know it's commonly called foreplay, and anyway, it's like this *regard*. Revere. Esteem.

The esteem Micah has for me. Yeah, he loves me. But he likes me too. He's *so* into me. And he enjoys being with me. I told him I felt the very same way. It's not what we're doing at all, though I have a blast with Micah. It's simply the fact that we're together.

He is neither shy nor selfish. From my head to my toes, Micah goes bananas.

I'd cum so many times before he even entered me. Sometimes my orgasms were so intense that I could knock out in a matter of seconds. Orgasms so powerful they tore through my entire body. And I would be spent. Ready to knock the hell out. That made me feel bad because I wanted to take care of him, too, even though I'm still trying to figure out how best to do that. I'm not on his level. Yet. I was learning a thing or two. And one thing about Micah: he wasn't shy about telling me. Teaching me or showing me.

And Micah is an extremely attentive lover.

He is attentive to me in general. But he spends an incredible amount of time pleasing me. And doesn't rush about it. Ever. Not in a hurry. Ever.

Head to toe. Rooter to the tooter.

Yup. I said it.

Micah is thorough. My *entire body* is his playground.

I was still coming down from *that* experience. I remember the night he went between my legs from behind, and my eyes grew wide when he spread my ass cheeks and started licking me there. It's hard to describe the feeling, but it felt good. I was so shy when he was back there that it was hard to focus on that, distracted by how good it felt.

And I've become quite acquainted with his fingers. His hands are large, his fingers are meaty, and he knows exactly what the hell to do with them. I've cum all over them. Plenty of times.

There's something else too. Several nights ago, when I fell apart in his arms, missing my mom, he took such care of me. As he always does. But Micah mentioned wanting babies. I was a bit taken aback at first. I noticed he hadn't mentioned kids since the hospital blow-up. I realized that it was likely my fault. He likely hadn't planned to mention them either, but the moment was so emotional that it may have come out inadvertently. I planned to tell him it was still a possibility for me. And I still want that for us. I get the feeling this will make him so happy.

So, like I was saying. Me hiding from my man that day… I was being *silly*. I can look back on that and laugh. Crack the fuck up at myself.

Because *now*, literally right this second, I want him. *So bad*. Right. Now. And I'm trying to figure out where he is. I figured he would have made his way back up to his room by now.

Who knew? I am doing the exact opposite of what I did after the first time.

Something about those tables. They always turn.

I grew impatient. Driven by desire, I made my way down the stairs in search of my man. Drawn to him like a moth to a flame.

When I arrived at his office, the door was open—it was always open. I found him at his desk, typing away on his computer.

"Hey."

"Hey love."

I leaned into the doorway. He didn't look *busy*, busy. Then again, I couldn't say I even knew what busy for him looked like. It was Thursday evening. When we spoke at lunch, he headed home, saying he would work from here for the rest of the day. And tomorrow. I'd been here about an hour. I came straight here from work and took a shower. It was close to six in the evening now. So I knew he'd be making his way out of here soon. We'd probably talk about what we'd do for dinner. I could have waited…but the now persistent pulse in my panties beckoned me to my man.

I was beginning to love having my clit licked, and my pussy played with. And feeling his dick inside of me. The strokes he delivered. His warm body on top of mine, the way he held me in his brawny arms. His deep ass voice whispering in my ear.

Yeah. Right about now, she was dripping and throbbing at the very thought of what Micah's tongue was capable of doing.

"Baby." It came out in a sultry whine, which I didn't mean for it to. That got Micah's attention because he immediately looked over at me.

"Yeah baby?" His tone even.

"You busy?"

"Not at all." Micah quickly closed his laptop and then turned to face me. "Are you alright?"

I nodded with a sweet smile. Now that I was here, I was silently battling within myself. Whether I would say anything or not. Directly. Without preamble. But I was feeling shy. I could easily just ask him if he's coming up soon. But damn it, I wanted him.

"Good." He mirrored my smile and kept his eyes expectantly trained on me.

"So, since you aren't busy. Uh… can we…can you…" I paused. Embarrassed, of course.

"Can I what, love?" He gently pressed after a few beats. His smile was gone, and now his face was void of expression.

"Umm. Will you…" Shit. "I'm going to text you."

I'm almost sure his smile grew. It was quick, but I saw it. Then he released his deep chuckle I've grown to love.

"Text me. Alright." He nodded. "I think I have my phone around here somewhere." After spinning back in his chair to face his desk, he moved a few papers around. "Here it is." Phone in hand, Micah turned back toward me. "Go for it, sweetheart."

I quickly composed and sent him a message. Partly because I didn't want to change my mind.

Mostly because I wanted him without delay.

When I heard his phone chime, I immediately had regrets. I felt exposed, open, and vulnerable. Those were good feelings with him because I knew I was always safe in his care. But I was bashful anyway. As freaking usual.

Micah silently read my message and looked up, but not before I looked down at the ground.

"Destiney baby. Look at me, please." When I wouldn't look up, he made his way toward me. Within moments, his warm hands cradled my face. He lifted my chin ever so gently, and I finally gave him my eyes.

He was smiling at me. His thumbs caressed my cheeks. "You are so adorable."

I smiled too. That helped me relax. Got me out of my head. He held my gaze for a few breaths. Then, "You want *anything* from me. Anything at all. It's yours." He pressed himself even closer to me, and I felt the bulge in his joggers; the thin material pressed between my shorts didn't obstruct anything.

I felt all of it. All of him.

Micah was absently caressing my face. His right thumb ran over my bottom lip. The pulse in my panties stronger now. Damn.

"You hear me baby?"

I nodded.

"I need you to tell me you understand."

"I understand." I managed to whisper.

"Good. Now that we're clear." He kissed my lips hungrily. I moaned into his mouth as I felt him press himself into me. Growing harder. He broke our kiss. "You see how much I want you too." He pecked my lips. "I'll always want you." Another peck. "What can I do for you?" Peck. "Hmm?" He kissed me passionately. Our tongues found each other. His hands were around my waist, pulling me closer. My hands around his upper torso, our kiss deepened. After a good while, we broke apart again. "Tell me what you want Destiney baby?" He looked deeply into my eyes. His eyes were hooded with low lids.

I felt desired. I felt special. I felt safe.

Micah patiently waited for me to give him an answer. And when I did- uncharacteristically, I was blunt. Straight. No chaser.

"I want you to eat my pussy."

"Mmm." He nodded slowly. "I can do that for you beautiful." He had been caressing me all over, getting me going. Rocking himself into me. My hands were all over him too. He came down to my ear, "What else do you want?"

"I want your dick."

He nodded again. "I'll make love to your pussy with my mouth. Then I'll give you all of this dick. That sound good to you?"

"Yes. Please." I purred.

"Mmm. You sexy, sexy girl." Micah's hands were at my waist, and he slowly pulled at my shorts. "I want you right here."

"Okay." I was on the same type of time.

I wanted Micah. *Right now.*

He kneeled, taking my shorts and panties with him. I stepped out of them once they were pooled at my feet.

"I'm going to place your leg on my shoulder. Hold on to me so you don't fall baby."

And he did. Micah lifted my right leg and rested it on his left shoulder. I placed one hand on his head and the other on his right shoulder; no sooner than that did he start to lick me. It was seriously ridiculous the way he made love to my pussy with his mouth. *His tongue.* And Micah's flat tongue covered a gang of real estate. If he didn't cover it, he sought it out and found it. Wasn't nowhere he hadn't licked sucked or slurped. His arms were around me, securing me in place. And I needed it. I worried my leg would give out a couple of times. What he was doing felt so good. His dick game was wild, but his tongue game was unmatched. It seriously made no damn sense how well he could work that thing. I ain't been the same between the legs.

And he did that for a while. When I began to whimper, he returned to a standing position, capturing my lips again. While we kissed, he was unhooking my bra. He stepped back to pull both of our shirts over our heads. "Go to the couch baby."

I took my naked ass a few steps to the couch just as I was told.

Micah removed his joggers and was between my legs again moments later. Gently, he spread them, and once he reconnected to my center, I closed my eyes and sighed.

He took his sweet time. Licking my clit with a flat tongue. Then sucking softly. I rocked my hips, following his tongue everywhere he went.

It felt. So. Damn. Good. I didn't hold back my cries of pleasure. I couldn't if I wanted to. He was eating me up like he had something to prove.

"Mmmhmm. You like that baby?"

"Yessss." I drew out. "Oh my gosh."

"Mmm." He kept doing shit with his tongue. Nasty shit. Wild shit. His tongue followed every move I made. "Pretty ass pussy… is she all mine baby?" His lips were just a breath away from me. Then he was back. Lapping at me again.

"All yours." I purred.

Destiney Fulfilled

Micah made me cum twice before his dick was inside me.

And his strokes were perfection. Taking his time, in and out, with precision. Now and then, he'd pull out and tap my pussy with his dick. I fucking loved that. His dick was heavy, and he'd hit the perfect spot each time.

"You never have to ask for something that's yours, Destiney baby." He was still stroking me. Deep and slow. Looking at me right in the eyes. "You bring me my pussy whenever you feel the need. It's *always* a good time." Damn he felt good. "I'm asleep…wake me up. I'm on this computer… I'm in front of the TV. I have a book open. Come. To. Me... you hear me baby?"

"Yes." I managed as I felt another orgasm coming.

***

Saturday afternoon, I was sitting at the kitchen island engrossed in my sketchbook. It was a peacock feather—just the outline. I used a black pen on an off-white page and made thick lines, thin lines, and curves. I planned to add color later. I *love* peacock feathers.

I also had a napkin generously piled with hot Cheetos right beside me. Occasionally, I'd toss a few in my mouth and keep going.

Micah walked into the kitchen and, after a moment, "That's incredible."

I looked up briefly, smiling. "Thank you baby." And then I was right back at it again.

"Okay…" Micah began. Then paused.

163

I finally looked up at him. He was planted at the counter on the other side of the island. Facing me. I ate a few more hot Cheetos, waiting for him to continue.

"How are you eating those without a glass of water?"

My brows dipped. "They aren't *that* hot."

Micah shook his head in disbelief. "Them damn things. You see Chester breathing fire, don't you?"

I chuckled at that. "Maybe for people who don't eat them often." I nodded at him.

"Fair enough. You aren't worried that red stuff is all over your fingers?"

I shrugged. "This isn't important."

His eyebrows went up in surprise. "It looks important. I love it."

"Aww, thank you baby. But no, just trying to keep myself balanced. Sketching helps me do that. Think of it like a therapy session."

"Makes sense," Micah said. He turned to open the fridge, taking out fresh produce. Then moved the blender over.

"It's a good thing I love you. This could have ended so badly just now."

Confusion etched his face as he looked over at me. I bit the inside of my cheek to maintain my poker face.

"You don't interrupt an artist at work, Mr. Walker." I schooled my features but could feel a slight grin trying to show itself. When Micah turned completely to face me, I cracked up laughing at his cocked eyebrow. "I'm kidding. I'm just letting it flow." Hopping off the stool, I went to him, wrapping my arms around his body and kissing him on his chest. "If I'm ever in my zone, you would know it. When possible, I'd tell you beforehand."

"*Oh*, I get it. Never interrupt a master at work." He playfully jested, kissing the top of my head. "Tell me your wife is an artist without telling me your wife is an artist."

"Definitely one of those."

We both cackled.

"I love you Micah," I spoke into his chest.

"I love you, Destiney baby."

I faintly heard the buzz of my phone. Since Micah was facing that way I asked him to check it.

"Indie the bestie is asking *can I come over?*"

Turning to my side, I reached for my phone. Instead of texting her back, I called her on speaker.

"Best."

"Hey Indie. I'm not home. Everything okay"

"Yeah. Just need some fresh air." She sighed.

"Okay." I pecked Micah's lips as he released me and left the kitchen. Likely giving us privacy.

After hanging up with India, I found Micah in his bedroom. He was sitting on his bed, and I noticed he'd changed into workout clothes.

"Baby?"

"Yep?"

"Do you mind taking me home? India needs me."

Micah came to pick me up a few nights ago, so I didn't have my car.

"Of course. Is everything okay?"

"Yeah. She's just needing an escape." I mentioned Indie's situation in passing.

"Okay.

"I feel bad baby. I hate to disturb you."

"You're not baby. I was just about to work out. I can do that when I get back."

I snuggled up, kissing him. Micah held me in his arms and lay back, and I straddled him. After a beat. "But you look so *comfortable*."

"I mean. I can drive you, no problem. But you can take the Benz."

"What if I don't come right back?"

"I have my Range if I need to go anywhere." Right. Micah has a clean ass, all black Range Rover he takes around the block now and then.

"If you want me to take you home, I can. Just let me know what you need." He kissed my neck. Then, "Honestly, she can come here too." He shrugged.

"Aww. You're so thoughtful." I thought that over.

"I have an idea. Maybe we can go out to Homegrown. Solomon said the band would be playing tonight."

"That's a great idea. She'll love it." I rolled off Micah to grab my phone. "Let me check with her and see if she's down, " I texted Indie.

I draped Micah with my arms and legs, and he turned towards me, taking me into his arms. A moment later, Indie replied affirmatively.

"I'll take the Benz. Later on, we'll come back, and we can go from here. Will that work?"

"Works for me." Micah's lips were back on my neck, gently littering me with his kisses.

"Mmm. Indie is pretty special for me to leave your arms and this impossibly comfy bed."

He let out a lazy chuckle. "You're a great friend. I hope her situation gets better soon."

"Me too baby."

I untangled myself after kissing Micah's lips a few times. I rose from the bed, and he did the same, rounding the foot to meet me. We held each other for a while.

When I descended the stairs, he was right at my heels.

"You hurry back to me baby." Micah had to adjust the seats considerably due to our height difference. He kissed my forehead, then my lips. Then he stepped back as he pressed the button to lift the garage door.

"I will. See you in a little bit."

***

HomeGrownSol delivered a good time as usual. We chilled, grooved along with *Smoke*, and had some of their bomb-ass food and a few drinks. I was so glad I could get India out. At least then, she could forget about shit, even for just a couple of hours. Her parents were dealing with chronic medical issues. They've been extremely challenging lately — specifically, things with her mom.

And apparently, she and her boyfriend weren't in a very good space either. India told me they were on somewhat of a break right now. They've taken a few breaks before, but India said she's feeling like they were done. Like *done*, done this time. And she seemed content with that- on the surface, at least. They dated for over two years, so she may be harboring hurt feelings.

Still, I wasn't going to pry. She'll come to me when she's ready to talk about it. India could always come to me, and she knew that.

Micah was with us too, but he hung back some. And Micah introduced India to Solomon during their break. Anyway, we stayed for their whole set, and just before we left for the night, Solomon handed Micah a handful of tickets to the *Colour of Music Festival*, which was happening next month. Micah said it was a great time, and he'd been there before.

167

Color of Music is an eighty-piece masterworks orchestra and the only all-black Orchestra on the West Coast. I read about the festival once Micah mentioned it and was fascinated.

The orchestra is an acclaimed ensemble composed of some of the top classically trained musicians in the country. All of them are of African descent. Musicians who have trained at some of the world's most prestigious music schools, conservatories, and universities. Many of them playing since their early childhood.

It sounds amazing. The festival would be over nine days with various performances, and the passes Solomon gave us were good for the entire festival. I gladly would have paid for mine had I known about it. This was an annual festival, and I planned to support them in the future.

Solomon was incredibly generous in sharing them with us. They would be put to great use. *I love the arts—not just the visual arts but also the performing arts.*

Art is all around us. Everything begins with a picture—everything we see. Our daily luxuries were once an idea someone had to draw or design.

The arts use math and science. The arts are history. Foreign Language.

The arts are all these things.

Anyway, I couldn't wait to go.

seventeen

MICAH

I am so very in love with Destiney Evans, soon to be Mrs. Destiney Walker or Evans-Walker. Whatever she wanted to do, I was good with it.

My ass was drowning in this shit. Her love for me and my love for her was overwhelming. In the best way. The feeling was incredible.

I'd been in love once before, and I missed that. I could admit that. Honestly.

And not only did I miss it, but I had been craving that connection for so long. Being wanted by someone and wanting them just as much was a beautiful thing.

No doubt our connection has intensified.

Especially after we started lovemaking.

But it's more than that. So much more.

I loved being in her company and having her in my arms. Destiney told me she loved lying under me and being with me, too. She didn't want to be *anywhere* else.

I'm a happy man.

I keep telling her how beautiful she is. And she is. So very beautiful.

Last week, I asked her to come by. She'd gone to dinner with Daijah and India, so I had to pick her up. I went to the restaurant to meet them once she told me she was about ready. I pulled into a parking spot near the entrance and waited for her to come out. I happened to look up at the exact moment they emerged and *damn*. They were all attractive women, but Destiney stood out to me. *Of course.*

I loved the way she moved.

She was so fucking sexy, and if I was doing my job right, she had grown to believe it.

Yeah.

My woman was incredible. Her talk, her walk. Her kind, gentle spirit. The effortless way she made me feel.

I continue showing her how much she means to me. I felt compelled to do so as her man. Reminding her at every opportunity. Destiney was so very special to me.

And her unassuming innocence was adorable.

I was so glad she was mine. I thanked God for her.

I'm never letting her go.

Speaking of lovemaking, I've thought back to that night.

The first night we made love.

It was just as beautiful as I thought it would be.

But it almost didn't happen.

Destiney came to me, put herself out there, was open and vulnerable and I managed to get her upset at me.

We came in from Mal and Ella's. Took a shower. Together. Then we were in my bed, and we'd been kissing each other for the past half hour. Things had gotten hot and heavy as usual, and it was all good in my hood. For now, I knew this was as far as things would go, and I was just fine with that. My baby was a phenomenal kisser, and I could kiss her soft ass lips all night long.

Our kisses were wet and sloppy. Our tongues were quite familiar by now, dancing to their own rhythm and making love to one another.

So, we came up for air, and imagine my surprise when Destiney said, entirely out of nowhere, "I'm feeling like I want you to make love to me."

It wasn't dark in my room; my bedside lamp was on to the lowest setting, and I found her sweet doe eyes trained on me. I knew her nerves were all over the place, and she was shy, but I was so proud of her for sharing her desires.

"You sure you're ready for that?" I asked, not missing a beat.

I also regretted that as soon as it left my lips.

Destiney glared back at me. Her brows knitted.

I knew she probably felt a slight sting of rejection, but it wasn't that at all.

It wasn't a question of whether I wanted to. I suppose I didn't think she'd be ready right now. We seemed to be enjoying what we'd been doing. With our mouths. I didn't want her to think we had to do this just because that's what typically happened next. I could have come up with something better though.

"What does that mean?" she snapped.

Okay.

That was the first time she'd used that tone with me. But I couldn't blame her.

Destiney turned away from me, so I leaned over and kissed her cheek, speaking softly in her ear, "I'm not trying to upset you sweetheart, just want to make sure." I continued kissing her cheek and her neck. "I'm in no rush. I'm ready whenever you're ready." I planted another kiss on her neck and then leaned back on the bed.

She exhaled a frustrated breath.

She was probably irritated now, and I likely turned her off.

I saw her cover her face with both hands, so I cuddled behind her and held her in my arms, rubbing her softly. I heard her sigh again, but louder this time. She wasn't pushing me away, so that was a good sign. Still caressing her and kissing her shoulder, I

171

repeated, "We don't need to rush this baby. I'm here for the long haul. Ready whenever you're ready."

And I was thinking about what I'd just said.

It was mostly true. I was ready if she was too. I wanted her **bad**.

But. I wanted to do this right. Marry her before we take this step.

"Destiney baby?" She still hadn't spoken. She still hadn't turned back towards me.

I studied Destiney like she was the most intriguing subject; to me, she was. I made it a priority to be in tune with her. I already knew she was in her head. And I certainly didn't help responding the way I had. I sensed an internal battle, likely a mixture of nerves and embarrassment.

I ceased rubbing her and said, "I want your eyes, baby. Look at me, please." I gave her a beat or two, and she turned to face me. I regarded her. Eyes on eyes. Her expression wasn't very telling, but she didn't appear angry. I spoke gently, "Tell me, baby. Tell me **exactly** what you want, beauty."

"I want you. Micah. I want you inside of me."

"I want to be inside of you too baby. But only if you're absolutely ready."

"Yes, baby I'm ready." She quickly replied. "I've never felt more ready."

I nodded. "You're sure?"

"Yes. But…"

"But what baby?"

"I don't really know…I'm not sure what **I** need to do. For you."

I released a light titter. There she goes again with this. My adorable, sweet, thoughtful Destiney. I kissed her forehead. I kissed her lips. Then, whispering in her ear, I told her, "Do whatever comes *naturally to you. Whatever you want to do. You'll be fine. You sexy girl."*

I stood from the bed, then put my hand out for her and brought her up towards me. "We won't need any clothing for this." I began undressing her. Since we'd just taken a shower, Destiney was only in a t-shirt and panties. But I removed them both. Then I removed my t-shirt, basketball shorts, and boxers.

She stood before me. I stood before her. Both of us were naked as the day we were born.

"We don't have to sweetheart." I managed, grabbing both of her soft hands in mine.

Destiney stepped closer, eliminating the small space between us.

"You don't want to, do you?" I heard the slight air of disappointment as she peered at me with doe eyes.

I chuckled. "Does it look like I don't want to?" I was so damn hard that it was painful.

She chuckled softly. "I'm completely naked right in front of you, and I don't know when I'll ever work up the nerve to ask you again." She shook her head. "Please baby. Why won't you have me." It wasn't a question. She moved even closer, our bodies skin to skin, and my hard dick pressed between us.

"That's the thing. I want you so much. You have no idea how much." I ran my hand down my face. "But I want to marry you first. I respect you. I told you I'm not going anywhere."

Destiney searched my eyes. She placed her hand on my cheek and rubbed her thumb over my bottom lip. "I'm not going anywhere either."

And now here we were.

Been sexing each other like it was going out of style. I was pacing myself, and my baby was keeping up too.

We've made love all over this house.

A few nights ago, she came looking for me. Wanting some of my "good shit," as she likes to call it. She's so cute because she came all the way to my office but got too nervous to ask me at the last second, deciding to text me instead.

Beauty: Can I have you baby?

My baby was asking for it, and it was so sexy. And sweet. And just like her to text it to me. She was adorable, but at the same time, I didn't want her to ever feel bashful about anything she did with me.

And the other night, I'd let it slip that I wanted babies. And I do. However we could make that happen. Surrogacy. Adoption. I was open.

Mal and I had a conversation about kids just a few days prior, and I think it came out since it was fresh on my mind. The moment was so emotionally intense. Destiney didn't acknowledge it right then, but I got the feeling it was coming. I was ready to talk about it whenever she was.

But yeah. Mal and I were reminiscing about when he and Ella first had Gabe and later when Gabby burst on the scene. Rocking our world.

*"It would have been something special if we could have raised our kids together. Real close like we were." I said to Mal. I'd stopped by his house to shoot the breeze. On the way out to the car, I saw a few kids playing in the front yard across the street. "Your kids will be grown by the time I have some… **If** I have some."*

*"You'll have children baby brother no doubt in my mind." He stopped at the railing surrounding his wrap-around porch. "You'll have a sitter. Gabby would love to watch the kids for you and baby sis. Then you can go out whenever. You know Ella and I didn't have that. Mommy would keep them a lot, but we weren't trying to wear her out too much." Mal said through a chuckle. "That Gabby was such a crier, remember? **My Gosh**." Mal shook his head. "My baby was **always** crying."*

We both fell out laughing.

"My baby came out crying and didn't stop that shit for like three years."

I shook my head.

"I don't know why I thought they would both be super chill like Gabe was," I said with a chuckle.

*"Yeah. Gabe was **super-duper** chill. He was the easiest baby in the world. Dude was always chilling. Hardly made a peep, even if he needed to eat or be changed."*

I nodded at the memory. "Yeah, and he's still like that. Mature as fuck and cool as a cucumber. Gabe being so low-key may be why you guys had Gabby so quick."

"Hell yeah. Ella always said, if we'd had Gabby first, that may have been it!"

I roared with laughter at that.

Lately, something hadn't felt right in my spirit, and I didn't like how I felt. The more I mulled over it, the more I realized I was conflicted with something. Something major. It wasn't even deep. But it was complicated.

After sitting with my thoughts, I figured out what was giving me pause.

I wasn't all the way all right with having sex with Destiney. Like this. Outside of marriage.

Hear me out. I *knew* if we had intercourse, we would create a soul tie. Not that I took issue with that. I knew Destiney was my forever. But just the same, I know how I am and how easily I attached myself if something like that happened.

Generally, men can differentiate sex from feelings and relationships. Typically, women confuse the two.

Men can sleep with a woman and not even think of her again.

Women can't do that. A select group of women like to say they can, but they're lying, mostly to themselves. It's biology. Men and women are not the same.

Also, men can guard their emotions and feelings the same way women are with their sexuality.

But the caveat is that *I* have issues separating the two. I'm man enough to admit that. I would only be physical with a woman I deeply cared about. A woman I loved.

As much as I enjoyed making love to Destiney -and we did it a lot... man, it was like once we started, we couldn't seem to keep our hands off each other. Continuing to connect with her outside of the institution of marriage didn't sit right with me.

I wanted to wife her. Needed to. And not *solely* so I could sex her.

That was my dilemma. And I would work that out.

※※※

I pulled into the gas station to fill up. We were about seventy miles away from Pismo Beach. A coastal town just outside of San Luis Obispo. We were making great timing. Pismo Beach was a four-and-a-half-hour drive southeast of Sacramento.

For the most part, we'd been doing what we did best, conversing. Destiney had fallen asleep forty-five minutes ago, so I'd been cruising to the music and enjoying the beautiful scenery. The Central California Coast was breathtaking. The water, the beaches, the beachfront homes.

I surprised Destiney with this quick getaway just last night. I told her to pack a bag, and we'd be away for a few days. She mentioned having a few days without any commitments, so I was quick about asking my assistant to block my calendar and set this up.

She was so excited. I felt the same way.

While Destiney was asleep, I listened to the radio. Eventually, I turned on SiriusXM since the stations were so spotty out here.

Eventually, choosing *SiriusXM Love*. It just felt so right. I'd been driving more than two hundred miles with the love of my life right beside me. Just the two of us.

Then the Isley Brothers "For the Love of You" came on, and I got to thinking… it was crazy how much a love song spoke to your soul when you were in love.

It was as if every love song was about your special someone.

Driftin' on a memory
Ain't no place I'd rather be
Than with you
Loving you

Lovely as a ray of sun
That touches me when the mornin' comes
Feels good to me, yeah
My love and me, well

Smoother than a gentle breeze
Flowin' through my mind with ease, soft as can be
Well, when you're lovin' me
When you're lovin' me

I wanna be living for the love of you
All that I'm giving is for the love of

you

Paradise I have within
Can't feel insecure again
You're the key, well, and this I see
Oh, I see

Now and then I lose my way
Using words that try to say
What I feel, yeah
Love is real
Our love is real

Yeah.
I couldn't have said it better.
I am so in love.
Once I cut the engine, I leaned over, kissing Destiney's forehead, then her cheek. She stirred just a little as I softly spoke in her ear, "I'm going to fill up and grab something from inside. What can I get you baby?"

"Purple Skittles." She languidly spoke with her eyes still closed.

"Purple Skittles. Okay."

As I opened my door, Destiney said, "Blue works too. Red is a last resort."

I looked over and saw that her eyes were still shut. I chuckled, "Okay baby."

After getting the pump situated, I headed inside the store. I only needed some jerky. We had plenty to drink in the cooler I had in my trunk. After grabbing her Skittles and paying, I went back to the car. I placed the bag on the backseat and returned the pump to the cradle.

"How much longer?" Destiney asked as I settled inside.

"About an hour or so. Everything good?"

"Yeah. Debating if I should go pee or not." She sat up and removed her seatbelt. "I better."

**

"It is beautiful out here," Destiney commented, letting her window down. We were on our way again once she used the ladies' room.

I nodded. "Indeed. I'll bring you back when it's a little warmer." The coast was beautiful any time of year, even during October, but the spring and summer were amazing. Also, we'd be able to go to the beach. It would be too cool to get close to the water right now.

"I just want to be with you Micah. You can take me anywhere."

"You got it. Do you have a passport?"

She shook her head. "Never needed one."

"We'll get that taken care of." I'd since tore open my jerky and ate a few pieces. "Also, I planned on tonguing you down, but now I wonder if you'll let me after having all this red meat in my mouth."

Destiney roared with laughter. "That wouldn't bother me. You kiss me anytime you want."

"*Oooh, lucky me.* I love kissing you."

"I love kissing you too baby."

We continued cruising down US 101-South. Traffic picked up a bit more recently, but it was a relatively easy drive.

"Should be about twenty more minutes," I told Destiney once we'd exited the freeway. We only had a few miles until we reached our Airbnb. We passed through the quaint beach town nearing our destination. No doubt coastal towns are charming. Prime ocean access. Beachfront homes, seafood restaurants, and tiny shops.

"Micah, thank you so much for bringing me out here. *I'm so excited.*" She squealed, dancing in her seat. Destiney reached over, grabbing my hand. "I love this. This aesthetic is giving me so much life right now! The landscape even seems serene. So glad I brought my sketchbook. I can't say I'd get tired of the sound of these waves either."

"You're welcome baby. Thank you so much for joining me." Destiney may as well get used to this. I'm setting the standard, and I was going to show her something. I love her so much. I'd give her the world. "I lived right on the coast for four years. I never grew tired of it either."

***

We settled in at our Airbnb. The house was quaint and cozy, like a small cottage. High on stilts, the back of the house faced the ocean, the beach just a few feet away. And the view was amazing. There were two bedrooms, one bathroom, and a tiny kitchen with a breakfast nook. This would be a perfect home for us for the next few days.

I drove nearly three hundred miles, so once we got settled, I lay on the bed for about an hour. Destiney lay next to me, reading on her Kindle.

It was early. Hardly noon. We left Sacramento just before seven a.m. and missed all the traffic.

"Destiney baby?" I reached for her, draping my arm across her and around her waist.

"Yeah."

"We'll need to get some groceries. You coming with me?"

"Of course, I am."

I chuckled softly. "Indeed."

I was taking her to dinner tonight, but we will cook breakfast and dinner at home tomorrow, so I'd need to grab a few things. Fresh fruits and vegetables were a staple in my diet. I had a green smoothie at least twice daily, so I packed some essentials in my cooler in case I didn't find exactly what I needed.

"Anything in particular planned?" Destiney asked me.

"Besides chill with you?"

"Yeah." She released a soft giggle and gently nudged me with her shoulder. This was a king-sized bed, so we didn't have as much space. Not as much wiggle room. But we would make it work. I liked being close to her.

"As a matter of fact, I do. Two concrete plans. The rest is up to you."

"What did you plan?" Her eyes were bright in wonder. She placed her Kindle beside her.

"Dinner tonight. Wear a dress if you packed one."

She nodded. "And tomorrow?"

"Tomorrow, a scavenger hunt."

"A scavenger hunt?! *Really?!*" Destiney squealed in excitement.

"Yes. You said you'd prefer a scavenger hunt over an escape room. I think that would be a fun thing to do while we're here." I'd arranged one through *Let's Roam Scavenger Hunt,* a company I found online.

"Wow! *I can't wait!* I've never done a scavenger hunt before."

"Neither have I."

"So, this is a first for both of us? That's so special baby." Destiney leaned over and kissed me.

"Indeed. Our first trip together and our first scavenger hunt. I look forward to many more firsts with you, my love."

"Me too baby."

Later that evening, Destiney and I were about to head to our dinner reservations.

There was a restaurant just a few miles from us with great reviews. I waited for Destiney in the living area and stood immediately when she came out of the bedroom.

"Wow. Baby… you look… my goodness. You look amazing. Beautiful."

"Thank you, Micah." She smiled shyly. "I won't be overdressed, will I?" Destiney wore a sleek plunge-neck halter gown. It was long and elegant with a hunter and metallic gold floral pattern. She'd pulled her long locs from her face into a low ponytail. She looked absolutely gorgeous.

"I'm not worried about that. You shouldn't worry either. You look stunning." I took her hand in mine, kissing it softly

"Thank you, baby. You look *great*. You are so handsome." I was wearing a suit, so if we were overdressed, there would be two of us.

"I'm aight."

"Have you seen you?" She volleyed.

"Have *you* seen you?" I threw back, chuckling as I put my arm around her waist, pulling her close. "Seriously, you're very welcome." I took her into my arms. "Are you ready baby?"

"Yes."

"Indeed." We headed toward the front door. "Actually. One more thing. Sit down baby I'll be right back."

I went back to the bedroom, then returned with a small textured white gift box with gold lettering on the outside, wrapped with a white satin ribbon and gold star.

Destiney's eyes grew wide. I handed the box to her and said, "Open it, baby. We have time."

"Micah…"

"Go head baby." I sat down beside her.

She timidly untied the bow, slowly lifted the lid, and looked up at me with wide eyes. "This is beautiful."

"Not as beautiful as you."

Destiney closely admired the diamond tennis bracelet and matching necklace.

"*Dior?* I mean… Micah. This is… thank you baby. I love it." She placed the box beside her and hugged me. "Thank you, baby." She said again.

"You're welcome. You wearing it tonight?"

"*Hell yeah I am!*"

We laughed. Destiney was still wearing her Tiffany bracelet. She put her tennis bracelet on her other wrist. I helped her put on her necklace. It all came together nicely.

"Alright. I think we're ready baby." I told her, shutting off the lights in the living area. "Let's get some dinner."

The restaurant was a short drive from our Airbnb and right on the water.

We were just in time for our reservation, and the hostess offered to seat us any place we wanted. It was an open-air restaurant. So, anywhere was a great choice. There were tables out on the terrace with a fire pit. There were tables inside, bar seating, a lounge seating space, and for a more intimate experience, there were cozy booths tucked back into the far corner.

In the center of the restaurant, an older gentleman sat a grand piano accompanying a woman dressed in a red sequin evening gown. Her voice was warm and lovely as she serenaded us with a cover of "Breathless" by Corinne Bailey Rae.

"Micah, this is amazing." Destiney crooned once we were seated. We decided on an inside table just off the terrace and had the best of both worlds. Our table sat near oversized windows from the floor to the ceiling, giving us a wide-open view. The sun had set, and I loved the ambiance of dark water and the sounds of crashing ocean waves. "Thank you, baby. I'll probably say this the entire trip. You'd think I'd never been anywhere or something." We laughed. "I just appreciate you. And I love being with you."

"I love being with you too, sweetheart. You're so very welcome. Thank you for joining me." Our server poured each of us a glass of water and promised to return shortly with our drinks and to take our order. "I'll be thanking you for joining me many times over these next few days." I winked at Destiney, and she smiled at me.

"That's fine. I love you, Micah. "

"I love you too, Destiney baby."

This place was the perfect end to our first evening away together and Destiney's first night in Pismo Beach. The lighting in the restaurant was low. Each table had floating candle centerpieces. Destiney was already beautiful, but the glow of the candlelight adorned her elevating everything. She sipped from her glass of wine, nodding slightly to the music surrounding us. I couldn't take my eyes off of her.

She was my beautiful goddess. My reason. *My Destiney*. My love of a lifetime.

"What?" She asked sweetly once she realized I was staring.

I smiled, nodding silently. "You."

She kissed her teeth and then smirked. It was so cute. "What about me?"

I nodded again. Still silent. Reaching across the table, I took her free hand in mine.

Usually, I'm not the type to be at a loss for words. Even when things are difficult to articulate, I can still deliver *something*. But now? I was stuck. "I can't explain it, baby…" I spoke. Suddenly, growing emotional.

"Aww. *Really?*" Destiney's eyes bore into mine, and I knew there was a depth now. Feeling how I felt in this moment, I was convinced there was.

And I wanted her to see me. All of me. It was perfectly fine with me to reveal the deepest depths of my soul to her. To speak from my heart.

"For you, I'll try." I avowed.

"Okay." Her voice held a comfort that I appreciated so much. Being vulnerable with her was never an issue, but something was happening.

Destiney placed her glass on the table, then reached for my other hand.

Silent, I held her eyes. And we remained that way. The lovely voice serenaded us with another love song.

"I was beginning to lose hope." It came out before I could stop it. Though I didn't have a speech prepared, this wasn't what I planned to say. But I knew I could bare my soul with no judgment. She had a small smile, her doe eyes glowing in the candlelight, and it was all good in my hood. "Then came you…" Her smile reached her eyes. "You're the answer to my prayers. I believe you were meant for me and the proof that prayers are answered." I gently gripped her hands a little tighter. "Your love is so beautiful. *Our love* is so beautiful. You've made me so happy." I felt like maybe I was rambling. "I'm here for the long run, baby; you're it for me."

"Micah. That's…" I could see her eyes welling up. Mine had already. It was crazy because we always spoke about our feelings for each other. *All the time.*

But there was something about tonight.

Something about right now.

Something different.

Maybe it was because we were away together for the first time. Or the fact that a woman was belting out love ballads, and the mood was just right.

Hell, maybe it was these candles.

"Thank you for those words. I feel the same way. You've made me the happiest… I've never been so happy. I never imagined I could be so happy… and you make me feel so free. So safe. Secure. Sexy…it's… I…" After a sigh, Destiney said, "I just love you, Micah. I love you so fucking much." She laughed, and a tear fell.

I chuckled. I understood her, undoubtably. My baby was feeling a lot like I was, growing emotional with so much to say and trying to find just the right words to articulate it. We'd established an unspoken understanding, and I knew her heart just like she knew mine. I gently wiped her tears. I was grateful for my long arms. She was sitting across from me. I usually preferred she sit beside me, but this was a sweetheart table.

Nodding, I returned, "I love you, my Destiney baby. I just want to keep loving you. Keep making you smile. Can I do that, sweetheart?"

"Yes, please. As long as I can keep loving you."

***

We returned to our Airbnb and immediately started getting changed and ready for bed. We showered before dinner so we could shower again in the morning.

The food was phenomenal. I had the Surf and Turf. Destiney had a Mushroom Risotto, and we shared a slice of cheesecake for dessert.

As I removed my clothing, I figured this was a good time to mention something I'd been thinking about. Now that we were intimate. And liable to be intimate again at any given moment.

"Baby?"

"Yes."

"We're all out of condoms," I informed Destiney. I loosened my tie to remove it. "We used the last one last night." I had been abstinent for two years, so I didn't have much of a stash, and we quickly depleted the small supply of condoms I did have. Once Destiney and I started lovemaking, we did that shit often, and honestly, it wasn't at the forefront of my mind to replenish them. I only want her. I'd be perfectly fine with shooting up the club raw. I knew she was my forever, but I needed her to be good with that. "I can make a run. But I was thinking since we're exclusive, maybe we could get tested; that way, we don't need to use them." Destiney had her back to me as she was removing her jewelry. "We can keep using them if that makes you most comfortable. But... just thought I'd mention it. You know." She said nothing. "Do we still need them love?" I quizzed after a few beats.

"Micah," Destiney said, her back still to me.

"Yeah, baby?"

Destiney turned to face me, and I was looking at her expectantly. She wore a small smile, but her eyes were glassy, almost like she was about to cry. *That* gave me pause, but I didn't have time to react. Finally, "We'll need condoms. I'm not on the pill. So. Unless you have a superb pull-out game..." She spoke evenly.

My brows knitted. *Pull-out game?* "Why would you need to be on the pill?"

She smiled wider this time. A tiny tear cascading. "Because. I could get pregnant."

My eyebrows promptly transitioned from furrowed to high on my forehead. "You could?" I walked around the bed to her side, sitting next to her. "I thought... didn't you have surgery?" I smiled too. Couldn't help myself.

She shook her head. "I had surgery, but not the one initially planned. I only had my fibroids removed." She spoke through a tearful smile. "I can still have babies." Destiney beamed as tears rapidly fell. I knew these were happy tears. I was growing emotional myself.

I loved this for her.

For *us.*

And as thrilled as I was to hear this news, it was only the icing on the cake.

"Wow. That's great, baby. *So great!"* We kissed slow and passionate for a long time. When I pulled my lips away, I pressed my forehead to hers. I needed to set the record straight.

We haven't spoken of children since our infamous conversation that day. And aside from letting it slip those nights ago, I avoided broaching the topic altogether. It seemed Destiney was moving the same way, as she never brought it up either, even after my slip-up.

But there was something I needed to tell her. And there was no time like the present.

"Sweetheart. Whether we had children of our own, had children through other means, or decided not to have them at all, I would still want you. Make no mistake, children with you would be a bonus for sure…" I gently held her face in mine, wiping a lone tear. "But you're all I need, Destiney baby." I kissed her softly.

Destiney looked up at me. Eyes on eyes. Her beautiful face held a glow and spread into a smile. "I know that, Micah. I knew that then. At the time, I was an emotional mess. You'd expressed your desire to be a father from the beginning and… I felt you would have been settling with me. You know?" She sighed. "We could have talked about it. I'm sorry. I wasn't thinking logically."

"I understand. That was an emotional day, baby."

"Micah?"

"Yes, love?"

"I trust you."

"I trust you too."

"So, it's all right with me to continue if, at some point, we don't have any condoms. I know you'll take care of me."

My mind started to process what she was saying, and I could surmise what she meant. Knowing Destiney, she was too bashful to say it directly, but she got her point across.

I'm a straight shooter, in any case.

"You mean you'll have my babies, Destiney?" I quizzed.

"Yes. I will."

"Indeed. I've seen a future with you from the beginning. You're my forever, and I want you to be my wife before we have babies."

"You're my forever. All of that is perfectly alright with me, too."

"Yeah?"

"Yeah."

I captured her lips again. "So. You tryin' to play this pull-out game or what?" I teased, murmuring against her lips.

Destiney's giggles were muted when my lips returned to hers. Her sweet tongue was in my mouth. Mine was in hers, and we fell right into our rhythm. Her dainty hands were around my hardness, and it wasn't long before she was moaning with need. She lay back on the bed, bringing me with her. When my fingers found their way into her panties and I discovered how slick she already was, I knew it was game time.

eighteen

MICAH

"So, what's up with India though?" Solomon asked me.

Sol, Mal, Ray, and I sat on the back patio at Mal and Ella's. Talking and having a few beers. The sun was setting, but it was still early.

I raised my eyebrows. "What's up with India? What do you mean by that?" I asked, the surprise evident in my voice.

"What you so surprised for?" Ray said. "Shorty is bad!"

India was beautiful. Stevie Wonder could see that. I was surprised to hear Sol express interest in someone. I didn't even realize he'd been stealing glances at her. We'd been here most of the day, and he was just now saying something. He was subtle as hell with that. Like me, Sol had a long-term relationship that had gone south some years ago, and he'd taken a step away from the dating world.

"I didn't realize you were back out here. You swore off relationships." I replied.

"Fine as she is, my ass would come up off the bench too," Ray said.

Everything with Ray has been pretty chill lately. At least for the time being. That was always a good thing. It was nice to have him around. If anything, we could always count on him to make us laugh.

Solomon nodded. "Yeah. I certainly didn't set out to meet someone. But India is beautiful. I mean, *damn*."

"Destiney is beautiful with a beautiful ass friend. The fuck are the chances of that." Malachi, you ain't bout to be known as the only one with a badass wife on your arm." Ray chimed in.

We all cackled. Malachi has been with Ella for years, and from day one, everyone was captivated by Ella's beauty. She seemed more beautiful as we got older too.

"Well, you've already been introduced to her," I told Sol.

"Gone in the house, she's still in there I think." That was Malachi.

"Sol man, you been out the game so long, you done forgot how to talk to a woman?" Ray said.

We all laughed.

"I know how to talk to women fool!" Sol said. He looked over at me. "She seeing someone? Does she have any kids?"

I thought back on what Destiney mentioned. "Pretty sure she's single, and as far as I know, no kids," I said.

"Hmm," Sol said, nodding his head. He threw back the last of his beer, then placed the bottle on the table, sitting back in his chair.

"Nigga you need to move a little faster than that. She's single, no kids and she *that* fine? Shorty ain't gone last. Better get yo ass to it!" Ray said.

Sol rolled his eyes, and Malachi chuckled. Ray wasn't slick. That was code, meaning he planned on shooting his shot. I wasn't stupid.

"Ray, you can forget it. That's Destiney's friend, and I wouldn't allow it."

"Man, what you talking bout?"

"I'm serious. Stay away from India, Ray." I gave him a look.

Malachi shook his head. "Don't do it man. You know you're still out here playing way too many games."

"Even if it ain't me, ya'll know what I'm talking 'bout." Ray spat.

I glared at him a second longer. "Long as it ain't you," I said finally.

Mal and Sol thought that was so funny.

"Well, that's my queue. Let me go find my wife. It's about time I gave her a few more kisses. Maybe I can give her something else since yall niggas ain't leaving no time soon. I'll be back."

We all laughed. Malachi and Ella fucked like some damn rabbits. I was surprised they only had two kids. She had to have gotten her tubes tied or some shit. I wasn't mad. She had been his wife for nearly two decades, and they'd managed to keep the fire burning. It was a beautiful thing, and it gave me something to look forward to.

"I'm gone head out man, but I'm going to ask India for her number before I leave," Sol said, standing up. I stood with him and slapped his hand. "Aight, man. Be good."

Sol went inside, and I sat back in my chair, finishing the last of my beer. I didn't mind getting between Destiney's legs myself. I pulled my cell phone out and texted her.

Ready to get out of here baby? I sent the fire emoji too, and Destiney knew what that fire emoji meant.

I leaned back in my chair as she replied.

Beauty: *Your place or mine?*

I'll sleep at her place tonight. Since I work from home, it will be easier for her tomorrow morning. I couldn't wait to get her home. I was going to make sweet love to her. In the shower and her bed. I could feel him waking up already.

Yours

Beauty: *Give me ten more minutes I'm talking to Gabby*

Indeed

"You done?" Ray asked irritably as I was putting my phone back in my pocket.

"Man, stop. You quit being nasty and you can get you one too."

"I tried! You and Malachi are blocking me."

I smirked and gave him a knowing expression.

"You know you ain't ready to settle down and be serious with anyone." Ray looked off in the distance. After a while, he said, "All this shit is just sex, man. That's it. Shit is getting old. I do want to settle down. But women play games too." Ray let out an exasperated sigh. Now, my interest was piqued. It was seldom that he got serious when it came to this topic. "Can I tell you something, cousin?" Ray was being vulnerable, which was rare as hell.

"Of course."

"I was sleeping with this chick off and on for some months. But then, I realized I was developing real feelings for her, which is something I *never* do. Like ever. I told her how I felt, and she told me she felt the same, so we decided to be exclusive. I was serious about that shit. Honest to God. I cut off everyone else and was only seeing her. I figured we could build something, maybe have a future. We even talked about moving in together. Well, I found out recently that she's still out there doing that same shit. I saw her coming out the washeteria hugged up with some nigga she was fucking. She'd been lying to me the whole time about all of it." He shook his head and then placed his face in his hands.

"Damn cousin. I'm sorry."

"I'm nothing like you and Malachi man. I wonder if I'm even capable of all that love and marriage and family shit."

"Sure, you are. It's all about timing. Sometimes, we meet the right people at the wrong time. Or the wrong people at the right time. Keep saying you will, and you'll find your person at just the right time."

"It's more than that. Ella and Destiney, they're perfect. Like a calm to a storm. The women I meet have so much emotional baggage."

"Everyone has some sort of baggage, Ray."

"Yeah. But older women have a different set of issues. Man, I outta get me some young snatch. They seem like the perfect type of woman. You got her right, man. That's what the fuck I'm trying to get."

"She's right where I want her," I spoke. "I wouldn't change a thing about Destiney. She's absolutely perfect for me." I couldn't help but smile. "When we first met, I had this idea of how I thought our relationship would go, but she got me all the way together man. She taught me so much. The proper way to court her. Patience in my pursuit." I rubbed my chin.

Ray furrowed his brows. "She the one that wouldn't see you for some months, and yall was just talking on the phone and shit?"

"Yes. The same woman. I unlearned all my bad habits. We spoke so much and learned one another inside and out before we even held hands. Let alone kiss or have sex."

"Wow."

"Maybe you should try doing things differently in your next pursuit. I don't think age necessarily has much to do with it. It's the person."

nineteen

DESTINEY

"This is going on my 'to be read' list! It's ever-growing, but I don't mind. I'll get to all these eventually." Gabby giggled. She did some clicking on her iPad, updating her Goodreads account.

I laughed. "It's the same for me, Gabby. Let me know when you're ready for that one. I have a copy I can pass you." We had been discussing *Jubilee* by Margaret Walker. African American historical fiction was a great genre, and Gabby was slowly embarking on her discovery.

I laid back on their comfortable couch, trying not to doze off. I was beyond full, first of all. We'd been having a great time at Malachi and Ella's for the past few hours. Eating Ella's delicious food, drinking, and enjoying each other's company. I hung out in the kitchen with Ella when Micah and I arrived, catching up with her and offering my help if needed. I took a quick FaceTime call from India, and Ella extended an invite to her. India's schedule is quite hectic, so I didn't expect her to be able to come on the fly. Surprisingly, she could. Before India headed out, Micah's friend Solomon came in, and they spoke briefly. Ironically, Micah had mentioned the cookout to him as well. They're both single, so I knew exactly what time it was when Solomon pulled his phone out and handed it to her. India was gorgeous, and I noticed the subtle glances he'd been giving her. Solomon seemed like a nice guy, and I was sure she'd fill me in if anything became of it.

Now, it was down to just Gabby and me hanging out in their living room, so we spent time bonding. I'm only about fifteen years older than Gabby, and she was seriously like the kid sister I never had. Gabby was such a sweet girl. Intelligent. Beautiful inside and out. Super silly. Gabby got it honest because Ella was much of the same. They were both so much fun to be around. My relationships with them both meant so much to me already.

For the past hour, Gabby and I nerded over books. I loved many titles across many genres, romance being at the very top of my list. I accidentally minored in African Diaspora Studies in college. I say accidentally because that's precisely what it was.

I needed to choose an elective for the upcoming quarter and decided on an introductory course on African American Literature. I love reading and figured it would give me a break from my intense linguistics courses. It was not at all what I expected but in the best way. Every damn thing blew my mind, and I *adored* my professor. As the quarter progressed, I was enamored with so many titles. The game changer was when I discovered books from the Harlem Renaissance Era, and that was when I knew. I couldn't change my major so late without adding at least another year before I could graduate; however, I was able to squeeze in a minor. *Cane River, Not Without Laughter, Blacker the Berry. Passing* by Nella Larson was another one Gabby and I talked about. It had grown in notoriety since the Netflix film, but I read the book several years back and enjoyed it.

Micah and Ray were still on the back patio. Not long ago, Malachi came in and pulled Ella to him from her seat on the couch, and they made out in the living room. Those two were always kissing. Not pecks, but that heavy kissing. It always cracked me up because Gabe and Gabby didn't pay them any mind, yet many kids their age got squeamish when they saw their parents being affectionate. I think one reason was that it was an everyday thing for them. I believe parents should show love and affection in front of their children. Hugging, kissing, holding hands, and even flirting create fond memories of your parents in love. I think it brings children security. It certainly beats the alternative of having memories of parents fighting all the time.

Once they came up for air, Malachi led Ella out the front door. They had an expansive porch complete with a swing and rocking chairs. The sun was beginning to set, and I was sure it was a romantic vibe out there. This wasn't even the first time. Earlier, Malachi quickly scooped Ella up, tossing her over his shoulder, and moved through the living room toward the stairs. I heard him smack her ass as Ella cackled.

"*Chiiii!*" Ella drew his name out. She was in a fit of giggles. "We have company baby!"

"Yall carry on. We'll be back. Or maybe we won't. I'on know yet." Malachi declared, strolling up the stairs with ease. With one arm, he held her securely, and with the other, he rubbed Ella's ass and thighs, giving it an occasional smack. Sounds of Ella's excessive laughter floated behind them. India and I shared a glance and fell into a fit of giggles.

Micah texted me about being ready to get going, and I was ready too.

"Alright Gabby girl. I'm going to grab your uncle so we can get out of here." I gave her a tight hug.

"Okay. Alone time with you is the best. We talk about so many things!"

"I enjoy our chats too love."

"I'm going to ask Uncle Micah if I can come by this weekend. You'll be there, right?"

I smirked. *I damn near lived there*, but I wouldn't tell her that. "Let me know when you're going, and I'll be sure to be there too."

"Okay!"

I'd already given her my cell phone number, and we occasionally texted one another.

I headed toward the back patio to tell Micah I was ready to get home. I was just about to open the screen door when I heard it. "Man, I outta get me some young snatch. They seem like the perfect type of woman. You got her right man. That's what the fuck I'm trying to get."

"She's right where I want her." I heard Micah respond. I stopped abruptly mid-step, and my breath was caught in my throat.

I couldn't believe what I heard. My heart dropped as I quickly spun around, walking straight past the kitchen and out the front door. Tears began to flood my eyes. *Right where he wants me?* The fuck does that even mean. Was his goal to get a young, innocent, naive girl to groom or some shit? I tore through the front door, almost colliding with Malachi and Ella as they returned inside.

"Destiney!" Ella exclaimed.

Seeing how upset I was, Malachi gently grabbed my arm. "Hey, Baby sis. You okay?"

I nodded quickly as the tears began to fall, and I didn't bother to wipe them.

"Why are you crying?" Ella asked, reaching out to me. I broke away from her and kept walking toward my car.

"Micah know you leaving? Why isn't he walking you out?" Malachi's voice dipped in concern. He tried to grab me, too, but I broke from his grasp.

"He doesn't know." I managed and continued down the driveway to my car.

"That's aight, I'm out here anyway," he said as he and Ella followed closely behind me.

I didn't respond. I jumped into my car, slammed the door, and sped off before I strapped in my seatbelt. I began to cry hysterically as the floodgates opened. I could hardly see as the tears fell freely from my eyes. I felt terrible for the way I'd treated Malachi and Ella. None of this was their fault. I hopped on I-5 northbound, ready to get home and into bed.

I knew he was too good to be true. I knew, at some point, the other foot would drop.

Everything had been going so perfectly that I had finally let all that go.

My heart was hurting. I heard my phone ringing. Glancing over, I saw it was Micah. He called again twice more. A moment later, Ella called me. I ignored her call but would text her once I was off the road.

Then, I would block Micah's number.

He can try that grooming shit with someone else.

twenty

MICAH

I called Destiney for what seemed like the hundredth time... but it went straight to her voicemail this time. Either her phone was off, or she blocked me. I was so confused.

We'd all had such a great time at Malachi's house.

Or so I thought.

Mal and Ella were great hosts, as always. We ate good, of course. Sol and Ray came through, and India joined us. It was great seeing her again. She was dope, and she and Destiney had such a great friendship. I loved that for Destiney.

Eventually, the men had all gone out to the patio, and the women spent time in the house for a while. Destiney was chilling with Gabby once India took off, but I knew she'd be ready to head home soon. It had been a long day. I planned to follow her home once she was ready. Sol had already headed out. I was sitting on the back patio with Ray, shooting the shit, when Malachi came in with Ella on his heels to alert me of what had occurred moments prior.

"What's going on with your wife man?"

"What are you talking about?"

"She left." I heard Ella say.

"Left?"

"She said you didn't know she was leaving. But she seemed pretty upset. Baby sis was crying." Malachi continued, "She wouldn't tell us anything. She just got in her car and sped off."

I stood immediately and headed into the house. Malachi, Ella, and Ray followed.

Now, I was confused as hell. And worried. Why would she be crying? And why did she leave without telling me? We planned on leaving together; otherwise, I would always walk her out. I grabbed my phone and called her. It rang through, eventually rolling to voicemail, so I called her again.

"You think somethings going on with her family?" Ray asked.

"I'm not sure. Seems she would have told me." After getting her voicemail again, I texted her, asking if she was okay and asking her to please call me as soon as she could. I knew she was still driving, but I was sure she'd get back to me once she was off the road.

"I'll try to call her too," Ella said, placing her phone to her ear. I grabbed my jacket and put my shoes on.

"Thanks Ella. Let me know if you hear from her before me." I wasn't even sure why I said that shit.

"Of course." She replied.

I hugged Malachi and kissed Ella on the cheek. "I'm out of here. Let me try to figure out what's going on."

"I'm out too, cousin," Ray said as we slapped hands.

As soon as I cranked up, I headed toward Destiney's house. I needed to get to my baby and make sure she was okay.

I made it to Destiney's house in record time and saw her car parked outside. I was somewhat relieved but even more confused, as I'd called her several times since leaving Malachi's. I sprinted up the steps and rapidly knocked on the door. I heard the locks disengage, and a few moments later, Daijah greeted me.

"Hey Micah." She seemed okay, so it was likely that there wasn't a family emergency. That was good news.

"Hey Daijah." I stepped forward but halted abruptly once I realized she wasn't inviting me in. "My apologies. Do you mind if I come in? Destiney and I were over at my brother's house, and she suddenly left in tears. I've been calling and texting her, but she isn't responding.

Daijah slowly shook her head. "She doesn't want to see you right now."

"She doesn't want to see me? Why not?" I exclaimed, then immediately felt terrible. My volume was too loud for comfort, and my tone was unfriendly. I wasn't the type of man to raise my voice to any woman. I took a deep breath and then exhaled. "I'm sorry for raising my voice at you, Daijah."

"No harm done." She reassured me.

"Do you know why she doesn't want to see me?" If anyone knew, Daijah did. She and Destiney were closer than close. Just as close as Malachi and me.

She paused for a moment. "It's best if the two of you talk about it."

"But she won't answer my calls."

"I promise you will at least get a text. I'll go back to her room right now and make sure."

"Thanks, Daijah. Have a good night." I said, turning to head back to my car.

"You too." She said to my back, closing the door softly.

She doesn't want to see me.

This shit is bizarre.

twenty-one

DESTINEY

"Are we really back here again?" You can't just ignore him, Des. That isn't fair. He has no idea why you're even upset with him. How do you expect him to fix it if he doesn't know what he did?" Daijah had come home right behind me, and I filled her in on the latest. We were in her room, and I was lying across her bed on my stomach. I hardly ever came into her bedroom these days because she was hardly home. She was lying right beside me on her back.

"He should know! How is that okay? *I have her like I want her*?" I imitated, pissed all over again.

"That's all you heard?"

"Yes. Well, aside from what his idiot cousin Ray said. I don't like him at all, Daijah. He's such a manwhore. He's always on these sexual escapades and dealing with multiple women at one time. He and Micah are nothing alike."

"That's his cousin. We got crazy ass cousins too. Hell, everyone does. But they don't have any bearing on who we are as individuals."

"Okay," I said, returning a blank stare.

"You just completely missed my point." Daijah threw up her hand and huffed loudly. "Since you're in your feelings, I'll let that slide." She sat up next to me. "You just said Micah is nothing like Ray, right?"

I nodded.

"That means there's more to be considered. You only heard *some* of the conversation. Just because Ray said that, that doesn't necessarily mean Micah agreed. He likely refuted Ray's stance, but you walked away before you could hear it. If Micah were that type, we'd know it. And I'm willing to bet you'd have a different opinion had you heard the entire conversation."

I considered Daijah's words. She had a point. Micah mentioned several times that Ray was a wildcard, but they tolerated him since he was family, loving him just the same. Malachi and Micah were close to Ray, Micah a little closer; nonetheless, Ray's lifestyle choices did not appear to have any bearing on Malachi's or Micah's in the grand scheme. They didn't even seem to have the same ideals and convictions.

"You see what I mean?" Daijah asked, bringing me from my thoughts.

"Yeah, I guess I do," I replied. Daijah was probably right. Knowing Micah, he likely didn't even agree with Ray. He was literally in the middle of a thought and pissed; I stormed off.

"Please reach out to him. I felt so bad. He stood on the porch looking like he lost his best friend."

I hung my head.

"I can text him, but I'm embarrassed at how I reacted."

"So, tell him that part too. Tell him everything."

I probably wasn't the best person for a relationship with Micah. I handled this situation like a damn teenager. He didn't deserve that, and I didn't deserve him. Who was I kidding? It was best I stopped while I was ahead.

I may need to end things with Micah.

twenty-two

MICAH

I got up to use my ensuite restroom. Just as I was washing my hands, I heard my phone ringing. I flew back into my bedroom to see it was Malachi. I sighed.

"Brother."

"Hey man. You talk to her?" Mal asked me.

"Not yet. I think she blocked me."

"Okay. I wanted to tell you that she texted Ella earlier. Ella just saw it though; she's never glued to her phone. Never knows where the thing is half the time."

"Really? What did she say?"

"Just that she's sorry for storming off and ignoring us when we tried to see about her. She didn't offer anything else. Ella figured she'd share if she wanted to talk about anything more, so she didn't press."

"Well, I'm glad she heard from her at least." I felt a little better about that.

"Yeah."

"I'm so confused man. I wish she would at least tell me what has her so upset. This is our first official argument, and whatever it is, she has completely shut down from me."

"You ain't cheat on her, did you?"

"What? No!"

Malachi chuckled. "I already knew the answer to that. I was just messing with you, man. But seriously, I'm sure she will come around eventually."

"You think so?"

"Yeah man. I can't think of anything that could be worse than that. She'll come around."

"Thank you, Brother. I love you man."

"I love you, baby Brother. One more thing. I won't keep you."

"What's that?"

"Romance the *hell* out of her. I know you already have been. You've learned from the best."

We shared a light chuckle.

"But seriously. You have her address. You know what to do."

"I gotchu."

"Try to get some sleep, baby brother. Everything will work out."

"Thank you brother. Goodnight."

"Goodnight."

I tried calling Destiney again just to get her voicemail. I let out an exasperated breath as I rolled onto my back, staring at the ceiling. I doubted I would get a wink of sleep tonight. I closed my eyes momentarily, hearing a light chime from my cell phone on my side table. I ignored it, keeping my eyes closed, trying to clear my head. Whatever it was, it could wait. I knew it wasn't my baby anyway.

Daijah said she'd make sure Destiney texted me, but that was hours ago. Maybe she didn't mean tonight; perhaps she meant eventually.

I'd give Destiney a couple of days. Three at the most. I was moving in if I still hadn't heard from her after that. Making an executive decision.

We were *not* going to have a repeat of last time.

No way, no how.

No sir, no ma'am.

twenty-three

DESTINEY

"Destiney!"

I looked up toward the voice just as Neeka excitedly waved, making her way toward me from across the produce section.

Great. I mumbled to myself, sighing inwardly. I didn't feel like talking to anyone, least of all Neeka. Yet and still, I remained in place, figuring I'd see what she wanted and then be on my way.

I stopped at the store on my way home from work. I only planned to be here for a few minutes tops. I could carry my items and didn't even bother getting a basket.

I needed more than the small bags of tomatoes, limes, and avocados in my hand. I hadn't been grocery shopping for my house in ages.

This store, in particular, was the one I frequented the most.

Back when I needed to.

Hanging out with Micah and being at his place so much meant I didn't have to.

But. I'd been back at my place for the past couple of days.

Just me. Daijah practically lived with Julian. Hell, up until three days ago, I was living with Micah damn near. I even had a key to the place.

Anyway, returning home meant I needed to cook for myself again. Last night, I had cereal for dinner, which was fine. I didn't feel like having anything else. The night before last, I had rice and spicy lentils. I eat lentils pretty often. They're a staple for me; they have lots of protein, and I always keep bags of dry lentils in my pantry. Micah even had a few bags for me at his house.

Micah.

Luckily for me, India was coming over tonight, and we'd be making tacos. Even though I didn't have much of an appetite, I loved taco nights with my best friend, and I was looking forward to it. Sometimes, we made them with black beans, but tonight, we were making them with *Impossible Ground Beef.* You cook and season it just like actual ground beef. It's pretty good. I still remember what real ground beef tastes like, and it's one of the best meat substitutes I've had. I've been a vegetarian for almost a decade and tried many.

Earlier, Indie told me she wouldn't be able to stay the night; she'd need to get back to her parents. But we'll try to link up again in a couple of days.

And speaking of a couple of days, I swear these past three days have been the longest three days of my freaking life. I was losing my mind.

Missing Micah.

"Hey stranger!" Neeka said with a plastered-on smile. "Haven't heard from you in a while. New man must be keeping you busy."

I stood there, silent. Deadpan. Looking Neeka in the eye.

I usually would have eagerly embraced Neeka and then filled her in on everything going on in my life. I didn't say a word. My silence was deafening and awkward. I guess she felt she needed to fill the space with something. "I mean.

You've been *super distant*." She was right. Neeka and I didn't talk daily, but several weeks had passed since our last conversation. We last spoke when she came to my house those weeks back. Ordinarily, I would have texted her by now. But I didn't bother to text her after that. Nor did she text me. Honestly, we'd only talk when I reached out first, anyway. Neeka continued, "I assume that's the reason." She cracked up. I didn't find shit funny, and her laughter was excessive, in my opinion. I'm guessing she was cracking up at herself, which was fine. I laughed at myself *all the time*.

Before I realized it, I started to laugh too.

At her.

Directly.

Neeka must think I'm stupid.

And at some point, maybe I was when it came to dealing with her wack ass.

I shouldn't have ignored all those red flags.

She was *never* my friend. Yet I treated her golden.

My desperation for a friendship with Neeka had me turning a blind eye to shit that most people wouldn't have tolerated.

"The phone works both ways." Her eyes grew wide at my even response. I know *that* took her off guard. I'd never spoken to Neeka like that. I didn't talk like that ever.

Fucking glass house. She can dish it, but it doesn't seem she can take it. It looked as if she almost clutched at her imaginary pearls but caught herself. Also, she'd suddenly stopped laughing—not a trace of a smile or mirth anywhere. I think right after I started laughing, suddenly, whatever she was laughing at wasn't so damn funny anymore.

"I'll need to get going. India's meeting me at my place."

211

"Really? What are you guys cooking?" She assumed we'd be cooking tonight, and she was right.

She used to be invited to these. But I ain't forget the last time I invited her; she had some fuck shit to say about my clothes.

"Tacos?" She asked, eyebrows high when I said nothing. *"I love Indie's tacos."*

"Me too. Bye Neeka." I said dryly. I turned to walk away without a second thought.

And I walk fast.

I was wearing a busted pair of sneakers covered in blotches of paint, so I got away from her faster than she could keep up. Neeka was impeccably dressed in her usual pencil skirt, tucked-in blouse, and pumps.

Anyway, the conversation was over. She was fishing, and I wasn't biting.

"Destiney, wait!" I stopped. Why? I don't know. But I didn't turn around. I was in the bakery section now, closer to the front of the store, which was a bit crowded. People busied themselves around us with their shopping carts and children. I honestly didn't want to hear anything she had to say.

"I don't have any plans tonight." Neeka offered once she was facing me. "Can I come by? I'll bring wine with me."

My eyebrows were high on my head.

That's bold as fuck. And desperate. I shook my head. "Honestly, Neeka, tonight isn't a good night."

"A good night for what? It's only me. Me, you and Indie. That's typical." She shrugged. Yeah, she was desperate. And eager. It was evident in her voice.

Meanwhile, I thought over just how blunt I would be with her.

I sighed. "It's not a good night for *you* to come over. I am anxious as hell whenever you're around. You're too much."

"Too much? I'm just being me." She chuckled at that. And I said nothing as she waived dismissively. "I'm your friend. Y'all are my girls, and I am *way* overdue. *Been bored out of my mind!* So, what time should I come by?"

I looked at her square in the eye. "You aren't invited Neeka. And you aren't my friend." Her eyes ballooned. Her lips parted. She wasn't getting it, so I needed to say it. "*I've certainly been a friend to you. I was so nice to you.* Too nice honestly." I shrugged. "A friend wouldn't speak like you've spoken to me. Or treat me the way you've treated me. I'm doing myself a disservice, giving you access to me." I gave Neeka half a beat, then, "And I know you're fucking Tyler." I lied.

I didn't know. But Neeka confirmed India's suspicions when she began to stammer.

"I... wha..." She snapped her mouth shut; her eyes narrowed to slits. "Tyler doesn't even belong to you!"

I slowly shook my head, rolling my eyes. Wow. *That's* what she chose to respond to?

"I need to spell it out for you, Neeka. Fine. It's not that ya'll are fucking. It's the way you choose to move about it. Sneaking around like that?" I gave her an incredulous glare. "Why hide?" I shook my head again, shrugging. "Friends wouldn't do that shit either. *We dated.* Why would you even... you know what? Never mind. Bye Neeka."

I turned to continue toward checkout, determined to leave everything right where it was.

Neeka caught me on the wrong day.

Or maybe it was the right day. It had been three days since the ordeal at Malachi and Ella's house, and I wasn't in the mood for Neeka's bullshit. Regardless, that conversation needed to happen a long time ago. I'm not sure I would have been so outspoken about that if I weren't in my feelings over things with Micah.

I've dealt with many toxic women. *Frenemies*. Plenty. More than I care to admit. Allowing women who are lackluster friends and just plain awful towards me into my life and my space was *my bad*.

But it's disgusting.

Repulsive how people think they can treat someone any way they feel like and then just sweep that shit under the rug as if it never happened and *then* be buddy-buddy in the next moment without even apologizing.

It didn't occur to Neeka to even hold herself accountable and ask *how* she's been a lousy friend so she can address it. And not the Tyler part, because honestly, that didn't bother me as much as how she treated me.

Neeka is toxic in general. And narcissistic. She invested too much time in the external, except for her academics and career. I'm no psychologist, but in my opinion, she never worked on developing her character. Or integrity. Neeka insisted she was looking for her husband, but the men she entertained only wanted to fuck her, so they'd never been able to tell her about herself.

And no man with sense would wife *that*. Not in *that* condition.

You can always tell when someone is speaking from a place of trauma. *Them motherfucker's* shine bright like diamonds.

You can hear when someone is projecting their feelings and opinions on the world because they are louder than everyone else—the loud minorities.

That's Neeka.

If she committed to seeing a therapist and did some serious work internally, she'd be okay.

But seriously fuck Neeka. I drove away from the store, pissed the hell off at her *audacity*.

I'm not the problem she is.

I'm like the mafia. It's hard to get in with me. My circle is curated, so when you're in with me, you are in. Like *in*, in. I am loyal. To a default.

Sometimes, I wonder if that works against me. Like, perhaps I've created a monster.

I realized I have a problem as it relates to people like her.

For the right people, I'm *exactly* the way I should be. Me.

***

I stepped inside and headed toward the kitchen. I dropped my backpack by the door and then placed my sack of groceries on the counter beside the roses I received yesterday.

Beside the roses was a sunflower arrangement I had received the day before.

They were so beautiful. The red roses were too, of course, but the *sunflowers*.

I'd never told Micah that sunflowers were my very favorite flowers.

And I love sunflowers. I love how bright they are, their big, beautiful boldness. They look like little suns, ready to lift your spirits. And when they were delivered two days ago, I cried all over again. Despite how ridiculously immature I was, Micah still thought enough of me to send my favorite flowers.

I barely hung my coat up when I heard my doorbell ring. I didn't think Indie would be here for another hour, but she knew she could come early if needed. I went to answer the door, and to my surprise, it was an *Edible Arrangement*.

After signing for my delivery, I thanked the driver and placed them on my counter. A note was attached, just as there were with the other two deliveries.

I'll always be yours, my Destiney baby. I love you. - MW.

***

"Neeka is wild. She doesn't even know what the hell she wants half the time." Indie said. We were sitting on the couch with some Tyler Perry movie on. I don't know which one. I was hardly watching.

When she first arrived, we'd briefly spoken about her and Solomon. Indie said he seemed chill, and she'd been chatting with him casually. She mentioned liking him a lot and seeing a future with him, but she was transparent about her recent break-up and wanted to be fair to Solomon. He was a good guy and didn't deserve her on some rebound shit. I respected that.

It was a trip too because Indie and I were both single for once.

We were *never* single at the same time.

Well, Indie was never single. Not for long, anyway; she was a serial monogamist. She's only had two boyfriends in the seven almost eight years since I've known her, but both of those relationships were years long. Before her most recent ex, she dated a guy she'd been with since high school. They dated for close to five years.

And I'd never been in a relationship.

This was my one and only, and… anyway.

I filled Indie in on what happened at the store earlier. And she was off on her tangent. Which often happened when Neeka did something to piss her off.

"I'm proud of you for standing up to her. I know she was flabbergasted." Indie chuckled hard at that. I did too. "I think she did well for herself, objectively speaking. If those things matter to you. But she leads with that."

India was right. Neeka is young but has accomplished a whole lot. She's a couple of years older than me but has a great career in Public Health Administration. Super smart. She skipped a grade, so she graduated from high school at sixteen and had two master's by twenty-four. She made great money, had nice things, and traveled the world.

But her conversation was limited, and somehow, regardless of the subject, she brought everything back to *her*.

Neeka was Neeka's favorite subject. She seemed one-dimensional on a good day. She only spoke about her academic and professional accomplishments.

"She's okay, I don't think she's a knockout." India said. She was still going. I was hardly listening if I'm honest. Neeka's ass wasn't my concern. "She likes to think she's the most beautiful thing you've ever seen. She's above average but her attitude makes her look bad. And that attitude and personality will repel a man every time. It seems some women who are high achieving have a harder time locking down a man. That's probably one of the reasons she doesn't have a man. She seems scattered and unsure of herself at times. She makes it seem that she has so many men that want to date her. Yet no one seem to want commitment. They just want to fuck on her. Like *all of them*. She used to say she didn't want anything serious but as of late, didn't you notice she's been commenting about wanting a husband? We *are* getting older so I could see why she change her tune."

India stood from the couch returning to the kitchen. Her words floated behind her. "I am so over that topic. And I really need to be nice." After a beat, "These flowers are beautiful Best." India commented. She was still back in the kitchen. Helping herself to thirds. I was stuffed, sprawled back on the couch, but I would probably have at least one more taco once I let my food go down.

I didn't have much of an appetite earlier, but I was ready by the time the food was ready.

"Yeah, they are." I sighed. "You see that fruit in the fridge? You're welcome to as much as you want. I can't eat all of it. Daijah may not be home anytime soon." That Edible Arrangement was massive. I'd already eaten quite a few of the chocolate dipped pieces. The pineapples were my favorite. Even then there was so much left of it.

"Sure, I'll have some." A few moments later, India put two plates on the coffee table then returned to her spot on the couch. One plate was covered with fruit, and one had two more tacos.

India could eat me under the table, but she always remained thin. "You know Des… there may not be too many more of these." Indie said, pulling me from my thoughts.

And they were on Micah. Naturally.

My response was delayed when I absently asked, "More of what?"

"I read his note. You broke things off with him and he's still fighting for you. Sending you these gorgeous flowers and expensive ass fruit." Out of my peripheral I could see Indie shaking her head. "I'm saying this out of love, Best. Micah may get tired of this. You don't want to lose him for good, do you?"

I hung my head.

Of course, I'd told Indie about the portion of the conversation I heard.

The night everything happened, I sent Micah a text message. Which I'd shared with Daijah and India too. They wanted to bite my head off for going overboard. Anyway, I did block him that night too but only for a couple hours. I thought that was a bit extreme after talking things over with Daijah. So, I unblocked him and sent him a text message. It was pretty late by then. I figured he'd gone to sleep. I wasn't expecting a response that night but after some time, Micah called me. I was still up so I answered his call.

I told Micah about the portion of the exchange I heard between him and Raymond. Micah went on to explain further and of course, it was taken out of context on my part.

Micah apologized profusely and despite that, for some damn reason, I stood firm on my brilliant idea to end things.

And since then, Micah has been sending me flowers. Beautiful flowers.

For the past three day's he'd also sent me *good morning, thinking of you, good night* and *I love you* texts.

The entire first day I left him on read, but by day two-yesterday, I was even more beside myself and replied to each one.

Good morning.
Thinking of you too.
Good night.
I love you too.

Micah hasn't tried calling me again. Anyway, I was such a mess behind this shit.

And it was all my fault. Again.

All of it. And I thought my breakup with him was apparent, but Micah wasn't giving up on me so quickly. On us. And I'm happy he wasn't. I miss him so much.

Why couldn't I have just gone to him, instead of rushing to conclusions?

Worse than that, making an impulsive decision. This misunderstanding could have been cleared up immediately if we'd just had a conversation.

I needed to handle myself better. Micah is a grown ass man and behaves like one. My lack of experience in relationships always shows itself at the worst times. It's embarrassing as hell. I wanted my man back and planned to call Micah as soon as India left.

And. Indie was right; this was strike two.

I'd be out of his life for good at strike three. No doubt in my mind.

***

I'm sorry baby.

India helped me clean the kitchen, and then she had to get going.

After shutting everything down in the front of the house, I headed to my bedroom to shower quickly.

I planned to call Micah as soon as I got settled. By the time I finished moisturizing my skin and settling into bed, I had received a text message from him. I figured he may be saying goodnight. He apologized. I sighed.

Micah had no reason to be sorry.

Desperately needing him- needing to reassure him, I called him. It rang once, and then I immediately felt the familiar comfort of his voice.

"Hey baby." His voice. It was smooth. It was familiar. And despite myself, it made me smile.

"Hey."

We were both silent for a beat.

"I'm sorry."

"I really am sorry."

We spoke at the same time.

"No Micah. I should be the one apologizing. *I'm* sorry. *I'm so sorry*. I'm sorry I didn't come to you." I was getting emotional, and, in a minute, I would surely break into an ugly cry.

"It's alright. I can see why you felt the way you did. Ray can have such a shit mouth. And I absolutely could have said that better than I did." He sighed heavily. "But... can we promise each other this won't happen again, and we'll always talk to each other first?"

"I promise baby." I avowed immediately. "I'm embarrassed as hell and angry at myself for how I reacted."

"No harm done beautiful. We learned from this, and now we can move on. I love you, Destiney baby."

"I love you too Micah. So much." I felt relieved. Immensely. And damn. I missed him.

The line was silent for a few beats.

"What are you doing baby?" Micah asked.

"Laying down. Talking to you. What are you doing?"

"Laying down, talking to you."

"Hmm."

"You tired baby?" He volleyed.

"Not at all."

"Same. I want you. I want to see you. I need to."

I glanced at the time. "It's late. Almost eleven."

"I need to put my eyes on you. Be near you. Hold you."

Same. I felt my excitement rising. "Baby… *please* be careful getting here."

"Let's talk while I'm on my way to you."

"Okay."

"Hang on about to change."

"Alright."

I heard shuffling. Then, "I've missed you so much beauty."

"I missed you too handsome."

I heard him moving about, then I heard the jingle of his keys a moment later.

"Alright. I'm headed your way baby."

I heard the garage door. "Can't wait. My days went so slow without you." I whined.

"Mine too sweetheart. It was torture."

I groaned. "It was like being cut off from everything that mattered."

"Same for me baby." I heard the car engine. After a moment, Micah said, "Don't take you away from *me* again. I need you."

The sincerity in his voice pulled at my heartstrings. I knew he wasn't trying to make me feel bad, but I did anyway.

And I needed him too. Even over these three days, the longest three days of my life, I needed him. "I need you too baby," I said finally. "Never again."

"Never. Ever."

Silence cruised through the line. I heard him quietly breathing as he listened to me do the same. I didn't even hear the radio on. "On the freeway now."

"Get to me safely."

"Indeed." Silence. "Baby?"

"Yes?"

"I've dreamed of you."

"Have you really?" My heart tripled in size.

"Indeed. You are the woman of my dreams. All my dreams include you."

"My gosh. Micah...I can't believe how sweet you are to me. And your words... they...you are *everything*."

"I'm just a man in love. *So very in love*. I love you, Destiney baby."

"I really do love you too Micah. So much."

"You mean so much to me."

"You mean the world to me."

More silence cruised through the line.

"Almost to you."

"Yeah?" My heart rate picked up.

"Yeah."

When I heard a groan, my pussy started to pulse. The groan was low but heavy and laced with desire, and I heard it loud and clear. I was on that same type of time.

"I'm here baby."

I got up from the bed and headed down the hall. I heard his car outside, and Micah was sprinting up my walkway when I opened the front door. He picked me up swiftly and began to spin me around. I tightly wrapped my legs around his waist as he hungrily kissed me with passion and fervor. I kissed him back just as eagerly, sensual moans emitting from us both.

He finally broke our kiss. Holding my gaze, he asked, "Can I make love to you, sweetheart?"

"Please do." I returned without hesitation.

Our lips connected again as he carried me to my bedroom, closing and locking the front door behind us.

He gently placed me on my bed and immediately began unbuttoning my pajama top, holding my gaze with low lids, undoing each one. After the final button, he gently pushed each side over my bare shoulders, peppering wet kisses down to my erect nipples and back again. I moaned in response.

Standing straight, he pulled his t-shirt over his head, tossing it to the side. I saw his dick print, and I reached for the waistband of his sweatpants, pulling them down. I was greeted with a head glistening with pre cum. My mouth watered as I went to lick it off the tip, but Micah gently pushed me back.

There was a subtle shake of his head. "Not yet." Going to his knees in front of my bed, he pulled my silk pajama bottoms and my panties over my legs as I lifted off the bed. "Lay back for me baby. I'm going to take my time with you."

Doing as instructed, my legs fell open as he settled between them. I would get my turn to please him eventually.

And I wanted to. Desperately. I wanted to make it up to him. Show him how much I missed him.

Micah had other plans.

"Mmm." He spoke against my pussy as he inhaled and rubbed my slick center with his fingers. She was throbbing for him.

"Damn… my pretty pussy was looking for me."

I groaned in anticipation. "You have her spoiled."

Micah lightly chuckled. "I'm here now baby." He inhaled deeply, speaking into my pussy, "Mine." Moans low and gruff, Micah swiped his tongue, and I damn near came right then. He rubbed my clit a few times and began to French kiss my lower lips, his tongue and fingers alternating inside of me; I started rocking my hips, getting lost in ecstasy. I cradled his face in my hands, watching him and spreading my legs as wide as they could go. In moments like this, I wish I was a little more flexible. But Micah made it work. His tongue reached everywhere it needed to. I gently caressed his jaws with my thumbs, enjoying the sweet torture his tongue was putting on me.

Knowing him, he'd want to get a few orgasms out of me before he took his first. I was good with that too.

We were finally reunited, and it felt so damn good.

twenty-four

MICAH

"Fuck… Destiney baby…You hear how she's talking to me?" I said between licks, sucks, and slurps. "Mine," I said it again.

"All. Yours. Baby." She purred. I could feel her orgasm rising as she continued to grind on my face. It wouldn't be much longer from here. She'd already come on my tongue a few minutes ago.

I made my way up her body, leaving a trail of kisses, and slowly pushed into her. I loved eating her, but I needed to feel her. I leaned close to her ear as I stroked her slowly, telling her all the ways I planned to love her. Confiding in her while making love to her was one of the best times to share my heart with her.

The energy surrounding us was just right. We were connected in the most intimate of ways, consumed with emotion, vulnerability, and passion. I maintained my pace, determined to slow stroke her to oblivion. She felt so good, but I concentrated.

This was not the time to fuck her. Maybe round two or some shit.

"Destiney baby?"

"Yes…"

"Does it feel good my love?"

"Yes… you know just what I like… you take good care of me. She's so happy."

"Hell yeah, she is. You hear how she's talking to me. She's so *loud."* My chuckle was a deep rumble. "I hear you baby. I like it too." Destiney was so wet that the sounds of her wetness filled the room with each move I made.

Destiney got *incredibly wet.* It actually blew my mind. Wetter than water. Shit was sexy as fuck.

I placed my hand on her clit, rubbing it a few times. My fingers slid back and forth with ease.

Destiney giggled.

"Oh, you're ticklish here too baby?" I asked her.

"Shit. Guess so… maybe a little bit." She giggled some, and it turned to a moan.

"Hmm." I spent some time there with my thumb. Rubbing her. Pressing her button. My baby liked that.

Yeah. I was already certain, but this confirmed everything. Laughing like we were doing, while we were lovemaking. Destiney was *absolutely* my wife.

I kept stroking her. *Slow.* Savoring her. I wasn't going any faster than this. I told Destiney I was taking my time and I was serious.

"You sexy girl. My beautiful Destiney baby." Still stroking her. "You mean the world to me. You're so special. I'm going to prove it to you every day for the rest of my life." I spoke closely in her ear, moving slowly and deliberately. Pulling out for just a second, I sat back up on my hunches, stroking my hardness. Destiney watching me with low lids. Looking like a beautiful fucking masterpiece.

My dick was oozing precum and glistening with her essence. Her fat pussy was swollen and gushing with a delectable combination of her juices and mine. I slowly pushed back inside. "Fuck baby, this is a beautiful sight." I was about to bust just watching the way my shit looked

227

sliding in and out of her slick opening. I was back in her ear again. "I can't wait to marry you baby."

"Hmm." Her faint moans were sexy as hell. "I can't wait to marry you either baby."

She was so wet. And she was so tight around me. She could take all of me now, and I filled her to the hilt.

"Baby."

"Mmmhmm."

"You almost there love?" I asked her.

"Yes."

I was close my damn self, but I needed her to go first.

Stroking her a few more times, I said, "Give it to me, baby. I got you." I'd be right behind her.

Later when I finally turned her loose, her mouth was around me, sucking my soul from my dick.

"Mmmhmm. That's right. You sexy girl." She was pleasing me so damn good, and I wanted her to know it. I learned Destiney liked praise, which kept her out of her head. I had no problem hyping my woman up. She loved it when I spoke to her low and slow. My voice was already deep but huskier when I got in her ear. Pillow talk with her was for anytime and everywhere she was. Not just between the sheets.

She continued sucking me, and she'd gotten pretty good at this. I'd told her so too. A few times.

I lifted myself into her slick mouth as I hummed. I knew she liked that.

We both enjoyed this, and that was the goal.

A deep rumble escaped me, and she moaned too. Destiney told me she loved it when I did that.

And anyway, we still had a few things to talk about.

And we would.

"Yeah… suck your dick baby."

Once we were done with this.

***

I stirred from my slumber, realizing I had dozed off. Deciding to try to get some sleep, I went to plug up my phone, and my heart skipped a beat when I saw a notification that Destiney had texted me more than an hour ago. I quickly opened the message, and just as quickly, my heart sank.

Micah, I am sorry for ignoring all your calls and texts. I heard a portion of your and Ray's conversation earlier, and I came to a conclusion that is likely not even correct. Based on how I have handled myself tonight, it doesn't seem I'm the right person for you. Relationships are just not in the cards for me. I don't deserve you, and I hope that you will forgive me.

I called Destiney immediately after reading that message. It was pretty late by then—maybe close to midnight—but Destiney answered my call.

And we talked about it. And I apologized profusely.

And since then, Destiney has uttered her embarrassment. Many times.

Truth is, I'm the humiliated one.

I have no clue why I needed to say what I said to Ray. The way I said it. Worse, my baby had to hear that.

Terrible.

I wasn't happy with myself. At all.

Mature men are extremely self-correcting. Inward looking. And the thing with inward-looking individuals is that we're always working to make ourselves better.

We can't help it. Like literally.

We know our value.

229

We know people hold us in high esteem, and we hold ourselves in high esteem. We are working to fix our issues *immediately*.

We will apologize *immediately* or fix things *immediately*.

We always represent our best selves in any space we're in.

Beyond that, I had Daddy and Malachi continuing to hold me accountable.

We hold *each other* accountable.

I expect to be called on my shit.

"Man, you fucked that one up yo." Or *"Man, I told you blah, blah, blah."*

And I was. As expected, Mal told me about myself. Called me on my shit.

After I spoke with Destiney and discovered the issue, I called Malachi and told him the next day.

"Nigga what?!?" *His voice was octaves higher.* *"I'm inclined to believe you are joking with me. I just **know** you lyin'."*

I snorted a dry ass chuckle. *"Wish I was brother."* *I shook my head.* *"I had one too many beers or something. That doesn't even **sound** like me."*

"No doubt." *Mal chuckled himself after a beat.* *"I would have walked out too, baby brother. Please tell me you cleaned that up."*

"I did. And I'm making it up to her in every way possible."

"Yo ass had better. Give baby sis whatever she wants."

A languid cackle left me in spite of myself. *"So that's it?"* *I posed flippantly.*

It was rhetorical. After that fiasco-of-a-blunder, there wasn't a damn thing Destiney couldn't ask me for.

For Destiney, I was willing.

"It's a start. The first order of business is to figure out **whatever** *the hell it is you need to do to get back in her good graces."*

"I'm already knowing, and I'm already on it." I returned.

Destiney seemed most concerned that her inexperience made her unequipped for a relationship with me. This being her first official relationship, she didn't feel she was cut out for it, and then there was our age difference.

I understood. But I disagreed, of course.

"Destiney... no..." I said the word firmly because I needed her to understand. I shook my head profusely, though she couldn't see me. This would likely be one of the few times I would ever tell her no. *"And I mean this respectfully, sweetheart. We aren't breaking up baby if you need a day or two. Space. That's fine. But we're not walking away from each other."* I'd told her. *"We're not just throwing all of this away. All the time we spent working this thing out, getting it just like we want it."*

No one is going to come behind me and step in and benefit from my hard work.

I'll be *damned*.

It wasn't going to happen.

I continued, *"We've gotten this to a great place. We built this beautiful thing together, and you had everything to do with it. Experienced or not."*

And I did give her space as much as I hated to. I gave it to her because that's what she needed.

And I continued to check in with her, missing her like crazy. Her laughter and energy were sorely missing from my home—our home. Her scent permeated my bedroom, and I spent all my time there, lying where she usually did, using the pillow she always used.

And I texted her.

And I sent her two floral arrangements.

When I perused the site and tried to decide, roses were an obvious choice, but that was too easy.

Destiney inspired and made me feel so many emotions; I wanted to step outside the typical. Sunflowers were a perfect choice because they reminded me so much of her. Destiney was like a ray of sunshine in my world. Her smile overtook her entire face. I was putty in her hands whenever she graced me with her smile.

"Everything feels so right with you. Micah." Destiney said, pulling me from my thoughts.

We were lying in Destiney's bed. I was on my back; she was on my chest. Her long, gorgeous locs splayed across the back of her naked body. It was dark in her bedroom, but her thin drapes let in the bright moonlight. My eyes followed the winding path of her body. A path my hands traveled many times. Her peaks and valleys. The rise of her plump ass. I loved her petite, curvy figure. Her naked body was alluring. She wasn't super trim or thin but fleshy and slightly toned. Soft and pretty. Lovely. Sweet.

I had my arms securely around her. Her arms were around me, too. It was late, after one a.m. now. We'd already decided neither of us was going to work tomorrow. We'd spend the day together. Not sure what we'd do, but I didn't care, just as long as I was with her.

It was completely silent until just a moment ago. We'd typically have music, but not right now.

"Like, my life has completely changed. In the best way. Since meeting you, I have seen everything differently. Myself included. It's like everything was black and white before. And now… everything is in color. Vividly clear and beautiful. I'm so glad I get to be with you Micah. It seems so surreal sometimes. Laying with you right now. Being loved by you.

As well as you love me. It's everything. You know? I never want to be apart. I love you so much." Destiney sighed a heavy sigh. "But love doesn't seem like a big enough word. The way I feel for you. It's a beautiful feeling. Something I can't describe. But my heart is yours."

I rubbed her back softly, processing her feelings and words for me. It was so sweet—all of it. "I'm the fortunate one," I was emboldened to say.

And I was. I don't know how I got her. But I did. Somehow.

Like my grandmother used to say, favor ain't fair.

"No way." I felt her chuckle against me. "I'm complicated. I am the *epitome* of self-sabotage. Men didn't get anything from me. My time or my attention. Occasional men tried to get at me, but it never went far." She took a heavy pause. "I used to think I wasn't deserving of a loving relationship. Until I met you. But I'm still learning, and I'm not so good at relationships. But I want to be better. I don't want to keep disappointing you. I may get on your nerves in the process… but I want to make you as happy as you've made me, if that's even possible for me. And I want to step outside of my comfort zone. And boldly take these steps. You've been so patient."

"Look at me, please." Destiney lifted her head from my chest as I told her, "You're doing just fine baby. You have no idea how happy you've made me. But let's discuss things. You can't make decisions for me, just like I can't make decisions for you. We can discuss them and make decisions together. I don't want you disappearing every time there's an issue. We can work through things together. I want to be here for you, but I need you to tell me when something's amiss. If you run away, I have no idea what's happening, and I can't be there for you. How can we grow?"

She slightly hung her head, looking away from me. "That's all I know how to do. Run away. Fight or flight. That's all I know."

"Baby." Destiney looked up again, and once I had her eyes, I said, "It doesn't have to be that way. Continue to show me how to love you, Destiney baby. If nothing else, I promise to take heed and give it everything I have. Everything within me. I've told you you're safe with me."

"I know." Her voice was small. Almost a whisper. Her head returned to my chest. "I need to tell you something."

"Anything. I'm all ears, my love."

"When I heard what I heard… which I know now I was *so* wrong about- but I didn't know that then… I was triggered."

I'd been rubbing her back. Suddenly, there was a shift in her energy. And I felt this tension.

That put me on alert. "Triggered?"

"Back when I was seventeen. There was a guy I knew. We were the same age, but he was much more sexually experienced than me… and he took advantage of me. It was my first sexual experience. He took my virginity." I heard her sniffle, and she started to wipe her face. Her head was still on my chest. But I wanted her eyes. At the same time, I tried to tread carefully. She was clearly speaking from a place of trauma.

"He took it?" My question was more of a statement. A statement I made as evenly as I could. "Destiney. *Baby*… were you…?"

She took a moment. A long moment. I heard sniffles and sobs. I felt her warm tears falling onto my chest. And I said nothing. Instead, I continued to hold her. Caress her.

I took a few deep breaths too because this made me angry.

"I mean. I don't think so. No. But I should have spoken up for myself." She was still sniffling but a little calmer now.

But me? My blood was boiling.

She gathered her bearings. "Anyway. I think that's what bothered me so much. It took me there. And I felt bad." She looked up. Her eyes were red and glossy. "Because I feel so safe with you. I was so frustrated with myself."

I held her in my arms. "You don't have to feel bad about any of that. Once we're triggered, our traumas show themselves whether we are ready or not."

"Definitely. And as much as I have wanted to leave that buried, I want to tell you everything. I want you to see me and know me. Inside and out."

"I want the same."

"I've never told anyone. Not even Daijah. I never spoken of it aloud. You're the only one who knows about that." She'd returned her head to my chest. I resumed rubbing her back softly. Trying to calm down. This shit with ol' boy had me livid. My chest was heaving in anger. I knew she could feel that my heart rate had picked up.

"Don't let this get you all upset," Destiney said, pulling me from my thoughts.

I was angry. I didn't know her then, but I was so very angry with that individual and what he'd done to her and taken from her.

"I'm sorry," I told Destiney.

Her eyes were on me again. "Micah. It isn't your fault. You have nothing to be sorry about."

"I'm saying it anyway. And I know it's not enough, but I'm so sorry. What you have is sacred, and he had no right to take it from you. Your virginity most of all."

"I appreciate your words and your heart."

"I mean it, love. Sincerely. Now that I'm a part of your life and you're a part of mine, I won't let any harm come to you. I'll protect you. I want to heal you of all of your hurts. Restore any insecurities."

"You're amazing."

"*You're* amazing." I thought about our conversation months ago when I told Destiney about the child that would have been. How much I grieved for them. I even shed a few tears. That's something I struggled with moving past. Especially now that I have the complete story. And Destiney encouraged me. *"Micah, your child is always with you, in your heart. And they're safe in the arms of Jesus. There's no better place for them. It's the only other place they belong".* I appreciated her being there for me and not judging me. I've since gone to therapy to better process my feelings concerning that.

My hands were all over her body. Rubbing as low as they could reach and back up again. "You know I'm not judging sweetheart. But why do you think you never told Daijah?"

"She's very protective of me. Even though I'm the big sister. And I know her. Somehow, she'll feel like she's to blame. I don't want to put that on her. None of this is her fault."

"None of this is your fault either."

"Most days, I can believe that." Destiney shared.

After a beat. "Have you talked to anyone about that? A therapist, a counselor?"

"I'd been to a few support groups. Years back. But that's the extent of it. I probably could benefit from seeing an actual therapist. But since I'm self-employed, I'm underinsured. I'd have to pay out of pocket, which can be pricey."

I waited a moment. Then I gently told her, "Find a therapist, love. I can request my assistant send me a list of some of the best in the area. Once you've found one, make an appointment at your earliest convenience. Use the card I gave you. Please."

"I promise I will. Thank you."

twenty-five

DESTINEY

"Baby."

"Yeah baby."

I sighed. Looking over myself in the full-body mirror in Micah's walk-in closet.

The outfit I had in mind didn't come together the way I wanted, so I changed into something else. Then something else. Then something else. This was my fourth outfit change, and I was no closer to being ready. I peered down at my cell phone, noting the time. I was going to make us late. I just needed to be comfy and casual. And cozy. We were closer to winter now, and temperatures had dipped.

We planned to meet with the crew: Daijah, Julian, Malachi, and Ella. India was coming out too, and she told me she'd asked Solomon to meet us. They'd been spending more time together. I could tell how much she liked him. Micah said Sol shared that he was really into her, too.

I love wine and a good conversation, and I looked forward to going out.

Tonight- if I could get myself together, we'd go to *Wine & Graze Taproom.* I'd never been, but Ella suggested the place. It's in the Delta Shores area of Elk Grove. I peeped at all the pictures on Yelp, and it was right up my alley. It looked like a chill, grown-ass vibe and comfortable atmosphere. Like a very sophisticated bar & lounge. There was music, flat screens everywhere, and plenty of comfy couches. Each person pays a flat fee, and there are self-pour taps with wines, beers, cocktails, and even coffee. The menu had typical bar options, and the food looked pretty good. If you want something lighter, you can build your own charcuterie board, which can be as small or as large as you like, with options to share with everyone.

"You alright?" Micah asked in alarm as he entered the closet. He was likely concerned because I took too long to respond. And he'd been ready a long ass time ago. He looked great. Wearing dark-washed jeans and a navy cardigan over a crisp white button-up. He was barefoot, but I saw the all-black Timbs he'd pulled out. Micah cleaned up very nicely, but I loved his casual look, too.

"Can we stay here?" I asked with a flustered sigh.

"We can do whatever you want to do." I saw him come up behind me in the full-body mirror I was still facing. He moved my hair aside and kissed my neck. My eyes fluttered.

"You always say that."

"I mean it baby. You're driving. I'm just along for the ride."

Chuckling, I asked, "But what do *you* want?"

"You." He lifted my hair, kissing my neck on the other side. This was an open kiss, so he left a wet mark.

"What do you want to *do*?"

"You."

"Besides that." I had just an element of frustration in my voice. He was so sweet, but this was burning up our daylight. Also, I was just a tad bit on the edge. I haven't been feeling very well.

I decided to keep that part to myself, though.

Micah tittered lightly before releasing me and sitting on the ottoman he kept in his closet. "Why do you want to stay here baby?" Micah asked in earnest.

I released an exasperated sigh. "I'm just in a funk. I didn't have the best day. And I don't like the way this fits." I shrugged my shoulders absently. "None of that made any sense, I'm sure."

"I get it baby. But first of all, you look great."

My smile spread as I looked down and back up at myself in the mirror. I had some high-waisted leather moto leggings on. A cropped slouchy sweater. It was one of my favorites. Dark grey with an embroidered tiger's face on the front. Lots of details and colors. I received compliments each time I wore it. White cami underneath. I'd probably wear my low-top, all-black vans. This was it. I felt good, and my man said I looked good.

"Your body is great baby. It's perfect, actually."

"Ain't nothing perfect about me," I said playfully, giving him a sincere smile. My sweet Micah said that all the time.

I stepped over to the built-in shelves in Micah's closet. Not long ago, he surprised me with an elegant emerald jewelry box. It had a glass lid, and the top opened like a chest, with various slots for smaller pieces. Two more layers, pulled out in the front like drawers for bigger pieces. It was so chic, and I was so grateful for it. I was beginning to acquire quite a collection. My man just kept decorating me. He'd given me a gorgeous pair of solitaire diamond stud earrings with the jewelry box. I hadn't taken those off since I put them on.

"I still think you're trying to get me fat." I joked sarcastically.

"What you mean?" He glared at me with a mischievous grin.

"We eat good. Often. Between you feeding me, taking me out. Mommy's. Ella stuffing us with her bomb-diggity food... I've probably gained ten pounds."

Micah laughed. "You're exaggerating baby. But you can work out in my gym anytime."

"I'm on my feet often, so I'm constantly in motion. I've realized that's not good enough for all this eating I've been doing. Somethings got to give."

"You're perfect for me baby." He stood again and came behind me. Turning me to face him as he wrapped me in his arms, he said, "If you want to get out, let's go. If you want to stay here, we can do that too. You look beautiful regardless."

"I'm all good now baby. We can go." I went up on my tiptoes, kissing him softly. "And I love you, Micah."

He pecked me a few times. "I love *you*, Destiney baby."

***

We had a great time at *Wine & Graze*. Stayed for a few hours. I'd definitely be back.

Micah and I were the last ones to arrive. I was sure we'd beat Mal and Ella. We'd met them many times before, and they were always fashionably late. We all knew how they got down.

Anyway, when we first arrived, everyone was coupled up. It was like a quadruple date. Eventually, the men congregated around one of the screens to watch a football game. We ladies sat around a nearby table and had girl talk. Laughing so damn much, of course.

Looking at them, I considered how thankful I was for these ladies.

I was. Truly.

And I loved each of them dearly for different reasons.

Day, my dearest sissy and very best friend. My sibling bestie. And always my voice of reason.

Indie, the bestie. My twin flame. A protector of my spirit and the calm to my storm.

And Ella, my sister-friend. Ella loved me and wished me well from the beginning, and she was quickly becoming so *precious* to me.

These ladies were my *tribe*, and they meant the entire world.

A chorus of *thank yous* sounded as our server delivered our charcuterie board. It was right on time. The four of us immediately began to dig in. We'd already started drinking since the beverages were self-pour. I had a sweet red wine in my glass, which was paired perfectly with the chocolate and cashews I started munching on. We also had crackers, pepper jack cheese, feta cheese, strawberries, and blueberries.

The ladies carried on chatting about something, but for a brief moment, I was distracted. I looked to my left to find Micah already looking at me. I smiled big and bright, and Micah did the same, winking too. I felt warm all over as he mouthed, *"I love you."*

Mouthing, *"I love you too,"* I blew him a kiss.

It was slight. A subtle gesture. I didn't make a show out of it. Just a little something Micah could see.

And anyone else paying attention.

Apparently, everyone was.

So, I surmise Micah was caught in the act. After our brief exchange, Malachi said something to Micah and all the men cracked up. Then, the sweetest chorus of *"Awws!"* broke the spell I was under. And I realized I'd been caught, too.

"You two are *so freaking adorable*. Hella sweet." India said, taking a sip from her glass. She had a red wine as well. Something drier than mine. Indie didn't like sweet reds as much as I did. "I love it Best." She was sitting right beside me and leaned into me, snuggling up close. "I am *so* happy for you!"

"Me too! I absolutely love Micah for you." That was Daijah. She had a white wine in her glass. The only one with white. Until recently, I used to drink white exclusively. I've gradually switched to red since Micah has so many wine selections. "I'm just glad you figured yourself out. Got out of your own damn way. Cuz... I love you, my dear sissy, but *oh my freaking goodness*." Daijah shook her head, chuckling lightly, and everyone joined her. Even me.

"Me three!" That was Ella. She sipped from her glass of rosé. Her favorite. I was bound to learn that detail since we often chatted over a glass of wine at Ella and Malachi's. "Des, you are *perfect* for baby bro. He's so happy. Love looks amazing on him. And it's no wonder. We knew there had to be something about you when he started telling us about you."

I couldn't help but smile. "I'm happy too. *So happy*. I love my man something fierce. He's amazing. Quite literally."

Ella nodded. "Oh, absolutely. I know a thing or two about the Walker men." Ella offered playfully, sipping from her glass again.

"It was the same for us Ella. Destiney never took anyone seriously. But then this guy named *Micah* came riding in on a horse. Sweeping her off her feet." Daijah said with a smile.

"*Right!* I knew there was something about him when she wouldn't stop talking about him." India chimed in.

"It be like that!" Ella said, laughing. "You ladies already know."

We all shared a laugh. "I love the way he looks at you." Ella continued.

Daijah and India nodded in agreement.

"Aww. So do I." I smiled again. Glancing over at Micah, I saw his back was to me now. The guys were focused on the game and having a lively discussion.

"Also, Ella, that lipstick is hella cute," India said. It was. It was a deep maroon, which looked gorgeous against her complexion.

"Thank you! You're poppin' too, boo!"

India laughed. "Thanks." Indie was wearing a scarlet red lip, which was her typical go to. It looked amazing against her complexion.

I took another sip of my wine. I was getting close to needing another glass, and I debated whether I'd get the same one or try another. I counted six different wine options. The next one would be my last. I wouldn't need more than two glasses.

"So, ladies," I began. Six expectant eyes looking back at me. Each of them drank from a stem wine glass. I had a stemless wine glass. I discovered recently that I'm not a good match for stem glasses. For some reason, I keep knocking my glasses over. Micah bought a set of stemless glasses for us to drink with at his house. I continued, "I need help planning Micah's thirty-fifth birthday." Nods of approval and words of confirmation sounded from each of them. "I'll probably do something at his home. It's the perfect place for it."

"Absolutely! What did you have in mind?" Daijah asked.

"Something small and intimate. That's his thing. He wouldn't want anything big and extravagant."

The girls nodded.

"Some food. Some music. Some drinks. A cake. Maybe a few decorations."

They continued nodding. "And his boys. Micah is guaranteed to have a good time as long as they're in attendance."

The girls agreed.

Micah had a tight circle around him. A *brotherhood*. A kinship.

Malachi, of course. The dopest big brother there ever was.

His childhood friend Solomon. His boy Tyson from college. His good friend Ellington from work. I'm sure he wouldn't mind having Ray there. And Julian, who'd been warmly welcomed to the pack.

And speaking of Ray, I didn't have any issues with him. I didn't take anything he said that day personally. Micah assured me Ray's comments weren't directed at me, and I trusted that.

But Micah was easy to please. He'd have extreme gratitude for just the thought.

I planned to invite Micah's parents, of course. As well as my dad and Ms. Natalie.

"What's on the menu Des? I'm glad to help with that." Ella offered.

"I love you, Ella, but no way. Not this time." I shook my head. You get a night off for once. You are always cooking for everyone for something or other, which we appreciate, by the way! I told Micah before we got here that your food is *bomb diggity!*"

Daijah and India laughed.

Ella laughed too. "Thank you! Are you sure though? You know I don't mind. I'll take that off your hands, no problem."

"I know. But really, not this time. All you need to do is show up and have a good time. Just like the rest of us."

I planned to have the food catered so everyone could come and enjoy themselves without worrying about the food. Since the party wasn't until January, I still have time to decide on the specifics.

We moved on to something else, and I looked down at my phone when it vibrated next to me.

I smiled at the text message I'd received from Mrs. Walker.

She is so sweet—just as sweet as she could be. I love seeing her and spending time with her. I sent her a screenshot of a pasta recipe I saw on Pinterest, asking if she'd like to try this next.

Mommy Josette: I'd love to! How about next week? It's a date

Mrs. Walker has already asked for my help with the coming holiday meals. Ella and Gabby will also help. Thanksgiving is swiftly approaching. We still have a few weeks, but it will be here before we know it. Then, of course, there is Christmas and New Year's.

I've been over multiple times helping Mrs. Walker cook different things and learning so much from her. We cooked homemade lasagna not long ago, and I was too juiced that day. I love lasagna, but I haven't had any in so long. I hadn't had any homemade entirely from scratch, ever.

And I was her proud sous chef. Her ambitious student. Eagerly soaking in everything I could. She's a prolific teacher. During our time together, we always learn more about one another.

So, it turned out that Mrs. Walker taught middle-grade English for the Sacramento Public Schools for over thirty years. Now that she's retired, she frequently volunteers with Friends of the Sacramento Public Library.

Suddenly, her love for books, stories, languages, and literature made sense. It was the sweetest thing to learn that we have a shared passion for those things, too. Mrs. Walker listened intently when I shared that my degree is in Linguistics. Many of my upper-division classes were cross-listed for English. I told her I always felt like the English and Linguistics majors were like fraternal twins. Many of the same courses were required. She found my observation funny, and after laughing heartily, she agreed. If you know, you know. I was *almost* an English major.

A course in Social Linguistics is what sold me. It's quite fascinating.

Mrs. Walker mentioned that she was surprised that I didn't have an art degree. Micah proudly shared pictures of my work with her. She told me she was so impressed. Considering I was self-taught.

I took a few art classes throughout my childhood but none in college. I told her at the time, I didn't think I could do art full-time and make a decent living. I figured I'd get a "real job" and do art for fun.

I couldn't have been more wrong. And it's truly amazing how God has continued looking out for me and providing for me. I've been working independently for nearly a decade now, but with plenty of work to do, I hardly have to look for work. I'm often approached, and sometimes, I have to turn things away because my schedule just doesn't allow it.

I'm not just surviving but thriving in the art space, and I'm so very thankful. I get to do what I love, keep my bills paid, keep myself fed, learn, grow, and network. I met my bestie, India.

It's why I can take on many volunteer positions or community gigs.

God is good all the time.

And all the time, God is good. *For real*.

Mommy also mentioned in passing that I should consider taking an art class or two at community college.

Because why not?

She planted a seed.

And yeah, I call her Mommy now and then. It slipped once, but it felt so natural. She certainly has been a mother to me these past few months. And she smiled so big at that. I did, too.

And I'm such a fucking crybaby. Of course, I cried right there. Right then. Happy tears.

Yeah.

And Mommy calls me her *sweet girl*. Mr. Walker calls me *sweet darling*.

And something else, I thought I knew how to chop and slice vegetables, but there was a much better way to do it. And yes, turns out there is a difference between cutting and slicing.

Mrs. Walker told me that cutting veggies roughly the same size ensured they cooked evenly and at the same rate. I learned to julienne carrots for the lasagna. We made one meat and one vegetarian. It was a deep pan too. We took the vegetarian one home, and it took Micah and me days to finish it. And it was even better the next day, too. Pasta is always better the next day.

We made a triple-layer caramel cake another day. It was scrumptious. I don't bake much, so I learned a thing or two, like using brown eggs as often as possible. For some recipes, let the eggs, milk, and butter get to room temperature to ensure they blend cohesively.

And we met Ms. Natalie some months ago and we've gotten together with her and dad a few times since.

She's *wonderful*. Dad is so happy. They're just adorable, those two. She seems just as fond as he is. I learned that she and Dad had a similar story and shared a similar pain.

Ms. Natalie was a widow. She lost her husband about six years ago in a tragic work accident. My heart broke for her hearing that. She has one grown son between Daijah's age and mine. He's currently stationed in Germany, and he'll be home sometime next year. We're excited to meet him.

***

India and I were starting our second week of working together. Working with Indie has always been a great thing.

A community theatre was putting on a few productions for the Christmas season, and we'd joined the Design Team to get the sets painted. We were formally hired as *Scenic Artists*.

The Set Designer, Mrs. Rose, was super talented and a visionary. I was beyond impressed with her. And the crew was dope as hell. They were a bunch of black hippie artists with *enormous* talent.

This was the first time India and I would work with a crew made up entirely of people of color.

Scenic Artist was something brand new to put on my resume. It was my first time doing scenic art, and I was learning so much.

It wasn't as straightforward as just painting the sets, though we'd do that, but rather creating visual illusions. We'd be painting on backdrops, and the scenery painted would create perspective. This week, we painted faux surfaces: rusty

249

metal doors, a colossal pile of stones, weathered wood grain, and a graffiti-covered brick wall.

We had an important job. Production costs can be very high when using those materials. Scenic artists can paint them on plywood instead at a fraction of the cost. Also, when it's painted, we can add additional details using different brushes, colors, and techniques. For example, we can use paints to create a rusty, aged, or worn look.

We'd be committed for at least the next six weeks. It would pay modestly, but I was perfectly fine with that. The experience was priceless. I appreciate the opportunity. And I love coming to work every day. I was having so much fun.

And the theatre was a hidden gem. Tucked away off the main road in a converted warehouse. You'd never know it from the outside.

The dear and delightful Dr. Giselle, founder and Artistic Director of the Village, is a beacon in the community.

Dr. Giselle is amazing. A Goddess.

Nearly seventy-years young and still teaching acting and dance.

A D.C. native and Spelman woman with a Degree in Theatre. She's graced many stages as a professional actress over the past five decades. A playwright. A thought leader. Industry expert. Fostering the black theatre continuum.

She has a theatre company based at the Village called *Imisi*, which roughly means inspiration in Yoruba. It is open to all ages and skill levels. She's created a space for young and mature black talent to grow and thrive as black actors, encouraging discovery, creativity, and scholarship.

Dr. Giselle welcomed India and me with open arms. Gushing over *her* excitement to work with *us*.

That's sweet and everything, but *we're* the ones so fortunate.

"Girl, I forgot just how huge this house is," India said as she stepped into the front door of Micah's home. India came here once before, but we didn't hang out here very long. That was the night we went out to *HomeGrownSol*.

She removed her shoes and left them by the front door. She never wore shoes inside, even when people insisted she didn't need to remove them. Her Indian culture wouldn't allow her to. I was already barefoot. Honestly, I've implemented no shoes inside since we first became friends. I've found that it stays much cleaner when you don't wear shoes in your home.

"Thanks, on *Micah's* behalf. It's a really nice house. Nicer than any place I've ever imagined spending this much time in."

India came by to assess the wall Micah wanted me to paint. We'd been off work for a few hours, but she went home first to check on her parents. Thankfully, they were doing much better these days. I wouldn't have bothered her with this request if that wasn't the case. This would take a while.

Micah asked me weeks ago to paint something on his wall, and I wanted to get started. That way, it would all be done in plenty of time for his birthday. The wall was expansive, so I asked India for her expertise and help. It would take much longer if I did it all myself. Besides, when India and I collaborate, we make fucking magic. I wanted to capture that here. I wanted this to be some of my best work yet.

My man deserved it. He took such care of me, and my mental health was of the utmost importance to him. He was serious about me seeing a therapist. Ms. Laurie, his assistant, sent me an email the following day. After some research, I found an amazing therapist. She was a black woman in her

251

late forties. She was a woman of God, a wife, and a mother. A Howard University alum, H.U. regalia tastefully decorated her office with crimson and cream Greek letters.

But all of that was secondary.

Dr. Jemma Robinson was a whole vibe. Trust-building. Inquiring. Compassionate. Kind. And she gently shared pearls of wisdom with me.

She shared one about relationships and striving to be the best version of ourselves for the person we care about.

*"We're the best **we** when **I'm** the best **me**."*

That had to be the most profound thing I'd heard in a while.

At the moment, I saw Dr. Jemma, and she insists I call her that every other week. That was a great cadence for now.

India stood in front of the wall, looked up and down, and touched it just like I had. I remember that puzzling Micah and he even chuckled about it. For an ordinary person, maybe it was odd, but there was a method to the madness. The wall was our canvas, and the texture of the wall would tell us how we would need to prepare it to receive the paint.

A great mural begins with the surface it's painted on.

"Stucco. And there's a glossy paint on top. Okay, so this will definitely need to be primed," India said.

"Right."

"How high up were you thinking?" She asked, looking up again.

"Probably seventy-five percent. Micah said this is an eight-foot wall." The wall didn't reach the ceiling, but the ceiling in this portion of the house was ten feet high.

She nodded. "We'll need two ladders."

"Yeah."

"It will cover the entire width?" It was approximately fifteen feet across.

"Yes."

She nodded again. There was an electric fireplace on both sides of the wall. That would save us a significant square footage of painting.

India walked around the partition wall, returning on the other side. "We're painting both sides?"

"*God, no.*"

We both cackled at that.

"Girl… I love you but *shit*. I was bout to lose it."

We laughed all over again.

"Since you won't let me pay you, please tell me what we can do for you instead. This will be a lot of work. We'll already be painting all day at the Village Theatre. So, after work won't be practical. Not every day. This will likely be a weekend thing." Micah still wanted to pay India. I agreed. And we would. She was crazy if she thought for a second we wouldn't.

"That's what I'm thinking." India nodded. "We can do occasional days after work. Once a week maybe. That gives us at least three working days a week. Let's put tentative dates on the calendar week by week and play it by ear. We can always move the weekday slots."

"Good idea Best. Let's sit down so I can show you the sketch I came up with. We can talk colors too." India followed me to the kitchen island.

Eventually, Micah came down to say hello and thank India in advance for agreeing to work with me. He also made dinner for us and then headed to his office. India and I watched part of a movie, and then she had to get going. I'd see her at the Village tomorrow bright and early.

When Indie left, I took a shower. Micah had already taken his, and he lay in bed reading when I finished my skin moisturizing and face routine.

I sighed heavily when I finally lay down beside him. I'd be asleep in two-point-five seconds, I was sure.

"You good baby?"

"Yeah. Just tired. It was a long day." I cuddled up beside Micah, and he closed his book and placed it on his side table. He also lowered the lamps to the lowest setting.

It had been a long day, but I still wasn't quite feeling very well. It came and went in waves. It's hard to describe exactly how I felt, but it wasn't my normal self. I hadn't mentioned it to anyone since it was sort of infrequent. In fact, I felt fine all day. It wasn't until I got in the shower that I began to feel sick. "How was your day, baby?"

"Good. Thank you love. Busy, but productive."

Micah had me in his arms from behind. He snuggled closer to me.

"That's good." I yawned. "I love your bed. I get such great sleep." I said absently as I closed my eyes.

"It loves you too."

I was tickled at that.

Micah held me tighter. Moments later, his hands were beneath my shirt and had risen to my bare breasts. He gently rubbed over my nipples, and they peaked immediately. My nipples are super-duper-sensitive to his touch. It felt nice. His firm, warm hands always felt nice wherever he ventured.

"I have no problem expressing myself." Micah began.

My response was a bit delayed. I was tired, and his gentle caress put me deeper in the zone. His deep timbre in my ear would do it every time. My breasts were in his hands. They were a perfect fit. He cupped each one, his thumbs still grazing my nipples. "I know baby."

Micah moved my locs to the side and kissed my neck. After a faint moan, "I have no problem expressing my appreciation either… no problem complimenting you. You're my good thing, Beauty. By now I expect you're used to it. Me complimenting you."

A slow smile made its way across my face. He couldn't see it. And anyway, I wondered where all this was going.

I didn't have to wonder too long.

"I have a confession… I've never told you this before, but I'm telling you now…" He kissed my neck again. He never stopped. He'd literally been kissing there the entire time. "I'm convinced that you're the best sleeping companion."

"Am I really?" I pressed languidly.

"The *very* best."

"How so?"

"That's easy. You're the *perfect* little spoon."

A boisterous chuckle came up from my belly. I wasn't expecting that. My silly Micah could always get a laugh out of me.

Micah laughed too. "I'm serious. You aren't a wild sleeper. You're soft." Kisses. "You smell nice." More kisses. "You don't snore either. This bed is nice and all, but I've gotten some of the best sleep *ever* sleeping with you."

"Wow. Well thanks baby."

"Mmmhmm."

"You're the perfect big spoon," I told him after a beat.

"Thank you, love." Micah reached back and cut the lamps completely off, then settled back in. "Baby."

"Yeah?"

"Real quick before you knock out. We're having a Holiday Gala for work in a couple of weeks. Will you be my date for the evening?"

"I'd love to baby." I turned to face Micah. Finding his lips in the darkness, I kissed him tenderly. "Absolutely. Positively. *Definitely*." I settled in his arms again, facing him now.

"Great." Micah kissed my forehead. "It's a formal event. Black tie. I'll be wearing a tux. Take the card and get yourself an evening gown. I'll wait until you get it to coordinate my tie and pocket square."

"Alright baby."

"High heels… one of those tiny purse thingies..."

My light titter floated into the darkness around us. "It's called a clutch."

"A clutch huh?" His chuckle was light, but I felt it. We were so close. I felt his every inhale and exhale. His massive hands were in my shirt again, wrapped around my bare back. Rubbing and kneading my skin. Something he was so damn *spectacular* at, by the way. "Some earrings. A necklace if you want…" His voice was slowing down as he started drifting. I was right behind him too. "…maybe nails. Toes. Or whatever else... get it, sweetheart."

"Thank you, baby."

"Thank *you*. Goodnight, my love."

"Goodnight.

twenty-six

MICAH

"Man, the fuck Lewis was doing! Fumbling like that."

"Right," Mal uttered.

We were die-hard football fans. Me, Daddy and Mal. The game was on, and Mal and I were watching it while shooting the shit on the phone. I could get to Mal's house from mine in eight-minutes flat. Sometimes, when the game was on, I would go by to watch it or vice versa, granted we weren't busy with something else. I continued, "He knew we needed those points. Leave it to him. Fucking Lewis."

"Exactly."

"We're up this season. Guess we may have a shot at the championship." We knew we weren't rooting the best team, but we were loyal fans, nonetheless.

I continued my sports commentary until I realized I had been carrying on for a while, and Mal was quiet. That was never the case whenever we talked about sports. "Mal?" My brows dipped. I had the call on speaker, so I glanced down to see if it was still connected. It was. "Mal?" Maybe he'd accidentally muted or something. "Mal?"

"Yeah."

"Everything good?"

"…Yeah… baby brother… umm…let me…let me call you back…"

"Mal, for real? You couldn't wait for us to hang up. Man, I swear!"

Shaking my head, I went to disconnect, but not before I could hear Mal chuckling, "My bad, dude…"

I shook my head again but couldn't help myself as I chuckled, too.

I tossed my phone beside me on the couch and laid back to continue watching the game. About an hour went by when I felt it vibrating beside me. It was Malachi calling me back.

"You better not be calling me in the middle of nothing man."

"Quit hating nigga. When my wife climbs on top of me, I'm gone rise to the occasion. Literally and figuratively. She wants it, she can get it… *Touchdown!!!! You see that shit man?*"

"*Yes!* That's what the fuck I'm talking about!" I cheered right along with Mal. It was a great play. Perfectly executed.

"What you needed though? You said you wanted to talk about something."

I lightly sighed. It was the irony for me.

That is what had me calling my brother in the first place. I'd initially called Mal to get his advice on something, but since we both had the game on, it was easy to get distracted.

I had the place to myself so I could speak freely. Destiney was out with Daijah looking for a dress for the Gala in two weeks.

Anyway, there is absolutely no doubt that Destiney is the woman God had given me.

My wife. The mother of our future children.

Knowing that I wanted to do right by her. I have to. I'm convicted.

I haven't been okay with continuing to make love to Destiney outside of the covenant of marriage. It's almost like I feel as though I'm violating her. And she deserves better.

I prayed for her, and here she was. Continuing to connect with her this way just made me feel guilty. It was hard to explain. Beyond that, there was nowhere I could go mentally to escape the integrity and morals Mommy and Daddy raised us with. The more I tried to drown it out, the louder that damn voice was in my head.

I really need Destiney to be my wife.

That way, I can make love to her.

Or fuck her.

Whatever she wanted.

In peace.

Being in my damn head so much has gotten me in a funk plenty of times. Like, I've mastered Destiney. I'm *very* in tune with her. But she's in tune with me too. I worry she may already be sensing something.

"I stopped initiating. But we still engage because *she's* initiating now."

I explained all of this to Malachi. The very best I could.

"I see." I knew Mal was processing it all. I let him rock.

I already felt relief just getting this off my chest. I'm glad I decided to run my situation by my big brother and pick his brain about it. I didn't think he'd see my position any differently.

Where I hesitated was bringing it to Destiney.

For fear of her feeling rejected. My baby is sensitive. Her feelings are fragile.

I quickly added, "Instead of denying her, I figured I'd just stop entering her. But that only worked once."

I knew what Mal was silently thinking, so I offered, "I try to hold out and give her a *few* the other way, hoping she'll be good with that, but she'll still ask me. I can't say no to my baby. A couple of times, she put that nigga in herself."

Mal chuckled at that. "I see." Then, "You need to talk to her about this. Like yesterday. If you hold this in and continue doing what you've been doing, baby sis will notice. She likely already has. When she notices, she'll convince herself something is wrong with her or your relationship. Getting ahead of the situation and discussing your position would be much easier, especially if you want to avoid hurting her feelings. Women notice these things because they're extremely sensitive. Even the most confident women have a level of sensitivity regarding this. If you fumble this, and she brings it up, it will be from a place of hurt or exasperation. I guarantee you. It won't be pretty."

I understood. "Yeah, I see what you mean. I need to figure out the best way to present this. She may feel shafted or even rejected. That's the last thing I want for her. I never want to hurt her. Even unintentionally."

"Right. Bring this up for discussion expeditiously, baby brother. Do not let this ride because it will cause a greater conflict than it needs to be. I believe she'll understand as long as you explain well. Make it make sense to her. That way, there won't be any room for feelings of rejection."

"Right. Appreciate you man."

"You got it. Always."

I will bring it up for discussion as soon as I can get my words together.

Mal had a great point; Destiney may have noticed the shift already and was possibly already in her head about it. I will bring it up soon.

I just hoped it wasn't too late.

***

I'll be headed out to Chicago right after Thanksgiving and be gone for eight days.

I'd go to Destiney's father first, but I planned to propose as soon as I returned from Chicago.

I hated that Destiney couldn't join me. She was just as disappointed. She wanted to come; she'd never been to Chicago. I'd been once, and it would have been pretty cool to show her around. I told her I'd be glad to take her there when her schedule allowed. She was committed to a community theatre project and was so excited about this gig. She'd been given tickets to some of their matinee shows, and we planned to check them out together once performances started.

I enjoy the magic on stage. As a kid, I was a thespian of sorts, eagerly participating in small productions at school and church.

But these days I prefer to experience the sights and sounds from the audience.

Especially musical theatre. I saw Hamilton twice. And the Lion King in San Francisco.

Life-changing.

So, I had it in my mind to ask Destiney to marry me in the coming weeks.

The guys and I talked about it when we were at Wine & Graze.

Malachi, Solomon, Julian, and I huddled around a tall table, watching a football game on an oversized flat screen. We'd been clowning around, drinking beer, and pigging out on a massive platter of wings.

The women, Destiney, Daijah, Ella, and India, were sitting around a booth just a few feet from us.

Looking regal and classy. All four of them. Chatting, laughing, sipping wine, and snacking on cheese, berries, chocolate, and nuts.

It all started because I got caught stealing glances at Destiney.

My baby is so beautiful. My goodness.

In a crowded room, I would always search for her. The guys were cracking jokes at me, but I knew it was all in jest. These men adored their women just as much as I loved mine.

Well, except for Sol. But I knew he was making something shake with India.

"You're staring again man." Mal teased, taking another swig from his beer.

I shook my head, chuckling. I couldn't help myself. I wouldn't even try.

"She wifey or what?" Sol asked, slapping me on my shoulder.

*"She is **certainly** wifey."* I returned. Resolute. Without pause.

"When you asking her?" Julian queried.

"Soon man. Before the end of the year, for sure."

I proceeded to show them my phone. I had been looking over some rings I had in mind for her. I narrowed it down to a few styles, and I'd get Daijah's expertise before I made a final decision. I'll likely ask her to meet me at the jewelry store.

The guys hooped, hollered, and whistled with wide eyes and high brows. I nervously looked at the women, but they were preoccupied and chatting away. Not paying us any mind. They probably thought we were carrying on about the football game.

"Shiiiittt! I need some sunglasses for some of these." Sol joked. Gesturing his hands in front of his face as if he was seeing something bright and blinding.

We all cracked up at that.

"No doubt!" Mal said. "I see you baby brother. These are *genteel*!"

I didn't mind their playful banter.

Julian nodded once he'd had a look. "She must be worth it, man." He'd just gone through this himself when he proposed to Daijah early this year. We didn't know him then but were excited about their upcoming nuptials. January was just around the corner.

Julian was my newest friend, but he was swiftly becoming more like a brother. Such a solid dude. Mal and Sol fucked with Julian too. They met Julian for the first time some weeks back when Mal and Ella hosted a game night.

And Destiney shared with me how well Julian treated her.

I appreciate that. Tremendously. More than he knew. I certainly make an effort to treat Daijah just as well as I treat Destiney. I know that mattered a lot to her. She and Daijah were inseparable and extremely protective of each other.

"She's worth this and so much more." I declared. "She's priceless."

***

Tonight was the Holiday Gala.

This year, it was being held at the Library Galleria. A premiere event space in downtown Sacramento.

There would be a live jazz band as our entertainment for the evening, an open bar, and a plated four-course meal.

That all sounded nice, but I got the feeling the food would be subpar.

For some reason, these events always failed miserably with food selection.

Everything else was always top-tier. The venue, the décor, the entertainment.

But the catering was always a miss. Never a hit.

Such a damn shame.

I didn't eat fast food, but every blue moon and tonight, I wasn't above rolling through a late-night drive-through if necessary. The Wendy's closest to me was open till one a.m.

I also secured a driver for the evening so I could drink to my heart's content. I didn't plan on being sloppy drunk around my working constituents, but I didn't want to have to think about driving tonight.

I was dressed and ready, hanging out at the kitchen island, waiting for Destiney. I'd cut the television off not long ago; I knew she'd be making her way down here soon. Daijah came by to do Destiney's hair and to help her get ready. She'd taken off about a half hour ago.

I glanced at my watch. We were doing pretty good on time.

My phone illuminated on the kitchen island beside me. It was a notification that our driver had arrived. He was punctual, and I appreciated that. The company I booked through were friends of the family, and they gave me a great price.

I gave him a quick call, assuring him we'll make our way out soon. He'd been paid to be our driver for the rest of the evening. I planned to tip him handsomely too.

I entered the living area and sat on the couch as I faintly heard my bedroom door open. I stood immediately.

Destiney descended the stairs like a literal angel. Floating. Taking my breath away.

From head to toe. Everything was just...

I felt like Johny Gill. *My, my, my.*

Destiney was striking in her gown. This was my first time seeing it. I only knew it was navy once she told me what color I needed to get for my tux. And the navy blue looked stunning against her chocolate skin.

Anyway, Destiney was luxurious. Exquisite.

The top was a tailored fit. Following her every curve like a second skin. Sitting tastefully close to her body. Perfectly lining her chest and waist. Sheer at the top. Boat neckline. Elegantly embroidered gold details with beads and sequins. Graceful sheer three-quarter sleeves.

It was a floor-length gown. Finished with a flowing skirt. The perfect touch of allure. This gown was *so her.*

She wore gold heels, which I saw peeking out as she continued descending the steps.

I loved her locs too. They were freshly retwisted, and it looked like they had taken two locs, stranding them into one, with all of them pinned and draped to one side.

I approached the stairs to meet her, immediately taking her into my arms. Embracing her close.

"Hello, beautiful," I spoke into her ear. Lining the side of her face with kisses, then kissing her forehead. I remained there for just a moment, taking in her scent. I could smell a subtle grapefruit, or maybe it was mango coming from her hair. Her hair always smelled nice; she used shea butter all over her body, including her hair. I loved the way it mixed with her natural pheromones and the body oil she used.

But tonight, she was wearing a different scent.

Something I hadn't smelled on her before.

I liked it.

It was warm and spicy with notes of musk and amber.

My hands remained at the small of her back. I never disconnected us as I stepped back to get another look at her.

"Hello handsome." Destiney returned. She seemed shy. Just a little. She was likely extremely nervous since she'd be meeting many people tonight. I'd make sure she felt safe. And comfortable. "I'm so glad you like it, baby." She told me.

I took her hand in mine and gently lifted it above her head. "Turn around baby." Destiney gave me a twirl, and I loved everything I saw. Wow. "I *love* it. Thank you for being my date. Last year I went alone. I would have skipped if I could. But I'm expected to attend as a VP."

"I'm honored to be your date, baby. Thank you for all of this. Everything I'm wearing." She looked down at herself.

"You're welcome. You look great baby. And you smell amazing."

"Thank you baby. And for that too. It's a new perfume I picked up. For special occasions." She gave me a wink.

"I love it baby."

I brought Destiney back to me, kissing her forehead again. Then her neck. Finally, her lips. We kissed a few times. Pecks at first, but then we began to get carried away.

"We should get going, baby," Destiney said, breaking our kiss.

"Yeah. Before we don't." I chuckled.

We headed toward the front door, and I picked up the plastic container I'd left sitting on the coffee table.

"Do you mind pinning my boutonniere on me?"

"Of course, I don't mind, baby."

I'd gotten Destiney a matching corsage. White rose with baby's breath.

"I haven't seen one of these since prom."

I snickered. "People still wear them. Weddings, of course. Most formal events, really." After she'd pinned me, I placed her corsage on her wrist. "Have I told you how much I love seeing my pretty wife wearing pretty things?" I asked Destiney. I kissed her hand.

She gave me a sweet smile. "No, you haven't baby."

"Well...*I love seeing my pretty wife wearing pretty things.* Or nothing. I like seeing that too."

She giggled at that as I opened the front door, allowing her to step out in front of me. We seldom ever entered or left through the front door. Always using the garage to come in and out. I paused to lock the door behind us, and before I could get the key in the door, Destiney was squealing behind me.

"*Micah!* Oh my gosh, is this limo for us?"

I was worried for a second. I almost dropped my keys. Destiney squealed so suddenly and so loud I thought something had happened.

I locked the door and met her as we descended the walkway leading to the sidewalk.

"Yes baby. We have a limo for the night."

"Aww, Micah, this is so sweet. I've never ridden in a limo before. Thank you for this baby."

"You're welcome love. I'm glad." Our chauffeur had since exited the limo and waited for us at the passenger door. After Destiney and I got settled inside, we were on our way.

***

We were having a *ball* at the Gala.

Ellington and his wife Jayla had been hanging with us most of the evening. The four of us chatted extensively during the cocktail hour. Jayla is lovely. She and E seemed to be tailor-made for each other. This was my second time meeting

E's wife. I met her briefly once before when she came to the office to take Ellington to lunch. She had their cute little one with her that day. Jade was so adorable. The perfect mix of them both. Just precious.

Once dinner was served, E and Jayla sat beside us at the same table. The banquet table seated ten, and a few others from our department, and their dates sat with us, too. We enjoyed our meal. They had a vegetarian option for Destiney. I was sure to mention that when I submitted my RSVP. But the food wasn't half bad. Better than I expected, actually.

Destiney and Jayla took to each other right away. Since Destiney is considerably younger than me, she and Jayla were around the same age. At one point it seemed Destiney and Jayla forgot Ellington and I were there. Chatting like old friends. E and I laughed about it.

Anyway, Destiney met dozens of people this evening. My boss, some colleagues, and a few direct reports of mine. They were all so glad to meet her.

And speaking of my boss, I'd heard that E was doing phenomenal work in his new role. Since Ellington no longer reported to me, I wasn't exactly privy to his performance. Of course, I wasn't surprised to hear that. We wouldn't be talking about work this evening, but I'd be sure to tell him to keep up the great work next week.

I'd managed to avoid Erica. So far. And anyway, I hadn't seen her at the office much, which was a great thing. But I knew she would be here. There was no way she would miss an event like this.

I was on high alert to stay away from her. And keep Destiney away from her.

I'd heard that some transplant from another department would be her date. He probably agreed to it because he hadn't heard about her reputation. Or maybe he didn't care. Either way, it wasn't my business.

The five-piece jazz band was great. They called themselves *The Flipside*. There were two ladies and three gentlemen. They played jazz covers during cocktails and dinner. After dinner, the dance floor was open, and the band did jazz covers of modern songs. Destiney and I danced quite a bit.

We were in the middle of a mid-tempo jam when Destiney alerted me that she needed to use the ladies room. Since Ellington and Jayla were still dancing Destiney didn't want to interrupt them, asking Jayla to go with her. I always noticed that ladies went to the restroom in twos. Or in groups.

"I'll escort you baby, no worries."

I hung out in the hallway. Not long after Destiney went into the ladies room, I felt the unmistakable presence of someone.

"Ahem."

I lightly sighed, obliging her. Expressionless.

"Micah."

"Erica."

I saw her once the dance floor opened, and people began congregating. She wasn't dancing, though. More so, walking around. And talking to people who were trying to dance with their spouses or dates. Victor steadily followed her around. It was funny because he looked pathetic.

We exchanged pleasantries when I saw him at the bar earlier this evening. That was it. But the dude had a smug expression on his face. I don't know who he was trying to fool.

Victor, looking smug, was hilarious. I think he thought he was doing something with Erica on his arm. It's obvious when a man isn't used to dealing with an attractive woman. They do all sorts of *clown shit*. Pandering is one of them. Agreeing to anything just to feel accepted.

Meanwhile, Erica was treating Victor like a damn doormat. Hardly acknowledging his presence. I was embarrassed for him.

She looked great, I'll admit. And just because I wasn't going there with Erica didn't negate that she was an attractive woman. But that was the extent of it.

She was an attractive woman on the outside.

Beauty was only skin deep with her.

And Erica didn't hold a candle to how gorgeous my woman was. Destiney was beautiful inside and out. I noticed all the fawning these men were doing.

According to office gossip, Victor had pursued Erica since he'd transferred into our department.

Months ago. Erica never gave the poor guy a second glance.

I guess she needed a date, and he was available.

Victor looked comical even now. Standing behind Erica like a lost puppy.

Just then, the door to the lobby swung open. As Destiney emerged, I saw the look Erica gave her. Erica whirled her head my way. She was so swift that I was sure she'd get whiplash.

"Alright Micah. I'm ready." Destiney told me as she linked her arm in mine. She didn't even seem to notice Erica standing there. And good for her. Erica wasn't even worth the energy.

"Indeed. Let's get back to our table. I think dessert is being served now."

Erica reared her head back as if her death glare wasn't enough. And she stood there, continuing to glare at Destiney for another moment.

"Wow." Erica drew the word out. Then, "So *this* is why you're not giving me a chance? You've been keeping company with... with... *her?*"

I didn't appreciate the infliction.

Destiney and I had already taken a few steps. We were almost to the door leading back to the reception. But I was putting an end to this shit. Right now. Once and for all.

"Erica. *I will not* stand here and allow you to disrespect me or my woman. I have already explained that we will not be more than colleagues. Should you allude to anything further *again*, I'll have you relieved of your duties. *Effective immediately.*"

Her eyes grew wide.

I turned to Destiney. She was looking at me expectantly with that beautiful smile that I love. "Shall we, baby?"

"We shall."

Just as we exited the hallway to the ballroom, Destiney stopped and turned back toward Erica, who was still planted in the same place. Her mouth was agape. Victor still standing there, looking... *confused?* Hell, I didn't know.

"You know Erica. It isn't very becoming of you to be so nasty." Destiney spoke in her usual tone.

Light. Airy. Pleasant. The voice I fell in love with. "Then you're steadily pursuing a man who has already made it clear he isn't interested. You've been informed of this two years ago. No woman of class should do such a thing. Especially in front of your date." Destiney shrugged. "You're a beautiful woman." Erica's expression visibly softened. And

271

if you could believe it, I saw the faintest trace of a smile at the corner of her lip. "Have a good evening," Destiney said, commencing her stroll, her head held high.

I was so proud of my baby.

Speaking of class, after Destiney was insulted, she handled Erica like a *class act*.

And I was confident that this Erica shit could finally be put to rest.

twenty-seven

DESTINEY

I really needed my sister.

I felt something off with Micah, and I trusted that he would come to me about it. That was his M.O. The thing was, though, he still hasn't, and it's been a couple of weeks now.

We had a great time at the Gala last week.

An amazing time.

I'd never been to such a fancy event before. It was nice.

Satin drapes hanging from the ceilings. Banquet tables galore with elegant place settings. Astonishing centerpieces.

Everyone seemed to enjoy the flowing drinks. The bartenders were top-tier. I had a bomb-ass white sangria.

I felt beautiful. Rode in a limo. And when Micah and I arrived, we had such a good time.

Good food. Great company. We Danced.

I met a host of people from Micah's department. Everyone was so friendly.

Well, except Erica. When Micah and I returned to our table, I sent a condensed version to the group chat with Day and Indie. The next morning, I called them on FaceTime and brought them up to speed. They were *rolling*.

I'd already told them about Erica when we had that run-in months ago.

I get the feeling she won't be trying me anymore.

As Tamar Braxton would say, *"girlfriend needed to get her life."*

She was too pretty to act like that, especially at this age. She had to be in her thirties. Too old for that. Erica reminded me of Neeka. They didn't resemble one another, but they were the same type. Pretty and pretty *damn* confused. Acting ugly because they're frustrated with their lives since they aren't bearing the fruit they want.

Acting out certainly won't fix *that* problem.

And anyway, I finally met the famous Ellington. Micah is a huge fan of Ellington. E's a good guy. He's about ten years younger than Micah. So, I'm just a couple of years older than Ellington and his wife.

I loved meeting his wife, Jayla. She said they were college sweethearts. Both of them are from Sac but met up at Chico State. About an hour and some change north of here. They've been married for just over three years now. They're a complementary couple with a lovely dynamic.

But seriously, Jayla is the folks for real. We spent the majority of our time hanging out and talking. A few ladies at the gala were shocked we were meeting for the first time.

Jayla and I talked about making plans to get together. We may invite the guys. We may not.

I'm kidding.

And Jayla showed me pictures of their beautiful baby. Jade is just about a year old. *So cute.* And such a happy baby. Chubby cheeks. Bright glittering eyes. A mound of dark auburn curls on her head.

Anyway, I assumed that we would finish the night when Micah and I got home. And just because we didn't, that *ordinarily* wouldn't cause me alarm. We didn't make love every night.

Sometimes, Micah would be too spent. Or I would be.
But this had been happening for a while. Weeks.
Micah didn't seem to want me.
And that scared me.
But he did give me a massage. Man. It was so relaxing.
As soon as we stepped in the front door. Micah knelt to remove my shoes. After his shoes were off, he carried me upstairs. Once we were in his bedroom, Micah got me out of my dress, bra, and panties. Sent me to the tub to soak in oils and bath salts. After that, I took a quick shower, and as soon as I got out, he met me with a plush bath towel. Dried me off. Then he brought me to his bed and got to work massaging me from head to toe.

Micah laid me on my belly first, straddling me. Then he rolled me onto my back. I felt his warm touch on every inch of my body. I told Micah a long ass time ago that he had the skills of a masseuse.

I moaned so much that I moaned my ass to sleep.

So, I was home alone, lying in my bed. I showered and did my moisturizing routine a while ago, and now I was relaxing. Or at least trying to. My head was about to explode.

Micah was going to pick me up in the next two hours, and we'd head back to his place.

And I knew Day would make me feel better. I texted Daijah when I got out of the shower, asking if she could talk tonight. Of course, I didn't need an appointment, and I could call my sister anytime, but since she was with Julian, I wanted to be considerate. I knew the conversation wasn't going to be quick. She was the same with me now that I was seeing Micah. She'd text ahead if she ever needed to talk.

On the rare occasions she came home, if she saw Micah's car parked outside, she'd let me know she was home and asked if it was alright to come in. She didn't want to walk in and catch Micah and me in the middle of something. I would do the same if I ever came home and saw Julian's car.

Daijah replied a few minutes ago, saying she'd give me a call shortly, and as promised, she was calling me on Facetime about fifteen minutes later.

"Hey Day." I chirped. I propped my pillows behind me as I sat up against my headboard.

"Hey Des." She was just as peachy, looking vibrant and beautiful as always. I told her so, and she brushed it off after thanking me, saying I was beautiful.

She always said that, and she was so sweet about it. "Hold on sister." Daijah leaned over and then returned to view, sitting in bed. "I needed to mute this TV. We're binge-watching some Hulu series."

"Yeah? How is it so far?"

"Pretty good, actually. You know I'm not much of a TV person, but this one has me hooked."

Daijah and I weren't much into TV. Growing up, we watched a lot of black sitcoms, but as we've gotten older, we both prefer to read or watch a great movie now and then.

"That's what's up. Text me so I can add it to my list. Not sure when I'll get around to it, but..." I shrugged my shoulders. We both laughed. She already knew how it went.

"*Exactly!* Julian didn't think I was serious when I asked him to pick us something to watch. He was too juiced to start this new series with me."

"You probably made him turn on them damn subtitles."

"*And did*! They stay on, thank you very much." We were both cracking up again.

For some reason, Daijah insisted on watching everything with captions. She's been doing it for years. Daijah could hear just fine, but she said it helped with making sure she didn't miss any of the dialogue. I guess I could see that, and after years of practice, I hardly noticed them anymore. Julian probably had the hang of it by now, too.

I've heard that people who don't watch with subtitles regularly would often get caught up in reading the subtitles and miss the action happening. Or read them moving their mouth. Only a people watcher would catch that. For the record, I am *not* a people watcher, but Daijah is, and she would point that out anytime she saw it.

She saw Neeka doing it during a girl's night when we watched a movie and nudged me, gesturing in her direction. It took a few minutes for me to realize what she was showing me, and all I could do was shake my head.

Once our laughter calmed, Daijah asked, "So, what's up, Des? Everything, everything? It's just you, and I. Julian is in the living room. I told him we needed to chat."

I nodded and sighed at the same time. Asking her about this would make it all real.

Part of me felt like maybe I was imagining things, but yesterday left me no doubt. It was hard to explain it even.

Forging ahead, I figured that whatever I said and however I said it, Daijah would understand.

She always understood me.

Thankfully, Daijah spoke fluent Destiney.

"Somethings off with Micah and me, Day. Whenever we're intimate, I literally have to ask him to penetrate me."

Daijah had a confused expression. "*Ask him?*"

I nodded. "Yes. But not in a sexy way. I'm literally saying, "Please put it inside." I have to ask him because, for some reason, he's avoiding that part. I tried holding out to see what would happen but realized he wouldn't do it if I didn't ask."

"Hmm." Her brows were furrowed. "And this is new?"

"Yeahhhhh." I dragged the word out. Confused as hell. And anxious. "I mean… initially, he waited for me to be ready. But once we started going all the way, it was fair game. Lately, though, it's like… I don't know. I feel like he's holding himself back. Emotionally and physically. There's like a block." I huffed. "That probably didn't make any sense."

"No, I follow you, sister." Her brows were knitted as she silently pondered. Then, "Do you think he's having an issue getting hard?"

Shaking my head vigorously, I responded, "No. No, no. Not at all. He's hard as hell within seconds. All we have to do is kiss, and he's ready to go."

Daijah nodded. "Maybe he's worried about finishing too soon?"

I shook my head again. "Micah doesn't have that problem either."

"Okay… maybe it's something at work? Or with his family? And he can't compartmentalize. Know what I mean?"

"I know what you mean. But family or work stuff seems like something he'd come to me about."

"Yeah." Daijah nodded in understanding. The two of us were both silent for a beat. "Well, Des, I am just as confused as you. *But you know what I'm going to say.*" She sang that last part and looked at me knowingly.

And I did. She never wavered in encouraging healthy communication. I appreciate that about Daijah immensely. "Talk to him about it."

"Yeah… I'm just hesitant."

"Why?"

"I mean. There's the "don't ask the question if you don't want to know the answer." And that's how I'm feeling. This whole thing is making me anxious. Shit Daijah. What if he's having sex with someone else, and he doesn't need it from me anymore? I know I'm not the most experienced. Sex with me is probably vanilla."

"*Woah!* Where in the hell is this coming from? Are you kidding me Des?" Daijah jested. "We both know that isn't it."

"What else could it be? We went from ravishing the shit out of each other to nothing. We were so connected before. He always wanted eye contact. It made the moment so much more intense. Now… he's like in his head someplace else. Certainly not in the present with me. Not even looking at me. What the hell is going on with him?"

"I don't know. Why don't you ask him?" Daijah said sarcastically. She stood up, going out of view. "One second, I have to pee really quick." Once Daijah was back in view, she said, "Talk to that man Destiney. Talk. To. Him."

twenty-eight

MICAH

Destiney was at my place. We were about to have lunch and planned to take a walk before the sun started to go down. It would be too chilly once it got dark.

I loved neighborhood walks with her and the quality time it afforded us. This had become a sweet moment with her that I always looked forward to. So, this was an excellent opportunity to talk things over. My talk with Malachi was almost two weeks ago and I knew I was pressing things waiting as long as I have. We'll discuss things today for sure.

We made grilled cheese on honey wheat with pepper jack and provolone and a delicious salad with spinach, arugula, avocado, walnuts, and strawberries. I hadn't tried strawberries on salad until Destiney introduced me and I love it.

Recently, I've cut back on meat even more than I had. These days I only eat chicken and fish. Red meat is very infrequent. Destiney never made it a big deal, and she had no issue coexisting with carnivores, but I welcomed the change. I could eat a little cleaner.

We'd eaten and cleaned up and were hanging out on the couch. I noticed Destiney was a little quieter. Not talking much while we were eating. She also seemed distant. She usually sat extremely close to me. If she wasn't in my lap. Right now, she was on the other end of the couch.

I wasn't even surprised. Mal was right. I shouldn't have waited to bring this to her.

The TV was on, but neither of us was watching.

Destiney had YouTube on with someone cooking something, and she was pretending to watch, but I peeped at her earlier. She was distracted. She'd been consumed with cooking channels on YouTube since she'd spent time with Mommy learning to cook different things. Mommy even gave her a few cookbooks, and Destiney was excited about them.

I had my laptop in front of me, checking a few things to prepare for my trip out to Chicago. I flew out three days after Thanksgiving. About a week away.

I hated that Destiney couldn't join me.

I looked over at her again, and I sensed some tension.

The way she sat, arms folded. Her absent gaze.

I sighed inwardly. Despite my plans to talk to her about this when we took our walk, I had the feeling we wouldn't get that far.

Something was up with her. I'm pretty sure I knew what it was, but she wasn't doing a good job masking it. Though she was trying, I knew her.

I studied her. And something was amiss.

We needed to talk right now.

I closed my laptop. I could do this later.

I walked over to the kitchen island and placed my laptop there. I returned to the living room and asked Destiney, "You alright love?"

She was silent for so long that I grew nervous. I made it back to the living room, and I sat on the couch right beside her. "Baby. Everything okay?"

Destiney sighed. "Honestly?"

Urging her forward, "Please do."

"I don't know if everything is okay. You tell me." She tried to say it evenly, but I heard the emotion there.

I nodded.

I grabbed the remote, turned off the TV, and then moved to sit on the coffee table directly in front of her. I held her gaze for a moment. She never wavered.

"Alright love. What's giving you doubt?"

She looked away from me briefly, and I could see gears shifting. When her eyes were back, she said, "Micah. Is there someone else? Are you cheating on me? Are you sleeping with someone else?"

I drew my head back. My eyes grew wide as saucers, and my mouth dropped open.

"No," I said firmly and definitively. I wasn't expecting *this* at all.

Where would she get the idea that I was cheating on her?

"We're being honest with each other. Please tell me the truth, Micah. I can handle it."

"That is the truth. Destiney, I wouldn't cheat on you. I *couldn't* cheat on you." My tone was pleading.

She crossed her arms, shaking her head slowly. "Then why don't you want me anymore?"

Ah. There it was. "I do want you baby. You're all I want. For the rest of our lives."

"Micah." Her tone was deadpan. She chuckled too, but there wasn't an ounce of mirth. "I don't feel like you want me. You never want to make love to me anymore. *You used to want me.* I know I'm not the most sexually exciting. I know I'm not the most experienced. But I thought... you said... we would learn together..." Destiney sighed an exasperated breath. She was absolutely on the verge of tears.

Meanwhile, I felt terrible.

Horrible.

Awful. Mal was right, and I could kick my own ass for this shit.

"You don't seem to want me anymore, and I get the feeling you're getting it from someone else," Destiney said after a moment. This time with an ounce of confidence.

"No baby. I swear. It's not that at all." I was frantic but told her in the most comforting tone I could muster.

I wanted to hold her, but her arms were still crossed. That told me she didn't want me any closer to her.

I needed to fix this immediately.

"Destiney baby."

When she wouldn't look at me, I leaned in closer. My lips were just a whisper from hers. She hadn't pushed me away, so that was a good sign.

"Destiney."

She looked everywhere but at me, and I couldn't blame her. Her heart was in my possession.

She'd given it to me hesitantly but willingly, and *I messed up*. That was my bad. I was going to fix this.

"Destiney, my love..." Placing my hands into the folds of her arms, I gently brought them down. I captured her hands, threading her fingers in mine, grateful she allowed me to. "Look at me, sweetheart. *Please*. I need you to know something."

She slowly peered up at me, and I saw her eyes pooled with tears.

Fuck me man.

I was supposed to be so much better at communicating. I'd caused her distress, and we could have avoided all this.

I needed to do some serious damage control.

"Baby. As God is my witness, I'm not seeing anyone else. All I see is you. You're the woman I want. You're it for me. *Please* believe that."

I took a moment to gather myself so I could make the rest of my dilemma make sense to her.

"So. Making love to you." I felt the corners of my mouth lifting and I didn't try to stop them. I couldn't even if I wanted to. A cheesy grin was across my face in nanoseconds.

"Being intimate with you is a privilege beyond description. You're a queen, Destiney baby. I don't take you for granted, and I don't take this lightly. You please me above and beyond anything I could describe. Your body is perfect. Your taste, your smell. The way you express your love for me whenever we come together. You satisfy every single one of my needs."

I'd been absently caressing Destiney's fingers, and she'd been caressing mine. That, coupled with the things I'd begun to express to her, was getting a rise out of me.

This wasn't the time for him to be bricking up, but he didn't know the difference.

Clearly.

After a moment, "Lately, I've felt conflicted." I gently told her. As I expected, her eyebrows were high on her head. "Baby. I love you, and I care about you. You are precious to me. And the truth is, I haven't felt right about being intimate with you outside of a covenant. Without a ring. I want to make love to you, but you deserve that within the covenant of a marriage. I wanted to talk to you about it. I was trying to figure out how without you feeling like I don't want you anymore or I'm rejecting you. That couldn't be further from the truth. I'm sorry for causing any stress or hurting you. I should have just come to you. I'm sorry baby."

Destiney nodded. I said so much to her, and I'm sure she needed to process it. So, I continued caressing her soft fingers against mine. I was semi-hard, too, still. I knew she could see it since I was wearing basketball shorts. Nothing was hidden in those.

"Where do we go from here baby?" Destiney asked me sweetly, around her adorable smile.

"That means you believe me? And you forgive me?"

"Yes baby. I believe you, and I forgive you." She leaned into me, kissing my lips softly. "I'm sorry for waiting until I was so upset about this to say anything. I was in agony, and all I had to do was ask you about this."

"It isn't all on you love. We both could have said something sooner."

"I understand your hesitation. But we can discuss anything and everything. Let's say something right away next time."

"Indeed." I moved from the coffee table back to the couch beside her. Pulling her toward me. She nestled her head into my side. Her favorite place to be when we were sitting on the couch.

I was glad to have her there. And glad this was finally off my chest. And I was so glad she felt better now.

"So, baby."

"Yeah?"

"You never said. What happens now?" Destiney asked.

I sighed lightly. "Well. I think we should abstain. Now that I've tasted you, it won't be easy. No doubt about that. But… the next time I make love to you, I want you to be Mrs. Walker."

"Mmm." I felt her vibrations in my side. "You've awakened the monster, and now you're putting her back in hibernation." Destiney playfully jested.

I released a boisterous chuckle. "We can do it. I know we can."

"We absolutely can." After a beat, she asked, "When are you planning to marry me?" We talked about marriage too many times to count. I told her she was it for me. I told her I wanted her for the rest of our lives plenty of times.

"Tomorrow."

"Micah. You haven't even officially asked."

"I assumed you'd agree." My tone was serious but laced with sarcasm. "And not just so I can get back in that pussy. Though that's a part of the reason. I want to spend the rest of my life loving you. You're all I need, Destiney baby." After a beat, "If I had a ring, and officially asked. What would you say?"

"I'd say yes."

My smile was wide. Hers too. Big, bright, and beautiful, reaching her celestial eyes. I could see every single tooth in her mouth. "Yeah?"

"Mmmhmm. *Yes.*"

Somehow, my smile grew even wider. "Yes?"

She giggled just a little, "Yes Micah. Absolutely. Positively. *Definitely.*" She murmured the last part as I connected our lips.

After many kisses, I pulled her back into my side, and we settled on the couch again. Destiney turned her cooking show back on, and I shut my eyes.

Content. Grateful. Excited. All the things, really. I hated that I'd have to be away from her, but I was already making plans in my head for when I returned. My first order of business was getting her a ring.

twenty-nine

DESTINEY

"Best. You okay?" India asked. Her brows knitted, concerning eyes surveying me.

I took a few steps out of the ensuite to my bedroom, and India stood to meet me.

I love Indie. She truly is the best.

So present.

Always there for me.

She just got me. Understood me. Never needing to explain shit- she just knew.

I flopped back on my bed. Stretching out a little. "Just not feeling well." I huffed. "And I miss Micah."

India sat beside me on my bed. "I know you miss Micah." She had her purse on her lap. I think she was digging around for something.

Anyway, I shut my eyes.

"When is he coming back?"

"Five more days." I groaned. I was barely halfway through these eight days, and I was already suffering extreme withdrawals.

For some reason, the few days before he left, I felt extra attached to Micah, and being away from him now felt *brutal*.

It occurred to me the other night that it was the conversation we had a few days before he left.

Yeah.

It was absolutely the conversation we had.

I can't even describe my feelings hearing Micah bear his heart to me.

Well. Relief initially.

I'd convinced myself, which is completely ludicrous, that he must have been cheating on me. I went to the most extreme rationale. But Micah talked me off that cliff.

And he's so good at that. Good to me.

He continues to prove himself.

How much he loves me. How much I mean to him.

He's taught me and *continues* to teach me what love is. I really didn't fully know before him.

He cares for me so deeply, loving me exactly the way I need him to.

A way I didn't even *know* I needed.

Effortlessly.

I love him so much. Words just can't explain.

So, I missed my man. *Something serious*. Micah keeps saying that he misses me, too.

We'd been texting and FaceTiming as usual, and though it helped, it wasn't the same.

India stayed at my place last night and will stay again tonight.

We were in full swing of our creative groove, working away at the Village, which was going well. The sets looked amazing.

And we'd been working away on the mural at Micah's house.

The wall had been primed with eggshell white, and then we outlined oversized leaves on it, some of them overlapping. The eggshell white was the perfect background color, as it was a warmer white that would make the brightly colored Monstera Delicios leaves pop in contrast.

We started adding color yesterday. Some of the leaves would be outlined, and some would be painted completely. Adding the color was my favorite part. I love to see the vision come to life, and adding the color does just that. Of course, I also love going to the art supply store, looking through all the color palettes, and picking out the perfect shades. I love the fun names they have for the various colors, too. It always seemed like the coolest job to be able to come up with the names for the endless hues of colors, like the names of the various scents at Bath and Body Works or Victoria's Secret.

So, we were working with four colors: a deep hunter green, a bright goldfish orange, a refreshing aqua blue, and a gleaming rich black. These colors were complementary, and I knew it would look great once we were all done.

The plan was to go back to Micah's in a couple of days. But that all depended on how I felt. I still hadn't been feeling well. It was growing worse. For the past few days, I've been feeling nauseous. Yesterday morning, I threw up.

Last night, I'd finally broken down and told Indie. Up until then, I hadn't told anyone. Partly because it wasn't unusual for me… once upon a time. Back when I had my issue of blood, I was constantly feeling sick.

Off. Tired. In pain. Not myself. And I just dealt with it. Not nauseated though.

"Try not to focus on that too much," India said, still rummaging through her purse. My eyes were still closed, but I could hear it. "Just look ahead." She told me in a comforting tone. "Your man will be home soon."

"Thanks Indie."

"You said Day would be home tonight, right?" She asked after a moment.

"Yeah. She said she'd just be stopping by though." I put my arm over my eyes. "Girl, what are you looking for?" She was still searching.

"My phone, but I found it."

I lightly shook my head. Indie carried a canvas tote, as most artists do, and sometimes, foolishly, she tosses her phone in there. I love India, but she really shouldn't do that. That tote of hers has a million and one things in it, just like mine. And it's always so hard for her to find anything. I've called her phone so many times only for her to retrieve it ringing at the bottom. I knew better than to ever put anything important in my tote.

A moment later, I heard Daijah's chipper voice. "Hey Indie!" India had called her on speaker.

"Hey Day. You headed this way yet?"

"Pretty soon. You guys, okay?"

"Yeah, we're good. Just need some clarity on something. Do you mind making a pit stop?"

"Sure don't. What do you need?"

"*I* don't need anything. But *Des* needs a pregnancy test. Make that two, actually."

I sat up fast, "Indie, what are you talking about?"

"A pregnancy test?" Daijah and I spoke at the same time.

Indie carried on with Daijah just like I wasn't there. "Destiney revealed she hasn't been feeling well the past few weeks. Feeling nauseous recently. Since we know she's been fucking on the regular…" She looked at me knowingly, "*It's quite possible Des is prego.*" Indie sang that last part.

"Des, why didn't you tell anyone you haven't been feeling well?" Daijah asked.

"I don't know. Just didn't think it was a big deal. I'm used to it."

"That was *before*," Indie said.

"After surgery, you said you've never felt better." Daijah pointed out. She was right.

"Precisely. Now you're feeling nauseous. Girl, you should have said something. We need to know. We were just drinking. Smoking hookah too."

That freaked me out. My eyes grew wide.

"When was your last period?" That was Daijah.

"It was several weeks ago," India's eyes ballooned. "But I don't have a period every month," I quickly added. "It's not quite monthly, but getting there."

My doctor said it can take a while for my cycle to be normal post-surgery, if at all. Some women never have a monthly cycle, which can make conceiving difficult when they are actually trying.

Were we trying?

No. We weren't really.

But… we weren't exactly *not* trying either.

We'd pretty much stopped using condoms altogether. Honestly, and now that I think about it, maybe that was incredibly irresponsible of us. Of me. Especially if I smoke hookah and drink on occasion.

"I'll grab a few tests…" I tuned out whatever it was Day and Indie were talking about. I had to think for a second.

Micah picked up a few condoms while we were in Pismo Beach.

We used those.

Then we got home and started playing the pullout game.

And Micah, being as thoughtful as he was, asked me if I was okay with that. Beforehand.

I was perfectly fine with that. I loved the way he felt.

He said he loved it too. And he'd been pulling out in time.

But since I'm not on any birth control, I guess there's always a possibility. Even if Micah pulls out. It only takes one.

Just one determined swimmer.

Wow.

Maybe I am pregnant.

Holy shit.

thirty

MICAH

"Hey brother," I said after I tossed my suitcase in the back seat and climbed into the front passenger side of Malachi's truck.

"Baby brother. You looking good. Feeling good?"

"Yeah. Glad to be back."

"Yup. Glad to have you back. Thank God for traveling grace." Mal pulled away from the curb, merging into the bustling airport traffic.

"Indeed. Thank you for picking me up."

"Of course. I got you baby brother."

The traffic flowed, and soon, we were on the freeway, making our way toward south Sacramento.

"So, how'd everything go? Productive? Accomplished?"

Mal asked. I was away on business for eight days.

"Yeah. I got to meet our new CEO. Had a few fireside chats with some counterparts in our neighboring regions. Appreciate the perspective. Things are looking well fiscally. Glad to be back though. It's too cold in Chicago for me."

Mal laughed. "No doubt." He sounded just like Daddy saying that, too. *No doubt* was their *indeed*. They both said it all the time. "We're just California boys, that's all." We both chuckled at that.

"Right!"

"I went up there a few times with the team." Mal played basketball when he was at Morehouse. "Couldn't get used to that. They don't call it Windy City for nothing. I think they get just about a month of an actual summer up there."

"Yeah. And long winters. Not my forte."

"Shiiiittt. Mine either."

We cruised through traffic, which, thankfully, wasn't too bad. The airport was just north of Natomas. It's about thirty minutes from our neck of the woods, but with traffic, it may take longer. I was okay with that. Hanging with my big brother was always a vibe.

"The kids okay?"

"Yeah. I meant to tell you, so Gabe had a group assignment he worked on earlier this week and his partner had to come over at some point so they could practice their presentation, which came out phenomenal by the way. Proud father."

I nodded. "*Very* proud uncle."

Mal nodded too. "So, it turns out his partner is this *girl*. And I am *certain* Gabe is sweet on her."

My eyes grew wide. "Oh yeah?" I chuckled at that.

"*Yes*. My boy was fumbling and stuttering. They were practicing, and he couldn't even get through his presentation." Mal and I were cracking up. "His calm and cool demeanor was nowhere to be found. That's what gave it away. He's *absolutely* got a sweet spot for her."

"Sounds like it. Nephew has a crush huh?"

"Man..." Mal rubbed his beard absently. "He's definitely smitten. You know Gabe. Not much else would throw him off his square."

We both cackled.

"I didn't want to make it a big deal, you know. But we talked about it. Gabe said they were just friends and that she was a cool girl. Smart. Friendly. He thinks she's pretty." Mal chuckled again. "She seems like a nice girl. So. All that sounds good to me."

"Damn." I shook my head. "We getting old brother."

"I'm saying. Gabe's going on fifteen. Gabby's going on thirteen. It's wild too. They aren't much younger than Ella and I were when we met."

"Right! Now that's bananas."

We cruised in silence for a few beats.

"Mommy and Daddy straight?" We usually shared the task of looking in on them, but I knew Mal was good for holding down the fort by himself.

"Oh yeah. Everything's straight at the blue house. G-squared and I went by yesterday evening as a matter of fact." (*G-Squared* were Gabe and Gabby girl). Mal looked over his shoulder as he veered into an open lane. "You planning to go by today?"

"Yeah, I need to run a few errands, so I'll stop by on my way out." It was hardly eleven a.m.; I took a red-eye flight out yesterday and flew directly back. Thankfully, there weren't any delays, and I was home early enough to have the rest of the day.

He nodded.

"How's my sis?" I was sure to look to my left when I asked. A silly grin made its way across Malachi's face just like I knew it would. It was the same grin I'd seen for the past 17 years.

"She's perfect. Can't wait to get back to her." After a beat, "Was in the middle of something and had to climb out my good shit just to come scoop yo ass."

"Mal, really?"

295

Of course, Malachi thought that was so funny. A deep rumble made its way from the pit of his belly as he filled the truck with his laughter. All I could do was shake my head.

"You gone find out baby brother. Believe me." Mal said once he calmed down.

I already knew.

This had been the longest eight days of my life, and I missed the hell out of Destiney. I couldn't wait to get back.

To see her.

As much as I appreciated Mal picking me up, I wished I'd arranged for her to greet me. But being so far away and for that long gave me room to consider my next move.

And it was time.

Before leaving for Chicago, I picked Daijah's brain on the best type of ring for Destiney. I narrowed it down to two, and when I couldn't decide between them, I asked Gabby girl to help me decide.

I knew Destiney would have loved either of them, but I'm glad I could ask Gabby girl. She was the reason I'd met Destiney.

So, I arranged to have a few things in place by this evening.

On my flight home, I mentally prepared what I was going to do for her and what I was going to say to her.

I wanted it all to be perfect.

I planned to visit Mommy and Daddy, then pick up a couple more things and get showered. After that, I'd pick up my baby and bring her home.

Yes. *Home*. With me. Where she belonged.

I was so fortunate to have secured a huge favor from Janelle, co-owner and executive chef at HomeGrownSol. Janelle graciously agreed that I could hire her to come and prepare a meal for us. I requested a few of Destiney's favorite things on the menu. She always raved about the roasted red potatoes with Brussels sprouts. And the roasted stuffed zucchini. The zucchini was delicious. Made with fire-roasted tomatoes, breadcrumbs, parmesan, mozzarella, basil, and garlic. Destiney loved it. We'd gotten it to go a few times.

We'd have some sweet wine. Candles. Also, picking up some flowers. Destiney may even want to soak in the huge ass tub in the master. I knew it would come in handy someday. I'd never used the tub, but I got the feeling Destiney would get plenty of use out of it. I had a stockpile of spa essentials for her.

Most importantly, I have already asked Mr. Evans for Destiney's hand.

I went by her father's home the day before my flight to speak with him.

"You take care of my baby. Give me your word that you will. She is precious to me and her late mother. Should you no longer wish to, you bring her back to me. Whole. Better than the way I am giving her to you." Mr. Evans spoke sternly. Much sterner than he's ever spoken with me. But I was perfectly alright with that.

I stood up straight, looking slightly downward into her father's eyes.

Sticking my hand out, I said, "You have my word, Mr. Evans. I will take the best care of Destiney."

He shook my hand firmly with a smile that reached his eyes.

"Call me dad."

"Baby brother?"

I looked over at Mal. "My bad… just in my head."

"Damn right." Mal cackled. "You thinking of your sweetheart?"

I grinned, and he cackled all over again. "You don't even have to answer that."

"Tonight is the night, brother," I revealed.

"Oh yeah? *That's* why you're in your head over there."

I chuckled. "I want things to go perfectly. Just running over it in my mind."

"That's all you had to say. I'll be quiet."

"You good big brother. I need the distraction." I was a ball of nerves.

"I know you. I'm sure you thought of everything." Mal chuckled. "Everything's handled. All you have left to do now is ask."

I nodded. "Yeah… you think she'll say yes?" I didn't plan on asking Mal that question, but I couldn't help myself. I wasn't too proud to reveal my feelings. We always spoke with complete transparency, after all.

"I think she'll say yes. You two…" he smiled, shaking his head. "The love I've witnessed growing between the two of you. It's explosive. She adores you, Micah. And likewise, you've shown her your heart and that it beats for her through your words and actions. It's been beautiful to witness. You did well, brother. Baby sis is good to you and for you. I think she'll say yes."

I felt better just that quickly. "You'll be the first to know," I told Malachi.

"I'll be here, baby brother. Looking forward to hearing the good news. Celebrating. Everything to come."

"Indeed."

I knew this was right.

It felt so right. And I knew this was what we both wanted.

Now, we'll make it official.

thirty-one

DESTINEY

Today was *everything*. Quite literally.

I was so happy my man was back.

He came to get me. And he took me *home*. To his house.

It's a fact that his place has been like a second home for me. And I've spent more time there than anywhere else. And that's just the way I like it.

So, we got home, and I don't know how or when he managed to pull it off, but Micah had the most romantic evening planned for me.

It was *everything*.

I stepped into the front door—Micah was right behind me—and was greeted with the beautiful sight of rose petals. At Micah's encouragement, I followed the trail, and the delicate pink rose petals led us from the front door to the dining room table.

The table was covered with a black satin tablecloth, more pink rose petals, lit candles, and two elegant place settings.

Then, I noticed the striking arrangement of sunflowers.

Even more striking than the last one. Bold and bright in a gorgeous vase.

I turned to Micah, looking up at him. He was right behind me and already wearing a knowing smile.

My smile was wide when I said, "Micah. This is all *so* beautiful."

"You're beautiful," He returned.

I fell into his arms, and he held me for a long time. Micah doesn't cease to amaze me. Ever.

I'd read about the sweet, romantic gesture of rose petals. I read all about them in my romance novels. Plenty. Seen them in the movies too. And honestly, I didn't think it would happen to me.

And...I was feeling emotional, but I didn't cry. I just held onto my man, momentarily losing myself in his sweet embrace, not wanting to sever our connection. I surmise he felt the same. Micah held me just as securely.

After a few moments—I don't know how many...softly, close to my ear, Micah said, "Been telling you love...anything for you baby." He spoke in that deep register I love so much—the one that gets me going every single time. And I held him even tighter, nodding silently.

My man is fucking amazing.

Micah loosened his grip but didn't let me go completely. "Sweetheart, there are some people here I'd love for you to meet."

I looked up at Micah in surprise. Then I looked just past Micah, and only then did I realize two women were moving about in the kitchen. Both of them dressed in a black chef's coat.

I briefly—only briefly—forgot that I was consumed by the savory scents of fragrant food when I entered the house. The delectable aromas emanating from the kitchen were even richer now.

My senses told me something delightful was being freshly prepared.

"Destiney baby. Meet Mrs. Janelle Bailey. The illustrious Executive Chef and co-owner of HomeGrownSol."

My eyes grew wide. My jaw dropped.

This is Janelle? *The* Janelle?

How did he get her?

That restaurant is *always* bustling. They probably were *right now.*

And she was *here*? *In Micah's kitchen.* Preparing a meal for *us.*

"Lovely to meet you, Destiney. Please meet my daughter Naomi, Sauté chef. She's been my right hand this evening." She smiled proudly as she shook my hand; Naomi followed suit, smiling shyly. She appeared about sixteen or so. Pretty, just like her mom.

"Sooo nice to meet you, Janelle. Naomi. I am fanning out right now. I *love* your food! Micah has got to be sick of me. He's *always* ordering something for me from HomeGrown."

"Hey, I don't mind at all. I'll usually get something for myself while I'm at it." Micah said.

We all shared a laugh.

"I appreciate all of the vegetarian options, too," I told them excitedly.

"That's what I love to hear! I'm so glad you enjoy it. " Her warm smile reached her eyes. Janelle continued, "Good food is great for the soul. I hope you find tonight's meal just as delicious."

"I'm sure we will! It smells great," I gushed.

"Your dinner is ready. Please be seated whenever you're ready for us to serve you," Naomi politely offered.

"Excellent. We'll go wash up and be back momentarily," Micah promised.

The guest restroom was just down the hall, across from the office. We both headed that way, and Micah pulled me to him just as we turned the corner.

"Hang on…give me those lips, baby." Micah gently backed me against the wall, and we kissed sweetly at first, but it quickly turned passionate. I started pulling away. Well, I was trying to, but Micah had a grip around my waist. "Where you going beauty?" He murmured against my lips, "…I'm not finished." His hand descended, and within seconds, he was inside my already damp underwear, and his fingers were moving just past my lower lips.

"Micah…" I moaned, trying to keep my voice down, "Baby..." He had two of his thick ass fingers inside me, and it felt so good. Not only had I missed him, but I missed this too. We'd only shared a few sweet pecks when he came to pick me up earlier. And this was nice. Mostly. I knew we were outside their line of sight, but I was apprehensive. Kinda paranoid. My moans were growing slightly in volume. And I was distracted because I didn't want either of the ladies in the next room to hear us.

"Ssshhh. You trying to blow our cover?" Micah teased, speaking against my lips. He was stroking me with his fingers. *Fuck.* Baby, you are slippery." His thumb was on my clit, gently rubbing…driving me fucking insane. "You like that sexy girl?"

"Yeah baby. I love it." Just that quickly, I'd released my reservations. Enjoying the strum of his fingers. They'd get an eyeful if they dared to come down this hall.

I wouldn't worry about that right now.

"Go head baby," Micah said, "Give me one right here. Right on my fingers." He was gentle yet persistent. Rubbing my clit with fervor. His tongue was *all up in* my mouth. Kissing me deep, slow, and nasty.

As if on command, I came undone, feeling an intense wave of pleasure making my eyes flutter. As I reached my peak, he swallowed my moans. Which absolutely would have given us away. I'm glad Micah's lips were still on mine.

"There it is," Micah praised. I loved that shit.

His fingers went into his mouth, where he sucked them clean, then kissed me again, and I tasted myself all over his tongue. I loved that shit too.

"Go on upstairs and get cleaned up, baby. I'll use this restroom and head back. I'll tell them you'll be a few more minutes."

"Alright." My voice was contented. And blissful.

I went upstairs to get a fresh pair of panties. These were done for.

***

So, dinner was absolutely delicious. Somehow, it tasted even better than it did at the restaurant.

First, they served Caprese avocado toast as an appetizer. This wasn't something on their menu. I'd have ordered it if so. Micah must have made a special request. He knows how much I love avocado toast. And it was so good. Perfectly toasted baguette topped with avocado, mozzarella, and heirloom tomatoes. Fresh basil. Fresh cracked black pepper. Olive oil drizzle. *Mmm!* The fresh pepper and fresh basil gave it a rustic flavor. For Micah, there was Italian turkey stuffed with portobello mushrooms.

Janelle made my most requested entree for my main course. I was so pleased. And I don't think I'll ever get tired of the balsamic Brussels sprouts. Micah had pan-seared Sea Bass over a bed of wilted mixed greens.

The food was stellar. Marvelous.

Janelle and Naomi quietly made their exit once they served us dessert. Each of them placed a generous slice of red velvet cake covered in light whipped frosting in front of us. Micah and I really could have shared a slice, and every bite was rich, moist, decadent, and heavenly.

Throughout the evening, Micah and I raved about the superb food prepared. We were thankful and delighted our chefs set the time aside for us. I was beyond satisfied with all three courses.

When we took our dessert plates to the kitchen, we discovered it was cleaned and restored to the tidy condition Micah kept it in. There was almost no trace of them there. Aside from the Tupperware, they packed the leftover food in. And there was still plenty for a filling lunch tomorrow.

I leaned against the counter, sipping from my glass of water. I was so full at the moment—past full. Lunch was the furthest thing from my mind, but I was emotionally full, too. My heart was so full. Yeah.

I closed my eyes, enchanted with the tranquil sounds of the soft music that had been playing, when something else occurred to me: I'm so glad I wasn't feeling too sick today. And able to keep my food down. I'd thrown up a couple of times, and that would have ruined everything. It would have blown my cover, too.

"Did you enjoy yourself, love?" Micah asked. He washed our plates and forks and then placed them on the dishrack.

I nodded eagerly, giving him a contented smile. "Thank you. I have. Today was *so*… it was everything, Micah. You're so thoughtful, baby. I'll remember today for the rest of my life."

"Indeed. I'm so glad to hear that. I missed you so much, baby. I could hardly wait to get back to you."

"I missed you too, Micah."

I could cry because I was so overwhelmed and appreciative of this man.

My man.

He continues to remind me of his thoughtfulness.

I don't travel often, but when I do, I'm exhausted once I get home. Micah did all of this for me after traveling the last several hours. It was the thought behind it all for me. He was so thoughtful to do this.

He turned toward the fridge and began loading the food.

During dinner, I extended my gratitude to Micah at least a million times. In true Micah fashion, he insisted it was no big deal, but I insisted that it really was. I told him I would have been just fine having peanut butter and jelly.

"Baby," I called.

"Yeah?" He moved a few things around but turned toward me when I didn't answer immediately. "Are you alright?"

I nodded with a lazy smile. My lids were low. "Thank you. I am."

"Good." He turned back toward the fridge. "Need anything, sweetheart?" He was likely wondering why I called out to him. He had checked in with me a few times earlier when I turned down a glass of wine with dinner. He didn't press, but I knew he would be bringing it up soon.

"I need you," I lulled.

"Do you?" His voice dipped. Micah turned back towards me, closing the fridge behind him. His lids low now. Just like mine.

"Mmmhmm." I placed my glass on the kitchen counter beside me and took a few steps towards him. Eyes on eyes, we were pressed together, body to body.

"Mmm. Tell me what you need, beauty."

I went for his belt buckle, then the zipper on his jeans, freeing him from his boxers. *Damn*. Micah was already hard as a rock. I stroked his hardness, then dropped to my knees. I could show him better than I could tell him.

"*Mmmmm*. I see."

"I missed you baby." It was muffled. I had his big dick in my mouth, after all. I commenced sucking, taking as much of him as I could. Giving it my very best.

"I missed you more... so glad to be back, my love..." Micah's fingers were threaded in my locs. Gently cradling my head in his large hands. Murmuring my encouragement and his pleasure. "There you go beauty. Damn, you suck me so good."

I pressed my hands against the cool fridge on either side of him. Anchoring myself for leverage as he began to stroke my mouth. Gladly relinquishing control.

My mouth was wet and slick and sloppy. I could taste his precum as he glided in and out like a hot-ass knife through butter.

Micah's strokes were slow and measured at first. Then, growing erratic the closer he got.

I fucking loved that shit.

"Destiney... beauty... you want this baby?" Micah didn't even have to ask.

I pressed myself closer. He understood my silent agreement.

When he released inside of my mouth, his beautiful sound surrounded us.

Micah helped me up, kissing my lips, my neck, and my chin.

"Thank you, baby. I needed you, too," He told me.

"Always a pleasure," I said in a flirty tone. Winking, I turned back to the counter, tossing back the last of my water. I washed my glass and placed it on the dishrack.

"You're so damn sexy," Micah told me, smacking my ass.

I yelped in surprise. Rubbing my ass at the mild sting. He was heavy-handed, but I liked having my ass smacked.

"Thank you handsome."

Micah nodded, taking me into his arms, and leaned us against the counter. After kissing my neck softly, "How about we take a shower, and I'll give you a massage?"

"Yes, please," I returned, pecking his lips sweetly.

"You got it baby. Head upstairs and get the shower started. I'll be right in behind you."

So, Micah gave me a massage. He's the best at them, and I was appreciative and excited. I loved being intimately close to him, as close as possible, considering we weren't making love right now. And this was good enough for me. It was perfect. We may have stopped having intercourse, but the intimacy hadn't gone anywhere. It was still living and breathing between us. I'd argue that we've gotten closer in these last few weeks.

And now we were *finally* dressed for bed.

That massage had me so relaxed that I would be down for the count soon.

But I needed to tell him the news first.

I'd been counting down the days while Micah was in Chicago. More than two thousand miles away from me.

Obsessively at first.

But then I thought better of it. Bearing in mind how much more difficult things could have been.

If Micah had been deployed or something, it would have been months, *not days*… with no guarantee he'd even return alive.

I had an *enormous* respect for military wives. No way I could do it.

That reality check got me through just fine.

I busied myself with work.

And the mural. Indie and I made significant progress.

In between time, I sipped ginger ale and kept ginger candy nearby, combating the nausea.

Yet still feeling a strong gravitational pull. Still longing for Micah.

I desperately wanted him home.

Not only because I missed him but I was grappling with the news.

The news was like a burning secret. Fiery. Scorching. *Ablaze* like an ignited flame.

Like a blaring alarm.

A declaration fighting to reveal its presence.

The news, warring to free itself from the containment of my lips.

Micah and I had been texting and talking on the phone, of course, and I came dangerously close a few times.

I wanted to tell Micah as soon as it was confirmed.

But I was sure I should share this with him in person.

And I couldn't wait. I was so eager to share this with Micah.

I sat on my side of the bed, checking in with Day and Indie. I shared a few pictures from the set-up downstairs in our group chat, and they asked a million questions. They also asked if I'd told him yet, and I said I was about to. Micah was in the walk-in closet, and I was sure he would be making his way out of there any minute. I promised I'd fill them in with all the details tomorrow and then wished them a good night.

I plugged up my phone just as Micah walked out of the closet.

"Can I talk to you?"

"Baby, I need to talk to you."

We spoke at the same time.

Micah was beside me in seconds. "Of course you can, baby, " his voice was laced with concern. "Everything okay?"

I nodded, "It is. I promise."

"Indeed. Well, you go first. I can wait."

"Okay."

Then, several moments went by. And I said nothing.

This was not how I imagined this would go. Because suddenly, and out of nowhere, I was nervous. I don't know why. Considering just hours ago, I was bursting with this news. Now I was feeling shy.

"Micah," I turned toward him. Looking into his expectant, warm brown eyes. He nodded, encouraging me to continue. He held his hand in mine, threading our fingers. "Micah," I looked away, but he was with me. Caressing my fingers. Patiently waiting for whatever this was.

"Yes baby? What is it?"

I took another beat, then, "I'm pregnant. I'm… we're…having a baby."

Micah's eyes were wide. His smile was even wider. *"Are you? Really?!"*

I smiled too. My eyes were filling up as I nodded silently.

"Baby! You're having my baby?"

"I am." Growing emotional, I sniffed, but my smile reached my eyes.

Micah moved to his knees in front of me. Lifting my shirt, he wrapped his arms around my waist, pressing kisses against my belly. His chuckle was deep, *"That's why you didn't want wine with dinner."*

"Yeah," I giggled at the ticklish sensation of his beard on my skin.

"Have you seen a doctor?"

"Next week."

I felt him nod against me. "I'm so happy baby." I would have known even if he hadn't told me. Micah's joy was evident as he continued scattering kisses all over my midsection. I closed my eyes, holding his head in my hands. He never moved from the floor in front of me. Rubbing my lower back, softly kissing me.

I couldn't help myself as I asked, "You promise you're happy, Micah?" I knew how much he wanted to be a father. But I also knew that he wanted to be married first.

I felt the same way, honestly.

Micah looked up into my eyes. *"So happy baby.* I wouldn't lie to you." I believed him. "How are you feeling?" He quizzed.

"I'm happy too." My tears finally fell, and Micah wiped them away. Holding his eyes, I continued, "But I know you wanted to be married before kids."

"Yeah." Micah nodded. "Which confirms I'm right on time with this."

My brows were knitted, "With what?"

Micah reached into his pocket, pulling out a small black velvet box. He opened it, and I gasped when I realized what it was and what he was doing. He took my left hand in his. "There are few things in this life I'm certain of…" He pressed my hand to his lips, "But when it comes to you..." Kiss. "Me. Us." Another kiss. "I am certain. I am so confident. Be my wife, baby. Will you marry me? Tell me you'll be my wife."

"I'd love nothing more than to be your wife, Micah. Yes," I replied through tears.

"Yeah?" He grinned.

"Yes baby."

He slid the rose gold diamond ring on my finger, and I peered at it in awe. Admiring the intricate details.

It was beautiful—an oval cut diamond in the center. Pavé set diamonds on the halo and along each side of the band.

Gorgeous. Radiant. Breathtaking.

I fell into Micah's arms. Right there on the floor. Kissing all over him. Holding him tightly, just as tightly as he held me.

"I love you, Micah."

"I love you, Destiney baby. I'm never letting you go."

Epilogue

One year later

"So, you ready to be an uncle?"

I remember when Mal first shared the news that they were expecting.

He was so proud.

I was too!

The question had caught me so off guard that I was stuck for a second. We weren't even on the subject. I don't recall precisely what we were talking about, but it wasn't remotely related. Anyway, the moment I realized what he was telling me, I looked up and saw a big Kool-Aid smile.

"Sis is pregnant?" In a matter of seconds, I was sporting the same smile.

"Yeah man. I can't believe it."

"Wow brother. That is great news! Congrats!"

"Thank you, baby brother."

I hugged him tight. "You already tell Mommy and Daddy?"

"Not yet. You're the first and only person we've shared this with. Do me a favor and keep this between us, baby brother."

"Your good news is safe with me."

"No doubt. You've always been that."

"Of course."

"We'll tell everyone at the end of the month. Ella wanted to see her doctor first, get her official due date and all that jazz."

I nodded. "Get ready. Mommy is going to be over the moon. She'll probably start buying stuff before you even know what it is."

We both cackled. I continued, "I don't know why you're so surprised anyway. The way you always pouncing on my sis."

"Aye man! My wife takes care of me. What can I say."

Months later, there was another moment I won't forget as long as I live.

It was a moment so very special to me.

I came to the hospital to meet my brand-new nephew, and when Mal placed him in my arms, he proudly introduced us, and that's when I learned my nephew would forever have a part of me, too.

"Baby brother. We're thrilled to introduce you to our son. Gabriel Micah Walker."

My eyes grew wide, "You serious man?"

Ella looked on proudly, "You better believe it. We wouldn't have it any other way. You introduced us, remember?"

I sure did remember that, but this was huge. My brother gave my name to his first-born child, a son who was already his pride and joy, a physical representation of his infinite love for his wife.

"Wow. This is... I am so honored. Gabriel is beautiful." And he was. Content and alert, his soft brown eyes looking right at me. I held Gabriel close, growing emotional. "Nice to meet you, Gabriel Micah Walker." I chuckled because I couldn't help myself. "Has a nice ring to it."

"We thought so too," Mal said.

"Indeed." I looked up at my brother and over at my sister-in-love. "I'm so proud of you. Both of you."

"Thank you, baby brother."

"Thank you."

They replied simultaneously.

I decided that day, right at that very moment, that should God bless me with a son, I would give him my brother's name, too.

313

***

I entered the room quietly to find Destiney sleeping. Making my way to the bed, I watched her sleep peacefully for a while.

I watched her sleep constantly, but I could pinch myself now.

I know this moment is real, but sometimes I still can't believe it.

Destiney is my heart. In human form. My heartbeat. Sharing this space and making a life together is such a beautiful thing. I express my gratitude every single day.

For years, I had been searching. For her.

And now, here we were. I'm her husband, she's my wife, and we're making memories we can cherish for the rest of our lives.

Destiney and I were married eight months ago. Our engagement was short—something we both wanted. We set a date, exactly a month after Daijah and Julian's nuptials and just *ten months* to the date we met.

Wild. When you know, you know.

Destiney was a beautiful bride. I remember when she entered the church on her proud father's arm. She neared me, and it was as if everyone else- everything else had disappeared.

As if time stood still.

For the briefest of moments, nothing else existed. Only my soon-to-be wife. When Destiney descended the aisle and we locked eyes, it was a moment of significant vulnerability. An unspoken connection. For us both.

I released tears of joy, trying with all my might to collect myself, and my big brother and best man comforted me.

"This is your moment, baby brother. Look at her. She's your wife. Everything you prayed for."

Malachi's firm, reassuring hand on my shoulder reminded me that he was right beside me and always would be. I knew this full well. He didn't need to tell me.

Like an angel, Destiney floated towards me. And all I could do was thank the good Lord above for his favor. For his sovereignty. For the best thing to ever happen to me.

The aisle was fairly long, and I saw Mr. Evans speaking to Destiney as they came into view. I couldn't hear him, of course, but seeing this sweet father-daughter moment between them was so special.

When they finally arrived at the altar, he said, "Are you ready, princess?"

Nodding, Destiney said, "Yes. I'm ready Daddy."

After firmly shaking my hand, Mr. Evans lifted Destiney's veil, kissed her forehead, and joined her hand and mine before taking his seat.

That was when Destiney grew emotional and Daijah, her matron of honor, helped make sure she didn't ruin her makeup, whispering encouraging words of her own.

Destiney was perfect—she couldn't have looked more perfect.

My wife had the wedding of her dreams. No expenses were spared. She wanted something intimate yet elegant and got exactly what she wanted.

The day we said 'I do' will forever be one of my proudest moments and no doubt one of the happiest moments of my life.

I continued to watch her sleep. She's never been more beautiful than she is right now.

She lay on her side with a body pillow propped between her legs. Lately, this was the only position she could sleep in comfortably. Her swollen belly had been growing and stretching, making room for our precious baby, and Destiney was such a great sport about it.

We've been waiting with such excitement for our baby to arrive.

We're about halfway there. Destiney officially made five months a couple of days ago.

We decided to keep our baby's gender a surprise.

It's been easy to do. We were just so grateful for this miracle.

We were pregnant late last year, but sadly we miscarried. It was an early miscarriage. A week after we confirmed the news, it was over.

And then we took some time away. We unplugged from everything else, focused on looking after each other, and took care of each other.

And I waited patiently for my wife to tell me when she was ready to try again.

And we did.

Then Destiney told me she was pregnant again, and I was elated.

This time, cautiously optimistic. But *so* happy. And grateful.

Leading up to that moment, we'd been trying ferociously. But not saying so out loud. Trying not to make it a thing. It was unspoken, but the synergy between us didn't require that we spoke it aloud. We both wanted this so much. And we both knew we'd have to stay the course.

When you have a few things working against you, *trying* to get pregnant is not fun, if I'm honest.

We had the challenge of irregular ovulation. So, we had to make love even when we weren't feeling up to it… if you catch my drift…for fear of missing the window. Taking a day off was a risk.

Anyone who had trouble conceiving the traditional way knows exactly what I am talking about.

Now, make no mistake. I love my wife. I'll always want her. I'll always desire her. But it got to be a lot for her. I knew that. And I wanted this *for* her so much.

But it finally happened.

I think back to the day she shared the news with me. I always smile at that memory.

I hovered over Destiney's belly, littering her mid-section with kisses, trying to manifest shit if I'm honest... I'd been trying, with all my might, to put a baby in her. I was sure to plant my seeds deep inside each time we came together. Placing a pillow under her hips. Reminding her to lie still and relax afterward. Let things take root.

And I was anxiously anticipating her telling me when it happened.

I was trying to be patient at the same time. I knew the situation was delicate, and I was sensitive to that.

"Is there a baby in here yet?" I asked her in jest, trying to lighten the mood. It had gotten to be a little heavy around here. Looming thoughts. Negative tests. Tears. Doubts.

I made my way up her body, kissing her neck and along her cheeks. Then I spoke softly in her ear.

"Wife...I've been planting seeds deep inside of you...I'm gone keep doing it. I'm giving you everything you need to grow us a beautiful baby." I kissed behind her ear and along her neck. "That okay with you sweetheart?" Two more kisses.

Destiney peered up at me with low lids, and I knew my plan was working. I was getting her ready for me. Ensuring she stayed out of her head would help, so I had a job to do.

I placed her hand on my hardness. I was ready too. She stroked me through my joggers. I needed these out of the way, along

317

with her shorts and panties. I groaned. "Like right now, I'm ready to plant some deep inside of you, baby."

"Husband," Destiney's voice was soft. Laced with need. But there was something else there, too.

However, I was unsure of what exactly.

I moved away from her neck, sitting back on my hunches. Eyes on eyes. Her lids were low, but I couldn't read her expression otherwise.

"Yeah baby?"

Destiney took my hand and gently placed it on her belly.

"There's a baby here right now." She smiled wide. That angelic smile of hers I love so much.

I smiled so big. "Is there really?"

She nodded silently. "Just confirmed today."

I took her in my arms. Holding her. Kissing her.

Then I went back to her belly, littering more kisses there.

Now, here we were.

I'm sure I was biased, but I didn't know a more beautiful pregnant woman. My wife is so beautiful—breathtaking—and she's all mine.

Speaking of miracles, I was so amazed watching her grow our child. There was something ineffable about seeing my wife carrying my offspring. Utterly indescribable, having the privilege of witnessing her grow a life from a seed I planted. And as you can imagine, I've grown even more protective of Destiney. My primal instincts are in overdrive.

And Destiney was so cute. Her skin was glowing. Her hair was growing.

She had been feeling less beautiful lately. She told me she felt as big as a house and was miserable, but I found her to be delicious.

And pregnant pussy was my shit.

Yeah. I said it.

I had a salacious desire for my wife that I couldn't explain. Yep. That pregnant pussy had a vice grip on my shit. I was always wanting to be inside her. She gushed for me without me needing to touch her. She was too uncomfortable to get on top now, but we did it from the back just fine. And if I wasn't entering her from behind, I was eating her. I spent so much time between her thick thighs, eating to my heart's content. I was delighted when I discovered how much her nipples had darkened and how much heavier her breasts were in my hands. I looked forward to having my wife back but was fine rocking with this for a while longer.

Oh, Daijah is pregnant, too! She and Julian are expecting a little princess, due any day now. Destiney and Daijah have grown even closer during this season. It's been so special. God has continued to bless us beyond anything I could ever imagine, and I am so thankful.

I was still beside the bed, admiring how beautiful Destiney looked carrying life.

Destiney is so precious. So lovely. *My good thing.*

Everything. Exactly what I need. More than I could ever want.

And this was love. An insurmountable love.

Immeasurable, vast, endless.

Unconditional. Absolute.

A love, sweet like honey.

Indeed.

Vivienne Paul

The End

If you enjoyed this story, please consider leaving a review on your platform of choice.

About the Author

Vivienne Paul is obsessed with a sweet, sappy black love story, and most days—with a cup of tea or glass of wine in hand—you'll find her reading or writing one.

A Northern California native, she's a wife and a mom embracing life's tender moments and it's beautiful chaos.

In the time between, she's an occasional artist and amateur chef.

She is currently writing her next book. Follow her for updates on upcoming titles.

IG: vivpaulwrites

vivpaulwrites@gmail.com

www.ingramcontent.com/pod-product-compliance
Lightning Source LLC
Chambersburg PA
CBHW050010120726
47903CB00006B/1716